A VINTAGE VACATION

MADDIE PLEASE

Boldwood

First published in Great Britain in 2023 by Boldwood Books Ltd.

Copyright © Maddie Please, 2023

Cover Design by Head Design

Cover Photography: Shutterstock

The moral right of Maddie Please to be identified as the author of this work has been asserted in accordance with the Copyright, Designs and Patents Act 1988.

Every effort has been made to obtain the necessary permissions with reference to copyright material, both illustrative and quoted. We apologise for any omissions in this respect and will be pleased to make the appropriate acknowledgements in any future edition.

A CIP catalogue record for this book is available from the British Library.

Paperback ISBN 978-1-80483-714-6

Large Print ISBN 978-1-80483-710-8

Hardback ISBN 978-1-80483-709-2

Ebook ISBN 978-1-80483-707-8

Kindle ISBN 978-1-80483-708-5

Audio CD ISBN 978-1-80483-715-3

MP3 CD ISBN 978-1-80483-712-2

Digital audio download ISBN 978-1-80483-706-1

Boldwood Books Ltd
23 Bowerdean Street
London SW6 3TN
www.boldwoodbooks.com

For Brian, very much loved.

1

I'd worked for XS – 'Finance with Heart' – for over twenty years. We were a perfect fit.

I'd risen through the ranks to become senior business manager and the next step up was director. Which on paper shouldn't have been difficult, because as far as I could see the board was filled with pompous nitwits more concerned with their golf and latest cars than business. Not that that stopped them steaming in at the eleventh hour and claiming all the credit, when in fact other people like me had sorted out all the difficulties of a deal.

That morning I stood in front of the mirror in the executive cloakroom, smoothing down the jacket of my scarlet suit. It stood out so well amidst the sea of grey that usually filled the boardroom. My hair was in its usual tight French pleat, my make up perfect. I rummaged in my bag to find my trademark 'Rouge Amazone' lipstick and applied a fresh layer. If Nick Crane, director of HR, wanted a chat, then I was ready.

My instinct, one that had been growing over the last few weeks, was that he was going to escalate the process he had mentioned during the staff '*Fun Sports Day and Tofu Extravaganza*' in Crawley. I was next in line for promotion, they were going to offer me a seat on the board. Now that the Olafsen contract was millimetres away from agreement and signature, it would be the perfect time. It had been one of the biggest deals XS had ever done, and my stamp was all over it.

I blotted my lipstick with a tissue. It was four minutes to eight o'clock. Exactly enough time to get the lift up to the fourteenth floor where Nick Crane had a glass-walled office, filled with his many meaningless awards and photos of himself with some of the other directors playing golf or in executive boxes at Twickenham.

On my way to the executive lift, I passed a couple of people who moved aside, respectfully murmuring, 'Good morning, Miss Harrington.'

I gave them a polite smile and hurried on. I tried to bite back a little thrill of excitement. This was it then, the moment for which I had worked so hard, for so many years. I'd known for a while that Howard Leeming was planning to step down from his post as director of business. There was only so much information that could be hidden in a company the size of XS, and Nina, my secretary, was a hotline to office gossip.

I reached Nick Crane's floor and took a deep breath.

Sheila, his PA, was waiting behind her desk: the gatekeeper. She barely glanced at me.

'Good morning, Miss Harrington. I think you can go straight in,' she said, after the obligatory ten-second wait for her to stop typing and look up from her laptop.

Nick Crane was sitting at his vast, blonde-wood desk, fiddling with some papers and files in front of him.

'Clover,' he said warmly, as though I was the only person in the world he had been wanting to see. Which was unlikely.

He stood up and came forward to shake my hand, which in

itself was unusual.

'Sit down. Can I get you coffee? Tea? Mineral water? Almond croissant?'

I shook my head. 'No, I'm fine thanks.'

'Big muffin?'

Yes, you are, I thought. *Tasteless and full of hot air.*

'No, nothing thanks,' I smiled sweetly.

I went to sit down, my heels catching in the thick pile carpet so that I stumbled a little and had to catch hold of the back of the chair. I cursed, *Why at moments like this one did I have to be such a klutz?* I really was safer sitting down behind a desk.

'Good. Good,' Nick said, as he sat down again, steepling his fingers in front of him and giving a huge sigh.

'Clover, Clover, Clover. I have a few things to discuss. None of them easy and none of them can go beyond these four walls for now. Is that okay?'

'Of course,' I said, folding my hands in my lap and adopting a professional expression.

He slapped his hands down on the desk in front of him. 'Well, I won't beat about the bush. XS – "Finance with Heart" – is being taken over. Yes, yes, I know it's a shock. It's going to be a shock to all the little people. XS has been in their sights for a while now, it's an American company, and the deal will be finalised on Friday.'

I'll admit I was completely poleaxed. None of this had reached my ears. Or Nina's, which was astonishing.

How would this affect me, I wondered, my thoughts whirling. As one of the supposedly 'little people', how would things change? Perhaps it would mean more trips to America? I wouldn't mind that. Better than Scandinavia, where I had spent a lot of time over the last year. It was a beautiful place and the people were lovely, but I'd been there in January; it was dark most of the time, and everything seemed so expensive.

'Really?' I said. 'How interesting.'

'Isn't it,' he said with unnecessary emphasis.

I began to get my thoughts together and feel a tiny bit optimistic. 'I've a great pipeline, plenty of opportunities, which could be very beneficial to the company. I've completed so many since I have headed up business, I can't remember exactly.' I noticed he had my personnel file open in front of him. 'Well, you can see in there. It must be dozens.'

Perhaps he was looking so uncertain because he wanted me to transfer to a new office, New York, or Washington perhaps. I wouldn't mind that either. I was in a relationship that was going nowhere, my only son was living in Canada. Perhaps I would be able to see him more often too? Which would give me the chance to...

He closed my file with a firm hand. 'Well, you see it's not quite that simple, Clover.'

For the first time I felt a little chill of doubt.

'You see, it's Water Cheeseman Pole. They are the firm taking over.'

I rummaged around in my memory banks. Water Cheeseman Pole, yes, of course I'd heard of them. The name always made me imagine some Dairylea cheese triangles floating down a river in a punt. One of the biggest finance companies in New England. Maybe Boston, I thought. No, they were in Hartford, Connecticut. That's where a lot of finance and insurance companies were based. So perhaps I would end up there.

'How exciting,' I said, 'what a marvellous opportunity.'

'I knew you'd understand,' Nick continued. 'They will be bringing in some of their best people. To work here, deal with the handover while things get settled. Get rid of the dead wood in the company.'

I nodded. 'Of course. I'd be happy to help with that. Once I get the Olafsen deal all wrapped up. And there are several other—'

Nick held up a hand. 'You mustn't worry about that, Clover. I'm sure after all the pressures of the last few years... what with one thing and another, at your age, you'll appreciate having more time.'

'Time for what?' I said, confused.

* * *

By far the most infuriating part of that morning, and the thing I later couldn't un-see, was Nick Crane's shoes. Why did they bother me so much?

I'd just been made redundant. I wasn't just one of what he had patronisingly called the little people, which was bad enough. I was also part of the dead wood.

As I'd been escorted, shellshocked, out of his office, I had hurried past the people waiting for the lifts and he had followed me down several flights of stairs. Almost at the bottom, I had turned to remonstrate with him one last time. He had stopped too, standing several steps above me, presumably to keep as far away as possible from the disease of my downfall.

His shoes were in my direct eyeline. They were a bright chestnut brogue, the leather laces neatly threaded and tied in a prissy little bow. They were narrow, like little model canoes, polished as bright as a showroom car and rather pointed. He had small feet for such a big, fat liar.

I guessed, knowing Nick, they were new, Italian, and very expensive. I had an overwhelming urge to pull my lipstick out and draw a smiley face on them with Hermès Rouge Amazone. But of course, I didn't. That would have been petty and undignified.

We both stopped for a moment.

'Sorry, Clover,' he said, in a voice that said *I'm not sorry at all*, 'these things happen, there was nothing I could do. Trust me, I wrestled with the board on your behalf.'

An unpleasant image of him in a black, wrestling singlet came to mind and I felt a bit nauseous.

'How kind of you to try. On my behalf,' I said through stiff lips. 'Yet here we are.'

'Now take care on the stairs, sweetheart, we don't want you to have a fall, do we?'

He gave one of his smarmy smiles. He was enjoying this.

I'd always known what an untrustworthy, sociopathic weasel Nick Crane was underneath his carefully tailored suits, overpowering aftershave and bright teeth. This was probably the most enjoyable thing he'd done since he caught his PA in the stock room with a junior accountant at the Christmas party.

'You're going to be such a great loss to XS,' he said, as people dodged around us on the flashy steel and glass staircase leading to the front doors, their eyes averted, keen not to be dragged into this. The brown cardboard bankers box Nick was carrying for me spoke volumes.

'I am, aren't I? Tell me where I have made mistakes? Where have I let the company down?'

He gave me a sad smile. 'Oh, you would never do that, I know.'

Patronising git.

'No, I know I haven't. I've brought in every deal I have ever made. Except this last one. And I would have done. I can't imagine what you will do now with the Olafsen takeover,' I said. I tapped my temple. 'It's all in here.'

'Oh, I expect we will manage,' he said smoothly, 'after all we will have your laptop. I'm sure that will help.'

'I hope—' I stopped.

I had been going to say I hoped the rest of his life would

morph into a long, disappointing nightmare, starting with his veneers falling out, but I didn't.

'I hope you will look after Nina,' I said. 'She is an excellent secretary. She's invaluable.'

'Of course,' he said, shuffling his vile footwear, eager to carry on with his task of escorting me out of the building like some sort of creepy nanny.

I couldn't help myself. I rummaged in my handbag, pulled out my Rouge Amazone and after giving him a furious look, daubed it all over the pointy toes of his shoes. He looked down in silent horror for a moment and then he started to bluster. His voice became rather squeaky.

'New... my mother bought... *birthday* present!'

I clipped the top back onto my lipstick. 'Perhaps next year she will buy you some Lego. Now, come on, hurry up, there's a good boy.'

He hopped about for a moment and then silently followed me. His mouth set in a nasty little line.

As we reached the front doors, he put my pathetic box of possessions down with a meaningful thump and made a great play of winding the lanyard of my security card around his fingers. It was only eight twenty and people were still arriving at the XS offices for work. They looked at me sideways, curious. *Schadenfreude*, I suppose you could call it.

Rather her than me.

Nick Crane tried to hide his feet behind a potted palm.

I looked around, wondering if I would see anyone else doing the walk of shame. No one. I picked up my box of possessions; it felt pathetically light. Over twenty years I had worked for XS – 'Finance with Heart' – and all I had to take away with me was a porcelain mug, a Manilla envelope stuffed with redundancy documents, a leather pencil case Jack gave me for Christmas, two framed certificates and a hideous glass award from last year's company event.

I was sixty-one, shouldn't I have more to show for twenty-two years than that?

I swallowed down my panic. Whatever happened, I was not going to cry in front of Nick Crane.

But what was I going to do? I wasn't prepared for this; I wasn't ready to retire. I loved my work; I always had. Without it I was lost. No one was going to employ me now, not at my age. Even though I felt and looked younger thanks to a lot of money and effort. I looked down at my newly manicured nails, which were immaculate. Trying to gain some comfort from them. I was effectively being retired against my will. To do what?

'Well, that's it then,' Nick said, fishing in his pocket for a handkerchief and making feeble attempts to clean the lipstick off his shoes without falling over. He was forty-seven: he had years left in front of him to fill with reports, complaints and dismissal procedures. He would have been eager to get back to his glass-walled office and his brass plaque and his shelf full of stupid trophies and start gleefully phoning around his friends to tell them how he had just ushered Clover Harrington out of the building. And adding embellishing details, no doubt.

'Yes, I suppose so,' I replied.

My right eyelid was itching, but I wasn't going to scratch it in case he started a rumour that I had broken down in tears.

'Well, there we go. Good luck with everything, and if there's anything I can do, you just have to ask,' Nick said, through his now-gritted teeth.

He had recovered some of his composure by this time, although I didn't think his shoes would ever be quite the same again. Perhaps his mother would spend the evening digging out the lipstick with a cotton bud.

I was suddenly very angry. *I used to wipe the floor with boys like you*, I thought. *I still could. Just come out with me behind the office building to the smoker's lair and I'll smack the smile off your face in five minutes, you utter twat.* His Ferragamo Oxford brogues would have been the least of his worries.

I remembered when he started here, wet behind the ears and thinking he was Bill Gates. And yet he had somehow risen through the ranks to become director of HR. A living, breathing example of the Peter Principle, where people were shunted ever upwards in a corporation until they found a role where their incompetence wouldn't be noticed.

'Just tell me the truth. Why?' I said.

He looked hunted for a fleeting second and then his layers of professional smarm washed over him again.

'Just one of those things,' he said. 'Blame the Americans. You know what they are like.'

I know what you're *like*, I thought.

And we both knew the real reasons although of course no one would have said them for fear of a lawsuit.

The first glass ceiling in life was being a woman, only broken through with a lot of hard work, persistence and determination. The second glass ceiling was age and that one seemed bullet proof.

'You could open the door for me,' I said, my voice very calm.

'Oh, of course,' he said, darting forwards, his knees rather high, treading carefully around me.

'How kind. I can't understand why everyone talks about you the way they do,' I said, and gave him a frosty smile.

His expression faltered as I walked past him and out into the world of the unemployed.

2

_____

Outside the building that spring morning was cold and crisp. There had been snow the previous week and dirty clumps of it still hung around. I picked my way through to the taxi rank at the end of the street, passing people hurrying towards the building, ecologically friendly coffee cups in hand. They were starting their day, off to punch in numbers, pore over spreadsheets, have back-to-back meetings in various offices where everything would be discussed, and nothing would be decided.

'Where are you going, Clover?' someone shouted.

I turned to see Gerry Sage, senior something-or-other. He was just arriving, a horrifying vision in red Lycra and a stupid cycling helmet to match his stupid bike. I couldn't think of what to say so I ignored him and just kept on walking.

I went towards the taxi at the head of the line, the pedestrians parting on either side of me as I approached them. Avoiding my gaze. Carrying my distinctive banker's box, I felt like a leper ringing a bell.

I was going home, back to my beautiful apartment over-looking the Thames, where I would sit in the quiet kitchen, make coffee with the complicated machine Jack had bought me for my birthday and watch the traffic on the river.

I thought of phoning Jack but of course at that moment I couldn't. Nick had confiscated my work phone and my personal one was left at home because I hardly ever needed it. I was a woman with no laptop, no phone and no job.

It felt as though I had lost some vital part of myself. My shoulder yearned for the weight of my laptop bag, the security of my iPhone 14 in my jacket pocket. I would have to dig out the old one and see how many phone numbers I still had that would be any use to me.

I felt a new frisson of fear mixed with panic. When the news of my redundancy filtered out, would the head-hunters contact me? How many companies would have a job for a woman my age? And what would Nick Crane say if he was asked for a reference?

A man in my position would be able to trawl round contacts at his club. The old boys' network gearing up at top speed. Non-executive directorships falling at their feet like confetti.

How would I talk to people if I didn't know their phone number and they didn't know my new one? I still had a stack of other people's business cards somewhere, perhaps in my desk at home. I would have to buy a new laptop too. My personal one had been stuck in a drawer for months; it had never been the same since Jack knocked a glass of wine over the keyboard.

And, oh god, what would my mother say when I told her I'd been made redundant? I could just imagine her expression. Sitting in her chair in the bay window, holding court over all the other residents. She'd enjoyed a lot of kudos off the back of my success in business.

What would my son think? What would Jack say? Nothing helpful, I was sure.

Our friends, old work colleagues? The prospect of telling

them all was ghastly. Before today I'd felt invincible, capable and valued. Now I realised I'd probably been an obvious target. I was over sixty. I had been expensive. I'd probably been near the top of the redundancy list right at the moment that XS had been cherry-picked by that cheesy, punting American company.

Three months' salary, a golden goodbye and – in case I decided to steal company secrets or contacts – straight onto gardening leave. What a joke. I didn't have a garden; I didn't even have a window box. I had a convincing but artificial rubber plant in the corner of my living room and some silk roses in a bowl on the landing. My 'gardening' was little more than a quick flick-over with a duster.

I rested my head on the taxi window as the crowded streets flew past.

I had been due to fly to Oslo in two days to speak to a room full of self-important people, the following week I was booked into a five-star hotel for a corporate dinner to celebrate the deal. I'd bought a new outfit too: a long, hand-beaded dress from Alexander McQueen. I hadn't eaten any carbs for a month because of it.

I hadn't ever been unemployed, not since I'd left university. Even while I was at school, I'd had Saturday jobs. I just couldn't get my head around it. What on earth was I going to do with my time?

* * *

'Sue them,' Jack said that evening. 'Take them to an unemployment tribunal. You didn't make any mistakes, you never upset anyone. You could screw thousands out of them. No warning, no discussion and dragged out of the building as though you were a criminal. It's humiliating and degrading.'

He had been sitting comfortably in his favourite armchair, one leg crossed over the other, one foot bobbing, a glass of eighteen-year-old Macallan in one hand.

'I have three months' salary and they have agreed to pay me an extraneous payment for the Olafsen deal,' I said.

Jack scoffed. 'Chicken feed. Get onto that solicitor friend of yours. Bill what's-his-name.'

'I can't, I don't have his personal number any more.'

'Well, just ring the office,' Jack said impatiently. 'Are we eating this evening or not? I worked through lunch. I know I said I would try and get away early and pick something up, but you know how things are. Step out of the office for an hour and you miss things. I'd be out of the loop in no time.'

'Thanks for that comment, so sensitive of you,' I said, knocking back my gin and tonic.

'No good going over it, Clover, it's done now. It's not my fault. Is there any food in the place or shall I phone for something? You'll never guess what happened in the office this afternoon? This will make you laugh. Remember Cameron Wallace? Tall bloke with glasses and a Lamborghini. He was telling me—'

I looked over at him rabbiting on, and felt a sudden, unexpected bolt of anger towards him. We'd been together for nearly six years, matched in our success and drive, and yet there he sat, comfortable in his Ralph Lauren casual wear, drinking whisky and ignoring my feelings.

I would have thought he could have spared me one evening to talk and commiserate. But no, as usual we were straight onto hedge funds, arbitrage and net market exposure as though nothing had happened. No wonder his wife had left him, if this was how he reacted to her difficulties. The feeling that I didn't like him at all, that I didn't even want to be in the same room as him, was growing.

'This is the worst day of my life,' I blurted out in the middle of his story about how clever he had been.

Jack blinked at me.

'It'll pass, petal,' he said at last. 'What doesn't kill you makes you stronger. Shall I order Thai?'

He pulled out his phone and dialled our local restaurant, placing the order he always did.

I sat there wondering if perhaps killing him would make me feel stronger.

I could almost imagine luring him out onto the balcony with the pretext of a Red Arrow flypast or a street brawl and watching him plummet twelve floors. Or perhaps it would be more satisfying to bludgeon him with his whisky bottle? No, then I'd definitely be arrested for murder: the perfect end to a perfect day.

'Here in ten minutes,' he said, pleased. 'By the way, petal, you haven't forgotten I'm going to be away for the weekend, have you? Off to Bonnie Scotland for golf with wee Alasdair and Raj first thing tomorrow morning.'

I tried to ignore his irritating take on a Scottish accent.

'Of course I haven't forgotten. And don't call me petal.'

'I can't wait...! It's going to be enormous fun – the boys on tour again. We've booked a car to take us to the airport... If we'd known you were free you could have taken us. Never mind it's too late to change it.'

He looked over at me and perhaps realised the depth of his insensitivity.

'It'll probably be good for you to have a few days on your own. Get your head round things. You've always sailed through everything. I can see this must be a shock.'

'I haven't sailed through things – I worked hard. I was meticulous. I have the spreadsheets to prove it.'

He wasn't really paying attention. 'We'll be back late Sunday evening. You could get some food in before then too. There never seems to be anything in the freezer but vodka. You might like to knock up something for when we get back.'

'What a treat for me,' I said waspishly. 'Perhaps I could iron some of your shirts too.'

'Don't do that,' he said absently, as he topped up his whisky glass. 'You don't do them properly.'

I sent him a hard look. 'You really don't care that this is the worst day of my life, do you? That I'm sitting here going absolutely crazy with what happened to me today and all you can think about is food and a whisky-swilling weekend with your foul-mouthed friends.'

'Of course I care,' he said, offended, 'but you'll be fine.'

'How? How will I be fine?' I spat.

'You could just retire,' he said. 'You're sixty-one. You're old enough for a bus pass. That was a joke! Calm down. You're financially secure, healthy... Your son will probably give you a grandchild soon. That'll distract you.'

'Ben lives in Vancouver. How exactly am I to offer to babysit?'

'Look, you are one of the most organised people I know. You'll work something out,' Jack said. The buzzer sounded. 'Ah, there's the food. I'll go down and get it, shall I?'

'Unless you think it's something *I* should do, you know, to start filling my time?' I said.

Jack got up, his eyes alight. 'There's bags of money in consultancy! Now – that's a brilliant idea! You know everyone, everyone knows you. I bet you could get a few people on board. I'll bet there are others who would like to leave XS or people who have been chucked out just like you.'

'So I round up all the rejects and try and make a thing out of it? Are you quite sane?'

Jack shook his head. 'That's not what I meant, and you know it. Come on, Clover, this isn't like you.'

'I am dying here,' I cried. 'I was assured, heaven knows how many times, that everything was going well. Once the Olafsen deal was done, I'd be invited onto the board. That I would be a director when Howard Leeming left. That nasty oaf Nick Crane lied to my face on at least three occasions. And once in an email. And then he has the gall to call me up to his office like some sort of intern and hand me this damn thing!'

I shook the Manilla envelope at him, and some sheets of paper fell out. Advice, help lines, a leaflet for the Samaritans. My eyes filled with tears, a mixture of anger and self-pity. I found a tissue in my pocket and blew my nose. I didn't think I had ever felt so alone.

Jack hesitated, his hand on the door handle. The buzzer sounded again, impatiently.

'I'll just go down and get the food and then I'll be back, and we can have a nice meal together and talk it through. You might like to open a bottle of wine. Okay?'

He trotted off towards the lifts, the door swinging closed behind him, and I sat, biting a thumb nail, and worried about what I was going to do with the rest of my life. And then I remembered Nick Crane's shoes and I was angry all over again. But at the same time I almost felt like laughing.

* * *

We didn't enjoy a nice meal together that evening because I didn't feel much like eating anything. I sat on my side of the table fiddling with my old mobile and being irritated and occasionally angered by Jack diligently chomping away opposite me. He worked his way through his Thai green curry, some prawn toast things and most of the roast duck, and then had a go at my Penang and noodles while I picked at a few oddments. I gave monosyllabic answers to his questions, and he didn't seem to notice.

We went into the kitchen with the dirty dishes, and I pulled another bottle of his favourite Chablis out from the wine chiller. He watched me open it and pour two glasses.

I may not have fancied the food very much, but I did fancy the wine and I knocked back quite a lot that evening. Half of the first bottle and most of the second. It didn't help as much as I'd have liked, but it did dull the pain a bit. Perhaps this is what I would do with my retirement: drink too much.

'I want to go on holiday,' I said at last when there was a break in the conversation.

'What do you mean? You want to go on holiday? Why?'

'I need a break, away from all this,' I said.

Jack looked at me, his face creased with incomprehension.

'I can't just swan off on holiday *now*,' he said. 'I'm right in the middle of stuff. Important stuff that's going to make me a lot of money if the dominoes fall right. I had a real breakthrough today; I was really cooking on gas. Everything was going brilliantly. In fact I'm hoping next week will see some real progress. You'll have to leave it for a few weeks.'

'I don't want to.'

I turned to look at him, sitting in his expensive clothes, his hair brushed sleekly back from his broad intelligent forehead. He was a very handsome man, it was true. Well-educated, successful, just muscular enough to be attractive. I could still remember why he had appealed to me, how he had won me round with his sparkling blue eyes, his easy charm and his grand gestures of opera tickets, birthday parties on the Thames, Christmas in Verbier.

We'd had a lot of fun to start with and he spent most of his time at my apartment, just going back to his occasionally when he needed some different clothes, when friends of mine came to stay or when he wanted to enjoy some 'me time'. This was generally to meet up with his buddies from work, drink designer beer and stay up all night watching American golf tournaments from Augusta or California. But now that this had happened, I doubted we had anything in common to hold us together. So far that evening, it had seemed unlikely.

'Where would you go?' he said at last, taking a sip of his wine.

'I don't know,' I said. 'I need a break from this blasted place.'

We went back into the sitting room.

'How can anyone need a break from London?' he said, genuinely puzzled.

'I don't know, but I do,' I said.

He sipped his wine thoughtfully, his eyes on the flickering gas fire with its poncey annoying white pebbles. He sighed heavily.

'I was going to arrange something later on, in May. As a surprise,' he said at last. 'I thought Mexico again or New York'

'I don't want a surprise. I don't want to go to Mexico or New York' I said, 'I want to go somewhere... beautiful and gentle and healing.'

Jack finished his wine and topped up his glass. 'Then I could find somewhere with a spa?'

'How sexist of you to think that all I need is a week in a spa, when my career is going down the pan.'

He sighed. 'Look I can tell this whole miserable business has really shaken you, but my advice is, get yourself straight back out there, networking, using your contacts, dropping the facts the news you are available into the right ears. Don't waste your time feeling sorry for yourself. I bet you'll have some of the head-hunters on the phone when the news gets out.'

'I don't have my phone, remember?'

'Well, perhaps you could email them?'

'I don't want to.'

'Oh, don't be so childish.'

'I'm not being childish,' I said through gritted teeth, realising I probably was. 'I am devastated, shocked and confused. How would you feel if it was you sitting there with a leaflet from the Samaritans? What the hell am I going to do? All I wanted was some sympathy, not some silly suggestions and yet more tales about what a great day you've had. Is that too much to ask? You're an insensitive clod sometimes.'

He looked offended. 'I'm sorry you feel that way, but you know I'm not one for encouraging someone else's self-pity.'

'I never asked you to. I just wanted one evening when you could show me some sympathy, some kindness.'

'I'm trying to make positive suggestions,' he said.

'No, you're not, you're just ignoring my feelings as usual.'

His eyebrows shot up. 'I've always been very sensitive to your feelings. God knows there are enough of them. Perhaps it's your hormones?'

'You have the sensitivity of a sawn-off shotgun, actually, Jack. *Sorry you're not feeling very well, sorry your father has died, sorry your car got pranged in the car park but let's talk about me.* Because that's all that interests you, isn't it?'

'There's no talking to you in this state.'

'Then don't. Don't talk to me. I'm sick of this. Look, Jack, I think it's time you and I called it a day. When you get back from Scotland, I want you to pack up your stuff and move out.'

'You don't mean that.'

'Yes, I do.'

I got up, poured myself a glass of water and stalked off to bed.

3
——————

The following day, Thursday, it was perhaps just as well that I wasn't going into work because I had a monstrous hangover. I supposed I deserved it but knowing that didn't help with my mood.

I had been hoping Jack would spend the night on the sofa but no. He sprang out of bed at six o'clock as though nothing had happened and straight into the shower in our en-suite.

He always made a lot of noise in the bathroom, sinus-clearing and coughing; you would think he smoked fifty a day. Then there was a lot of splashing noises which meant the wet room floor would be like a driving school skid pan when I went in there. At last, he came out, bringing with him the whiff of Armani Prive Indigo and three damp towels which he dumped on the floor next to the washing basket.

I lay on my side, looking at the towels and feeling furious.

Why? Why would anyone do that? How much more thought or effort was it to actually put them *inside it*? I suppose he thought the staff would clear up after him, i.e., me.

He whistled a few bars of 'Scotland the Brave'. He was obviously in a jubilant mood.

'Not up yet, petal?' he said cheerfully. 'Oh, I was forgetting. You don't have work, do you? Lucky old you. Well just stay there and enjoy a bit of a lie in. You deserve it.'

I raised my head, about to ask if he would bring me a cup of tea.

He looked out of the window to the street below. 'The car's here,' he said. 'I'm off then, I've got to get to the airport. Don't worry about me, I'll pick up some coffee on the way,' he said, grabbing his jacket from the valet stand by the bedroom door. He swung it onto his arms and adjusted his shirt cuffs. Then he blew me a kiss.

'Don't get up to mischief. I'll see you Sunday evening. Perhaps you could knock up something simple. Like a lasagne?'

'Lasagne is not simple!' I shouted after him.

I heard him bounce his suitcase down the stairs.

'I want you to leave,' I yelled.

Soon after I heard the front door slam shut.

No real mention of the previous evening, or of my upset feelings. Of the ultimatum I had given him. I felt odd, disconnected with everything, slightly panicky.

I lay there and thought about things and took a few deep breaths to calm down. I had a headache and a bad case of morning breath. I needed some paracetamol and a cup of tea. The last thing I wanted was to get out of bed and fetch them, but really there was no alternative.

Wearily I threw back the duvet and pulled on my dressing gown. I stood at the window watching a boat chug down the river. Those men had a job. My day stretched ahead of me. I had no idea how I was going to fill it. Perhaps I should go and tell my mother, as a first step.

I was used to sweeping into work, doors held open for me. Nina would be there handing me a sheaf of papers with pink post-it notes attached, quietly passing on the gossip and tid-bits of news that she thought might be interesting or useful. My head would be buzzing with an adrenalin high; I was respected; I had a purpose; I had a place in the world; and I fitted it perfectly. Well, not any more, obviously. None of those things.

I made tea and looked for painkillers. There was a packet in the bathroom cabinet that I pounced on with relief. Then I realised Jack had done his usual trick of putting the empty box back. Why? *Why* would anyone do that? It was just about the last straw.

I gave a quiet growl of rage, because anything louder would have hurt my head, and threw the packet into the bin.

About twenty-seven seconds later the answer came to me.

I did need to get away now. Not in a few weeks when it suited Jack. Now.

Far away. From here, from this flat, from Jack. From the chasms in our relationship that had now widened into a bottom-less pit. Soon, if not now, then tomorrow. I couldn't bear to be here surrounded by all the things that had once made me happy, but now just served to remind me of being on the scrap heap. I needed a proper holiday, the first one I had taken in years.

Well perhaps that wasn't exactly true because of course I'd had holidays. But even as I sat on a beach in Cancun or stood overlooking the ocean in the Seychelles, I knew those places and those holidays had been Jack's choice, not mine.

I'd never been the sort of person to just sit around drinking cocktails from hollowed out fruit, although of course I liked cock-tails as much as the next person. I'd never liked sunbathing. I hated trying to read my iPad, squinting against the sun, and I loathed lying on a sunbed, in a row of other sunbeds, with absolutely nothing to occupy my mind. But that was the sort of thing I'd ended up doing because that's what Jack liked. And as he had organised everything and paid for us to be there, it would have seemed ungrateful to complain.

He'd generally gone off and booked them 'as a surprise' and once 'as a birthday present', but the truth was that he had decided which holiday he liked the sound of, and then booked it in secret so that he didn't have to discuss it with me.

His idea of torture was wandering around the streets of a medieval city, visiting excavation sites of ancient settlements – basically anything that involved museums, art galleries or culture – unless they were the backdrop to a black-tie event with a few celebrities thrown in for good measure.

Well, this was going to be my choice, my holiday, my thing.

For inspiration, I went to look at the row of travel books arranged neatly on the bookshelf, but they too were Jack's choices. I needed something less 'sophisticated', less trendy, more grounded.

But where?

I went into the kitchen and opened a few cupboard doors, looking for biscuits now that my carb-fast was over. My gaze fastened onto some Rustichella d'Abruzzo spaghetti I had bought because it had a beautiful, rather baroque, pattern on the tin. I almost closed the door again. Even in an emergency, I couldn't eat raw pasta. Then I stopped.

Italy. I liked Italy. I liked the warmth, the pasta of course, the countryside, the red wine... It was years since I'd been there. I rummaged around in my memory trying to recall where I'd gone and why.

Of course, over thirty years ago I'd visited my cousin. Zoe Russell, now Zoe Rossi. She'd been getting married to Paulo. Tall, dark-haired, smiling all the time.

It all came back to me then: that long weekend in the Italian Lakes when they got married, Paulo's huge family, all those old aunts and uncles, a celebration, laughter, dancing, vines coiled around the pergolas, a fabulous view over a lake, the mountains in the distance providing the perfect backdrop. That's what I needed. That's what I was going to have.

I'd returned the summer after Casper and I had divorced, and that time I went on my own. Three-year-old Ben had gone to my parents for a week. The guilt and the grief my mother had caused me for years afterwards was worth it. The freedom and the occasion made for a wonderful few days. I could almost remember the feeling.

Zoe had visited me in London a few times since then, but why on earth hadn't I gone back there before now?

I picked up my laptop. Perhaps I would send Zoe an email, explaining I needed a break, asking if she knew of any little rental properties overlooking the lake. I'd suggested going there with Jack the year after we got together, and he had visibly shuddered. The next thing I knew, we were off on a 'surprise holiday' to Thailand.

Then, impulsively, I picked up my old mobile, which was still charging and connected to the cable, knocking a pile of unopened post off the worktop onto the floor as I did so. I left it there. Then I went looking for my address book, something I only ever used once a year to write Christmas cards.

'Zoe? It's Clover. Yes, it's me! How are you?'

4

Why had I been so nervous about telling my seventy-nine-year-old mother that I had been made redundant? It was quite ridiculous. But then she had always been the sort of mother who lapped up the good stuff and preferred not to know the bad. I hadn't told her that Casper and I had split up until the decree nisi had come through and I had engaged a Norland nanny.

I drove into the gravelled car park at Winchester Hall, stepped out and took a deep breath.

* * *

I found my mother sitting in her room reading, feet up on a tapestry footstool. She turned.

'What a lovely surprise,' my mother said, 'I wasn't expecting you until next weekend.'

I went over to kiss her cheek. 'You're looking well.'

She was too. She'd been stunning in her youth, and now at seventy-nine she still was. Her silver hair was cut into a beautiful bob; her blue eyes were sparkling and intelligent.

She waved me to a chair beside her.

'Do you know, I think I need a holiday. It's years since I had a proper trip anywhere. I'd love to fly somewhere but I'm guessing it's out of the question. I was sure my blood pressure was rocketing last week; it was a wonder I didn't pass out. The locum doctor gave me some new tablets, and he dared me, absolutely *dared* me, to go to my keep fit class. Oh, don't worry! I'm much better now.'

'That's good news,' I said.

'I think there is too much salt in the food here, that's the problem. I said to Janine as much – you know her, she's the old woman in the suite next to mine – and she agreed with me.'

I knew for a fact than Janine was only a year older than my mother, but I didn't labour the point.

'We were thinking of starting a petition.'

'Why don't you just say something?' I said weakly.

'Oh, that wouldn't work,' Mum scoffed. 'You have to put it in writing with these people. Otherwise, they take no notice. Sometimes it's as though we are just a nuisance to them, to the management.'

'The fees you pay to live here are astronomical. I would have thought they would listen to what you want,' I said.

Mum nodded. 'You would think that, and you'd be wrong. Janine said she wanted a visit from the chiropodist; she has bunions from all those years of wearing stilettos. Well, it was as though she'd asked for cracked cocaine. Or a visit from John Nettles. She said the girl – I won't call her a nurse – rolled her eyes so much it was a wonder one of them didn't fall out. Talk about a face crime!'

I could feel the energy draining out of me by the minute.

'But otherwise you are well?' I said after my mother had paused for a moment.

'Well, actually, all things considered I am. Oh, but what's the alternative?' Mum said. 'I'll be eighty in August. If the Lord spares me. That's a terrible age.'

'It's a wonderful age,' I said brightly.

'Really? How odd of you to think that. What are you doing anyway? Shouldn't you be at work? I thought you had some big contract on the cards. The Swedes.'

'Norwegians. Well, yes, but... well I'm not part of that any more,' I said.

She huffed a bit indignantly. 'Don't tell me they've moved you onto sort out something else. I bet they are trying to stop you getting a bonus, aren't they?'

'Well, no, not exactly—'

'It's disgraceful. But typical. Women do all the work and then at the last minute the men steam in and claim all the credit.'

'No, it's more—'

'You wait. One of that pack of hyenas will be turning up in a new Mercedes next month, crowing about how clever he is.'

'I've been made redundant,' I said, blurting it out when my mother paused to draw a breath.

'Nonsense,' Mum said firmly.

There was a long pause while the information sunk in.

'You've been made redundant?' she said at last, her voice lowered to a conspiratorial whisper. 'But how? Why? Surely not? I was having tea with Sylvia and telling the new woman, Peggy, about you only yesterday. Peggy was rabbiting on, showing off about her son who is some sort of minor official on the council. You would think he ran the United Nations the way she brags. *Eleanor, do you know, my son is responsible for county-wide recycling!* It's really quite sickening. I almost asked if he worked on the bin lorries. Instead, I told her all about you. Soon to be a director. That shut her up, I can tell you. I was so pleased.'

'XS have been taken over by an American company. It was all very hush-hush – I only heard about it the day I was made redundant.'

My mother rustled about in her handbag, pulled out a tissue and blew her nose.

'You've broken my heart, doing that,' she said at last in a small, tearful voice. 'How could you?'

'Well, I didn't make myself redundant on purpose. I'm not exactly thrilled about it,' I said.

'I suppose not. Oh dear. So, when did this happen?'

'Wednesday. I was escorted out of the building half an hour after I got there.'

My mother gasped. 'No! How terrible. Did anyone see you?'

'Well of course they did! Lots of people,' I said.

Her voice dropped to a secretive hiss. 'You should sue. Sue someone. I wish Daddy was still alive, he would know what to do. No, I take that back. It's just as well he's not alive, this would have killed him.'

I sighed. 'Mum, stop it. I'm not going to prison; I just don't have a job. How do you think *I* feel?'

This was why I had dreaded telling her. She had always demonstrated a startling lack of empathy when it came to this sort of thing. I remember when Casper and I got divorced, her only concern was what she would tell the vicar when she next saw him.

'Well, there must be something you can do?' she said at last.

'No. There isn't.'

'All that education and then this happens. I've decided I'm not going to tell anyone. Not until you have some good news to announce,' she said bravely, 'not until then.'

'I am sixty-one,' I said. 'That's the age a lot of people retire.'

'I've told everyone you're fifty,' she said. 'I can't have a daughter who is sixty-one.'

'You were a child bride,' I said.

'I was,' she said, slightly mollified. 'Eighteen! An *absolute* child. Do you know my wedding dress had a twenty-inch waist measurement? Smaller than Princess Margaret's.'

'Yes, you've told me many times.'

'And now look at me. A fat old woman living in a home for derelicts. I wish I could go on holiday.'

'Oh, stop it, you're nothing of the sort.'

Five years ago, after my father's death, she had moved her vast collection of clothes and shoes into Winchester Hall, a vast Georgian manor house that had been converted into luxurious apartments for the over fifty-fives. She was much envied for having the biggest and best ground-floor suite which had turned into a sort of gathering point for the aging glitterati. She seemed to hold court pretty much in the style of Jackie Kennedy in her heyday, and invitations to her occasional Sunday afternoon tea parties were much sought after.

'So, what on earth will you do now?' Mum asked.

'I rang Zoe last night, to ask if I could go and stay with them.'

'Dear Zoe. Such a shame,' she said.

'What's a shame?' I said, my hackles rising.

'Well, you know. All that education and then she goes off to marry some Italian gigolo and run a pub. She broke her mother's heart, you know.'

Hmm, I'd forgotten this cracked record.

'No, she didn't, Mum, and Auntie Gladys loved Paulo, you know she did. She went at least once every year to stay with them. You could have gone with her too; she always wanted you to. And he never was a gigolo.'

'Well, that's not the impression I got. Are they well?'

'Yes, she sounds very happy *indeed*,' I said pointedly, 'absolutely thriving. And they are not running a pub. It's a trattoria. Such a perfect setting, with a glorious view over the lake.'

My mother's sniff of disapproval spoke volumes.

'Do they have proper facilities?'

'You mean electricity and running water? Of course they do,' I said, exasperated. 'I'm sure there's a roof and indoor toilets too.'

You see, I did love my mother, but I forgot every time how she could make my mood slump, my optimism shrivel and my good humour disappear into stomach-turning irritation.

'Well how lovely for you,' she said sadly, 'to be having a trip away. Even if it is to the back of beyond. That's not going to find you a new job though, is it?'

I wondered how soon I could end this conversation; I was getting more depressed by the second. Why had I even thought that my mother would understand? I felt a tiny part of myself, my self-belief, shrivel even further.

I took a deep breath. 'I hope you have been keeping busy?'

'I have. We had a talk from someone who trained at the London Flower School. About table decorations. It was quite interesting although personally I always understood chrysanthemums to be very passé. Perhaps they are in vogue again.'

'That sounds marvellous,' I said.

'I don't care what she said, I won't be putting bits of stick in my arrangements. Or cabbages.'

'No. Well I'm glad you are enjoying life here,' I said.

At least one of us had a routine, some social life. Which was more than I had. Life in the last few months had consisted of going to work early and coming back late. Social occasions had been dwindling to either my or Jack's company events.

'Yes, I can't complain,' Mum continued. 'I have a musical event to attend this afternoon. Some students from the university are coming to entertain us. With songs from the shows.' She threw me a knowing look. 'The excitement here is positively feverish.'

'How marvellous,' I replied. I almost felt like crying.

'Well, I very much doubt it. Knowing my luck, they will be doing *Cats* or that awful French *Miserable* thing with all the flag-waving, and you know how I loathe that.'

'Fingers crossed then,' I said brightly. 'Have fun.'

'I'll try,' she said bravely.

5

So, I'd arrived in Italy.

To be honest, it was a shock after everything that had happened recently. Had it really only been days since I'd known what I was doing, where my life was going? Now everything was up for grabs, so to speak.

I wasn't just Thinking Outside the Box, now I was actually Outside the Box.

I had no job: that was the unbelievable thing. I still hadn't got my head around it.

I had taken an early flight to Bergamo, where I followed the herd through security to where all the officials seemed unfeasibly attractive. I was still able to appreciate a finely chiselled jaw and dark sparkling eyes, even at my age.

I pulled my cases off the carousel; the baggage reclaim area was the usual scrum of family groups and bickering couples looking for their luggage. Dads looking manly and heaving huge bags off the conveyor belt, mums muttering through clenched teeth at their travel-weary children. And me, on my own, finding my way to the arrivals' hall, hoping against hope that Zoe would be there to meet me as she had promised. She'd always been a bit scatter-brained; it was quite possible she'd forgotten I was coming.

I went on past a colourful wall – a mural of lovely Italian scenery – and out towards the glass exit doors.

I looked around for a familiar face. It was three or possibly four years since Zoe and I had met up in London, but she couldn't have changed that much surely? I supposed I was looking for someone my age, of medium height and build, but with red hair that always made her stand out in a crowd. There were plenty of women standing around, most of them guarding suitcases or children, but none of them was my cousin. There were a few drivers in dark glasses, holding up laminated cards with complicated names written on them in black marker.

I parked my cases against a wall and stood, shading my eyes from the bright sunshine. Well, that in itself was a bonus after the dreary weather I'd left behind in London. It was unexpectedly warm for March too: people were wandering around in light jackets, not muffled up in a thick sweater and coat like I was. I could feel the sweat breaking out on my top lip. Nice.

Out of the corner of my eye I could sense a man looking at me, and then walking in my direction. I turned away, humming under my breath; no, I didn't need a taxi, or any help, thank you very much.

I walked a few steps and then chickened out and walked back; there had been enough warnings about leaving luggage unattended, I didn't want the police taking my cases away and blowing them up. I had all my best underwear in there.

The man was still there, and I could tell he was focussing on me now that the crowd of people had thinned out. *Go away*, I thought, slightly worried. He was holding up a card too, not laminated and wipe-clean like the official drivers', but just a piece of corrugated cardboard. With my name written on it in felt pen. And a smiley face.

Startled, I took a good look at him. He was about my vintage, tall, with silverish hair. Very attractive in an Italian, tanned, finely-profiled way. He had bright, brown eyes under thick brows, which were now looking directly at me. I fidgeted a bit and clutched my handbag a bit tighter.

'Clover Harrington?' he said, pointing at the cardboard. '*Permesso*, I think this must be you?'

Mmm! Nice accent, I thought. And then I pulled myself together and went back to being suspicious.

'Yes,' I said rather warily.

His face cleared and he grinned. He had a wide, pleasant smile, which under other circumstances I would have found appealing, but I had no idea who he was or why he knew my name. I looked around, hoping to see Zoe.

'*Scusi*. Zoe Rossi has sent me to collect you, didn't she tell you?' he said. 'She had a migraine this morning, *nulla di serio* – oh, nothing serious – but it wasn't safe for her to drive. So, I am here instead. Gio Agnello.'

He gave a little nod, smiled again, and held out a hand for me to shake. Which I did. He had a nice handshake – firm, but not too fierce like he was trying to establish some sort of dominance. I was a bit of an expert in that field. Over the years I'd shaken hands with everything from limp fish to Indian arm wrestlers.

And Zoe had sent him to collect me?

A likely tale. I could just imagine the headlines.

ENGLISH WOMAN, 61, MISSING IN BERGAMO

Clover Harrington was last seen leaving the airport with Gio Agnello, a man now known to be an international terrorist and people trafficker. Polizia di Stato and Interpol have asked for any information concerning her whereabouts.

This would be accompanied by some grainy footage from the airport security cameras of me walking confidently away with him to my doom.

'But I don't know anything about this,' I said, using the same sort of tone I had occasionally used in meetings when someone had been incompetent. It worked there; it didn't seem to work here.

He pulled out his phone and showed me a photograph of myself. It was the one taken from the XS website. Senior Business Manager. Specialism: outsourcing and company streamlining. What the hell did that actually mean?

I was looking groomed and sophisticated in the same red suit I had been wearing when I'd lost my job. My hair was newly highlighted and pulled back into a tight, French pleat. My arms were folded because I'd been wearing a new and incredibly uncomfortable bra that day – I could still remember it. My smile in the picture was rather forced and insincere as a result.

Yes, it had hoiked up my bosom and given me more of a waist for once, so perhaps it was worth the effort and the expense, but I'd had to go and change in the executive loos when the photoshoot was over.

The man twinkled his eyes at me.

'She said she would tell you. *Permesso.* Check your messages?'

I tucked my handbag behind my cases and pulled out my new mobile, embarrassed that I hadn't thought of that already.

I held out one hand towards him a little way, palm outwards to keep him at a distance. My fingers fumbled on the unfamiliar phone: I'd only had it for two days and I wasn't used to it yet.

After a very long wait and numerous text messages welcoming me to Italy and offering me all sorts of deals on my call rate that I didn't want, a text came through from my cousin. Sent while I was over the Alps.

Sorry Clover, have just finished a spectacular migraine. Nothing too bad but I can't drive. I've asked a neighbour/friend to come and pick you up. His name is Gio Agnello I'll send you a pic. He's very trustworthy. See you soon, can't wait! x

Under that was a picture of the man standing in front of me, taken on a veranda somewhere overlooking a lake, his hair ruffled by the breeze. Unless some very sophisticated criminals had hacked into Zoe's phone, I was going to be okay.

I turned back to Gio Agnello, firstly thinking what a great name that was, and secondly being relieved that he was not intending to gag me with gaffer tape and stuff me into the boot of his car.

I checked the photo and looked up at him again. The same smile, the same well-cut hair, the same humour-filled brown eyes.

He was standing patiently watching me, his hands in the pockets of his dark jeans. I didn't know why, but I'd always found it rather sexy when men did that. Perhaps it was because it emphasised their—

'Okay?' he said.

I bleached my thoughts. 'Mr Agnello—'

'Gio,' he said.

'Gio. Thank you for coming to collect me; I'm sorry if I seemed a little suspicious,' I said.

'No, *va bene*, it's fine. Of course you would be cautious – a lady on her own,' he said. 'Can I take your cases and we will find my car?'

At least he hadn't said *old lady* on her own. Perhaps he was being diplomatic. He did look the same sort of age as me, so perhaps, like me on a good day, he didn't actually feel his years. Was this a good day? I wasn't sure. It was certainly slightly better than the ones that had preceded it.

* * *

Finally we reached his car, which was some sort of truck, muddy with a tow bar and a roof rack. With some relief, because the spring sunshine was suddenly very warm, I shed my heavy wool coat, bundled it up and went to put it on the back seat. There was a tatty cardboard box there already which Gio moved.

'Paint,' he said. 'I don't want to get that on your coat.'

'Are you a decorator?' I asked.

He gave a chuckle, 'I like to think I'm an artist.'

'Oh,' I said, embarrassed again, 'sorry.'

'There's nothing wrong with being a decorator,' he said, laughing. 'Sometimes I do feel I should put paint onto walls instead of canvases.'

He concentrated on the traffic for a while as we left the airport. Everyone seemed to be in a tearing hurry which meant no one was sticking to the speed limit. Nor did they have the same concerns that I had about overtaking, undertaking or lane hopping. Several of them had an apparent death wish.

I sank down a little in my seat and pressed my feet to the floor, searching for an imaginary brake pedal on the wrong side of the car, as we headed through a tangle of industrial estates and small towns.

'You've been here before, so you know it's not far, only about an hour or so,' he said after a few minutes.

'I don't really remember,' I said.

Yes, I'd been here when Zoe married Paulo, but Casper, my then husband, had been with me, and he wasn't hiding his reluc-

tance to be there. I'd come back once after that when I got
divorced, but since then Zoe and I had only met up a few times,
always in London when she came to visit me, and had occasional
WhatsApp calls when she always seemed to be busy and laughing. Could someone be that happy with the same man for so
many years? Was that possible or was she on medication? None of
my relationships had lasted very long: nine years was the longest.
Why was that? Perhaps it was me.

We flew past petrol stations and rather nice looking trattorias
with the obligatory tables and parasols outside on the pavement.
And always in front of us, there was the scenic promise of snow-
tipped mountains. Were these the Dolomites or the Alps? I'd have
to find out; it just showed what a rush I had been in when I left
London. I'd had no clear knowledge of what I'd find in Italy or
what I was going to do when I got there.

I shivered and wondered how long it would take for Jack to
realise I had gone. I'd left him a Post-it note on the fridge door,
telling him to pack his things up and leave, but not where I was
going. Now I thought perhaps I had been too angry.

Beside me Gio Agnello still wasn't talking much, just pointing
out occasional things to me: an ancient church or a place where
he had worked in the days when he was a teacher. Once, a
hideous, half-finished office block that he said had been built at
huge expense with European money and never been occupied
because of disagreements between the councillors. Some had
liked the design; some had loathed it.

'But maybe one day,' he said, with a tilt of his head. 'As we Italians say, Bisogna che si levi di buon'ora chi desidera piacere a
tutti. You can't please everyone all the time.'

'Seems a shame,' I said, craning round to look at the cause of
all the trouble.

'But here, look, we are at the lake,' he said. 'Now do you remember?'

Oh yes, of course I did. The view was just gorgeous, and even though I'd travelled a lot and seen many places which were beautiful or notable, this view was awe-inspiring. And then, as is often the way, it was spoiled by houses and more petrol stations. In between them, tantalising glimpses of the water and the rocky cliffs, little towns on the other side of the lake glistening in the sunshine.

'It's absolutely lovely,' I sighed.

'I'm glad you approve,' he said with a smile. 'What are you hoping to do while you are here?'

I didn't answer, I just made a non-committal sort of noise. The truth was, I had no idea. I was used to having plans and details and order in my daily life. Now, I had none. It was still making me feel uncomfortable. I liked to know what I was doing, where I was going. Preferably with a spreadsheet.

'Oh, catch up with Zoe and Paulo,' I said vaguely. 'Spend some time with them.'

'And how long are you here for?'

God knows, I thought. I hadn't even considered that. 'Oh, you know, see how it goes,' I said.

'Then we will meet up again I am sure,' he said.

He was trying to be pleasant, I could tell, to be friendly and charming. I knew I should be friendly and charming back, but I just couldn't quite get myself to do it. I just wanted to shut my eyes, be left alone. To think and perhaps sulk. Which was pathetic.

'That would be nice,' I said, trying to sound like a normal person having a normal conversation.

Really though, at that moment I felt like dropping my face into my hands and making some sort of howling noise while rocking backwards and forwards. But I didn't think my companion would have appreciated me doing that.

I looked out of the car window at the passing scenery and felt the annoying prickle of unwanted tears sting my eyes. I clenched my hands in my lap and took a deep, slow breath. In my experience, once a woman started crying, men shied away like startled ponies and got a bit patronising. I was not going to cry about this, definitely not. And certainly not here and not now.

I could see he was giving me little sideways looks as though he could sense I was upset, which in a way was vaguely comforting. I did a bit of throat-clearing and pretended I was looking in my bag for something. Eventually I brought out a tissue and blew my nose.

'Is it far?' I said at last. 'I really can't remember.'

'We are nearly there,' he said. 'You will be glad to rest after your journey, but perhaps we will meet later. Paulo has invited me over for a drink tomorrow evening. There, look.'

As he spoke, we drove into a tunnel, still running along the lakeside, but with open arches so that the view was not impeded. Then, suddenly into the darkness of a proper tunnel through the rock, which seemed to go on for a very long time.

The lorries coming towards us were huge and noisy, the lighting far too dim for my liking. And then just as I was wondering how much longer this was going on and how on earth it had been built in the first place – engineers really were amazing – we shot out of the darkness and into the sunlight again to see another fabulous view over the water. I gasped with amazement and Gio turned to me, pleased at my response.

'Lovely isn't it? Bellissima! I never tire of this place,' he said, 'never.'

I bit back a whimper as a lorry illegally undertook us and pressed my feet to the floor again.

I darted a look at Gio. *Just watch the road.*

There were more buildings ahead, more people, cars parked in laybys, and then a cluster of boats seemingly moored just beside the road. The road narrowed and twisted and with each turn the views became even more spectacular. The snow became thicker on the mountain slopes above us. How had I missed this when I came here before all those years ago, or how had I forgotten?

Perhaps I had been in the back of the car arguing with Casper, while one of Zoe's friends drove us to the wedding. Casper hadn't wanted to come here in the first place, he'd only been persuaded because it meant a rare trip without our toddler son, Ben, and throughout the journey and the whole of our brief stay he'd made no secret of this fact. No, it couldn't have been that. I must have been asleep or in a coma or just not functioning properly. Perhaps I had been working on my laptop. It wouldn't have surprised me. Why had I allowed my career to take over so much of my life and my thoughts? Why had I never learned to enjoy other things, people, places? What was wrong with me?

'Are we there yet?' I said again.

He laughed. 'You sound like a little child.'

I smiled despite myself. 'Do you have kids?'

'Oh, yes, I have two: a daughter, Isabelle, who is a doctor in London and a son, Francesco, who lives in France. So, far away. And you?'

'I have one son, Ben, who lives in Canada.'

'I miss my children. You must miss him,' Gio said.

I gave a silly little laugh to cover up the fact that I did. 'Sometimes, but it's difficult. I'm always so busy. I do – I have done a lot of travelling, with work.'

'Ah, I see,' he said after a moment.

I thought about it. That wasn't remotely true, what I had just said. In fact, it was rubbish. Why was I saying such ridiculous things? My pregnancy and Ben's arrival had been a complete shock to both Casper and me. The death knell of our marriage actually. I had wanted more children at some point, but Casper hadn't. He liked his life ordered and tidy, as I'd thought I did. White carpets and sleek fragile furniture were more important to Casper than Ben.

When we'd met, I'd been captivated by Casper's good looks and intelligence but, even when I'd married him, I'd known he would be a terrible parent. He'd left when Ben was two and a half, unable to cope with the Duplo, the stickiness, the noise. I plunged into the nightmare world of nannies and au pairs and pretending I was coping perfectly well, until in the end I believed it too. But deep down, I always thought at some point I would be found out: seen for the very ordinary person and imperfect mother I really was.

Had my career really been that important to me? As a working, single parent had I lost the more important plot?

It was a lie – I did miss Ben. I missed him terribly. And for various reasons, I hadn't seen him for nearly three years. But people at work didn't want to hear that.

All the mothers I'd ever worked with had been the same, or perhaps like me they hid their true feelings. Oh yes, of course we wanted and needed to be at work; we loved the cut and thrust of business; we were just the same as a man really – certainly as good, if not better. If you wanted to get something done, ask a woman. And then add a light-hearted laugh and a knowing look.

Over the years other women I'd worked with had managed to have a family, dropping out of the picture on maternity leave while the men had complained about them the moment they left. Then I'd seen how they had been treated by work colleagues when they returned. Worrying about childcare and school holidays and playdates while the child-free people, the men with stay-at-home wives and compliant grandparents, rolled their eyes.

I turned away, blushing at the memory of my own insensitivity, to look at the view of the lake below us now. The road wound up the cliff, each bend more acute than the last. Perhaps when I'd come here before I'd come a different way?

'I'm sorry you have had to do this drive because of me,' I said.

He shrugged. His eyes were on the road. For a while he didn't answer. It was as though a barrier had gone up between us.

'It's fine,' he said at last.

'How can you drive this road in the winter?'

'Sometimes you can't,' he said. 'This road was closed in January; we had wonderful snowfall.'

'Oh.'

Though he was talking again, I had the feeling I'd said something to annoy him, but I couldn't think what. My head was too full of worries at the moment. I was even annoying myself.

6

'Here we are.'

At last we turned off the road, into a small lane and down towards a town which was nestled in a grove of trees. There were a few shops, but everything looked a bit dusty and run down, as though nothing much ever happened here. A couple of the houses on the outskirts were even boarded up. And one – a beautiful little villa behind iron railings – looked as though it was falling down, a hopeful *Casa in vendita* sign tied to the front gate with orange string. House for sale. A scruffy-looking dog was asleep on the pavement in front of it, basking in the sunshine. A man in a blue workman's boiler suit strolled past, a newspaper under one arm.

The view from here grew even more spectacular; the lake below us sparkling, the mountain ranges in the distance brilliant with snow, balancing white clouds on their heads. We drove on and then took a little turning, through a five-bar gate, down a gravelled driveway.

And then I saw her, Zoe, coming out of the trattoria and hurrying towards me, her face one big happy smile. I felt a surge of relief. I was struggling with the seatbelt and opening the car door before Gio had turned off the engine.

'Clover!'

'Zoe!'

We embraced each other and stood hugging and rocking for a few moments.

'I can't believe you are here!'

'Nor can I!'

She pulled back and we looked at each other as she wiped away the tears from my cheek with a tissue. It seemed to me she hadn't really changed at all in the years we had known each other.

Yes, her hair, which used to be a brilliant auburn that cascaded down her back when we were teenagers, was now darker and cut into the functional bob she'd adopted some years ago. She was curvier than I'd remembered; her face more tanned and lined. But underneath it all I could still see the cousin I had grown up with, the one I had fought and played and plotted with. The friend who had shared a student flat with me at university, seen me through my divorce from Casper, visited me and offered advice. She had commiserated with me when things went wrong and cheered me on when I was promoted. I hoped I had been an equally good friend to her. I wasn't sure I had.

I felt close to tears again, that here was someone I could relax with for the first time in ages. She would not be saying one thing to my face and at the same time sneaking around behind my back, cosying up to the directors. She would not spitefully present me with complex financial problems on a Thursday to solve by close of business on Friday afternoon.

'Good journey?' Zoe said.

I drank in the sight of her, in her simple cotton dress, cardigan and flat sandals, her hair held back from her face with a floral hairband. She looked cheerful, uncomplicated, happy. In my heels and woollen suit, I felt awkward, hot and overdressed.

'Fine,' I said. 'What a wonderful place – such a view. I'd forgotten.'

'Fantastic, isn't it? Come in. Paulo is inside, dealing with the last of the lunchtime trade. Gio, will you join us?'

He held up his hands. '*Grazie*, no. I must get back.'

'But you must come over for dinner soon? Perhaps next week-end?' Zoe said.

Gio flicked me a look.

'That would be nice,' he said after a long pause. I had the distinct impression he'd been about to say the opposite. 'I hope you enjoy your stay.'

'Thank you so much for the lift,' I said as he walked back to his car.

'*Non è un problema.*' It's no trouble.

'Well! Come on in,' Zoe said, and she took hold of one of my cases and wheeled it towards the side of the house. I followed her with my hand luggage, my heels stumbling on the uneven stone slabs.

The trattoria was nothing like I remembered it. There was now a veranda tacked onto the front of the beautiful old stone building, and three cars were parked on a wide gravelled area where once I was sure there used to be a lawn and a fountain. There were a few tables outside, and one elderly couple were even sitting with glasses of wine, enjoying the view and the fine, bright spring day.

'Come on, we'll go in through the back door. I'll show you to the barn. Paulo has been pretty busy, but he'll probably be nearly cleared up now. He's so looking forward to seeing you again.'

It was many years since I'd met up with Paulo in person, and here I was dumping myself and my problems on him and Zoe with hardly any warning. I suddenly felt guilty and uncomfortable. I hadn't really thought this through at all. What would he think of me? If the tables were turned and Zoe had appeared at my apartment with little or no notice, Jack would have been furious.

'I'm sorry to land on you like this,' I said.

Zoe looked puzzled. 'Don't be daft – I'm delighted you're back. It's been years! I always seem to come and see you in your lovely London flat. It's far more exciting than here, believe me. Now come on, you must be hungry.'

We went into the back of the house, past some bins and a couple of empty plastic crates and through to the enormous kitchen where Paulo was standing at the stove, stirring something in a saucepan. A sullen looking young man in checked trousers was standing at the sink, prodding at something with a dishcloth.

Paulo's face lit up when he saw me and he came over, wiping his hands on a tea towel.

He kissed me briskly on both cheeks and gave me a friendly hug.

'*Bellissima! Benvenuta!* Welcome, you are so welcome. And as beautiful as ever! I'm sorry not to come and fetch you from the airport. Has Zoe explained?'

I hardly recognised Paulo, but it had been a long time since I'd seen him except fleetingly in the background on our Zoom calls. He'd been a cheerful wave over Zoe's shoulder, a call for a happy Christmas or birthday.

He'd had a head of dark curls when he was younger, now he was nearly bald with a neatly trimmed grey beard. I remembered him as a young man of course. Handsome, quite athletic actually. Now he was nearing seventy, and quite chunky. But that was reassuring too; didn't people say you should never trust a thin chef?

'It's fine. It wasn't far and Gio was very pleasant,' I said.

'Was that all, just pleasant? That's a disappointing reaction,' Zoe said with a twinkle in her eye. 'He's considered quite a catch around here with my friends.'

Catch? I didn't want and wasn't looking for a catch of any sort.

'Now let's take your bags through. Follow me.'

She led me through to a door at the side of the kitchen which opened onto a little courtyard and beyond that what must have been a barn which had now been converted into a self-contained annexe. It was all exposed beams and huge windows and filled with an assortment of mis-matched furniture, some of the armchairs covered in colourful throws. The linen curtains were drawn back, letting in the wonderful view of the trees stretching down to the lake below.

'This is lovely,' I said.

It felt peaceful. Quiet. Which was just what I wanted.

'Isn't it? We converted it for Nonna – Paulo's mother when she couldn't live on her own any more, and now she's gone, we keep it for guests or the kids when they visit. Bathroom through there beyond the little kitchen area. We sometimes rent it out too, for holidays.'

'Then you must let me pay you the going rate!'

'Nonsense, Paulo wouldn't hear of it and nor will I. You can help out in the trattoria if you feel the need to do something while you're here.'

I had no idea what I was going to do while I was here, that was the truth of the matter. I tried to imagine myself being helpful, but what did that involve? Cooking? Not my speciality.

'How's business?' I asked.

'It's been very quiet through the winter, well, and last year if I'm honest, but we are hoping it's going to pick up. We usually get more trade in the spring and summer months of course. Paulo has been busy renovating the other barn since January ready for a summer let. It's just about finished. At least he has had something to keep him busy. And we've been updating the trattoria too. Much to the annoyance of the regulars. They hate it when things change. But some of the bar stools were falling apart.'

'Marvellous, I'd love to help,' I said, although I wasn't sure I'd be any use, and if I was honest, I hadn't imagined myself serving in a wine bar. I hadn't done that since I was a student. 'I shall be very comfortable here; I can feel it. How is your migraine by the way, I forgot to ask?'

Zoe waved a dismissive hand. 'Oh, it's nothing now of course, but it was a bit of a nuisance while it lasted. I'll be fine.'

'And how are the children?'

'Hardly children any more! Leo is twenty-eight now and teaching in Rome, and Nico is twenty-six and working as an electrician in Florence. But they visit, especially around Christmas or if they need a break from the big city.'

'No grandchildren yet?'

Zoe held up one hand and crossed her fingers. 'Not yet but I have hopes. How is lovely Ben?'

'Fine, I think. I spoke to him last week. He's busy and happy. That's all you can hope for really, isn't it?'

'Of course. Now that we have all the small talk over: it's lovely to see you, but why are you here, out of the blue, on your own after all this time?'

'Straight to the point as always,' I said.

'Well, I can't count the number of times I've tried to persuade you to visit, but you've always been too busy with work.'

I sat down rather heavily on one of the chairs. 'Busy with work... Well, I'm not now. That's why I'm here. I've been made redundant. I was escorted from the building on Wednesday morning; my laptop and phone were taken and I'm on three months gardening leave.'

Zoe looked astounded for a moment and then clapped her hands.

'Redundant? You? How absolutely marvellous!'

I was momentarily rather shocked. 'Well, I didn't think it was marvellous when it happened, I can tell you.'

Zoe quickly composed her face into a sympathetic frown. 'No, really? That must have been awful then. But at least now, think about it, you can do anything! You could go and visit Ben after all the delays and cancellations. You're free! You can start enjoying life.'

I hadn't really considered this way of looking at it and her enthusiasm felt a bit misplaced. It certainly didn't tie in with my own feelings. How could losing my job possibly be marvellous? Not only the job, but everything else in my well-ordered life was in turmoil. I wondered how long it would take Jack to move out of my apartment...

'I just lost the plot when I heard, and Jack was no comfort. He was far more interested in his imminent golfing weekend. Things between us haven't been great for a while; I told him I needed a break, and I wanted him to move out. I needed to get away from him, from London, from seeing people from work and their mournful faces, when half of them are probably relieved it's not them.'

'Ah, poor Clover,' she said giving me a consoling hug. 'I'm sure that's not true; you're just upset. I hope they gave you a big, fat pay-out?'

'It wasn't the money,' I said. 'I just felt I'd been chucked on the scrap heap. Work is all I've known for so long. Without it I feel a bit of a... well, a non. A non-person.'

'Don't be daft. There's more to life than your job,' she said. 'You know, Paulo and I live a simple life here; it's not the rat race. And Paulo's favourite saying is *felice come un cane al sole*. We are as happy as a dog in the sun. A rather tired and bedraggled old dog at the moment though, if I'm honest.'

But what about me...? I thought. *My sense of myself?* How could I be happy with my life now? What defined me if I didn't have work? I knew I would retire one day, but I needed that to be on my own terms: gradually ease into it at some unknown point in the future, not be chucked out without ceremony.

'Look, you get settled in and come through when you're ready,' Zoe said kindly. 'I know travelling is tiresome at the best of times, and you look whacked.'

'Thanks, Zoe,' I said, grateful for her kindness. 'I'll get unpacked. I won't be long. For one thing, I need to change into something cooler.'

Zoe looked me up and down; my designer suit and cashmere roll neck sweater were perfect for work, for London, for hopping into taxis and holding people's attention in meetings. They screamed, *BOSS LADY: don't mess with me!* Here, I just looked ridiculously overdressed.

'Good idea. Take your time, you know where we are.'

Zoe went back through into the house and closed the door quietly behind her.

I suddenly felt very alone. Not just because she had gone, but because I felt my whole world was tilted off its axis. Everything I knew and was familiar with – my work, my son, my mother – was thousands of miles away. I didn't know what I was going to do next. What to think next. Perhaps that was the problem: I needed time to think things through. And help out in a trattoria? What use would I be there?

Perhaps Jack had the right idea after all. I could think about starting up my own consultancy. ...But how? My brain couldn't process that at the moment. It all seemed too difficult. I'd think about in in a few days when I'd calmed down. Perhaps I needed a spreadsheet? I was good with a spreadsheet.

The hairpins holding my hair up into its customary tight, French pleat were giving me a headache. I pulled them all out and brushed out the tangles. My mother always said hair should be kept shorter as one aged. Perhaps I should do that? I had a mental image of myself madly chopping away at my hair with some nail scissors in the hope of looking like Mia Farrow or Audrey Hepburn. Knowing my luck, I would just look like Albert Einstein. Without the moustache. So far anyway. Hormones in a woman of my age were very unpredictable and unhelpful.

I went into the bathroom, which was small and spotlessly clean but perhaps in need of a lick of paint. Folded over a rustic, painted towel rail there were pretty pink towels, the edges embroidered with white daisies. For some reason the sight of them made me want to cry. Was it the homeliness of it all? The feeling that here was a couple who lived simply, who were not interested in the sort of stylish nonsense that had filled my time? Who probably didn't give a thought to pensions or base rates or the latest exhibition at an obscure gallery?

I washed my hands with soap scented with lemon and that made me want to cry too. What on earth was the matter with me? When did I get so emotional?

7

I pulled myself together and took a few deep breaths. I wasn't here to sulk or fester over old resentments or – worst of all – carry on spending my time having imaginary arguments with Nick Crane, saying all the pithy and accurate things I should have said but hadn't.

I re-applied some mascara and a slick of red lipstick; that always made me feel better for some reason. It had become my trademark in the board room.

No, I wasn't going to think about the board room, I wasn't going to picture Nick Crane and his weasel face and lipstick-daubed shoes, or Doug Badderly and his body odour that after an hour or so in an overheated under-ventilated room caused even artificial plants to wilt.

I tied my hair back with a scrunchie, changed into a new white linen shirt, a cardigan and some jeans that Jack didn't like because he said they made my hips look big. Well, he too was going to be a part of my past. They felt comfortable, and no one was going to be looking anyway. Then I found some wedge-heeled sandals which were the nearest thing I had to sensible footwear.

I went across the courtyard into the trattoria where the scrubbed pine table was set with red-checked napkins and white china plates. It was simple and inviting and the aroma that was filling the kitchen was divine. It made my mouth water and I felt properly hungry for the first time in days.

Paulo, reassuringly substantial in his chef's apron, a striped tea towel slung over his shoulder, turned towards me and smiled.

'Ah, *Bellissima*! There you are! Come and sit down, come, sit. Please. Zoe is just finishing up in the bar – a booking turned up half an hour after we closed.'

This surprised me. 'And you still served them?'

He shrugged. 'Of course. They are friends. We can't afford to turn away customers. Anyone can be late.'

Oh, well, try that in London and you'd never close, I thought.

Zoe came in, pulling a face. 'Sorry, Clover, I just got the last few people out and I've locked up. Are you feeling okay? You looked a bit peaky.'

'Oh, it's just the travelling,' I said, trying to sound carefree. 'I'm fine. What are we eating? It smells delicious.'

Paulo put a long wooden board out in the middle of the table, filled with cold meats, piles of olives and chunks of cheese plus a rustic-looking loaf. Then he ladled soup into some bowls.

'Pasta and bean soup,' he said. 'The best thing for a broken heart. Zoe has told me what has happened.'

'Oh, my heart is not broken,' I said firmly with a little laugh.

'*Contusa*, then,' he said. 'Bruised.'

'So tell Paulo exactly what happened,' Zoe said, coming to sit opposite me.

I picked up my spoon and stirred the freshly chopped herbs into my soup.

'An American company took over XS and I was made redundant, that's the size of it. I didn't have the faintest idea it would happen.'

'How awful,' she said, slicing a crackling crust off the end of the loaf. 'Still, like I said, you should see it as a chance to do something else.'

'But—'

But what?

Zoe reached across to hug me. 'To start off, have a jolly good holiday here. I bet you haven't had any time off for ages. Take some time out, relax, do some sketching like you used to, go for walks, have long lunches, have an afternoon siesta, live like a native.'

I started eating. I didn't want to talk about work. More than that, I didn't want to talk about not working.

'This is delicious.'

Paulo smiled proudly.

...Go for walks.

I thought about this while I tucked into the assortment of meats and delicious and unfamiliar cheeses in front of me.

Walks... I'd never understood this as a pastime. I only walked to and from the car these days and my shoe choices reflected this. I didn't have anything resembling walking boots and I'd always joked that if I was invited to go somewhere where wellingtons were needed, then I wouldn't go.

Perhaps I was a softy. Perhaps I should rethink things.

Perhaps it had been a mistake coming here in the first place? Away from the city, the noise, my contacts. Everything that was familiar.

I felt a tremor of panic and my spoon shook halfway to my mouth, spilling beans and orange-coloured soup all down my white shirt. *Oh great.* It was the sort of mark that – despite any stain remover, repeated washing, bleach, scrubbing on a stone down by the lake – would never come out.

I dabbed ineffectually at myself while Paulo and Zoe chatted easily about the menu Paulo was thinking of putting on for next month. They hadn't seemed to notice the state I was in, or if they did, they were too polite to mention it.

'We are planning the usual afternoon feast for Easter,' Zoe explained, 'but Paulo can't decide what to cook although it's usually lamb. It would be lovely if you were still here. If the weather is good, we put all the tables together on the veranda and invite friends and family around. If not, we light the fire and close the shutters. It's such a lovely occasion. We are usually there until late.'

'Perhaps you could help us in the kitchen?' Paulo said. 'Are you a good cook?'

Hmm. If I were honest, I wasn't any sort of cook. I was used to eating out all the time: dinners with clients and business lunches, and of course Jack thought breakfast was for wimps. I'd usually grab something on the way to work.

'I don't cook much at all,' I admitted. Paulo's lower lip stuck out in disbelief or perhaps disapproval. 'But it might be nice to try,' I added.

I took an olive which was huge and dripping with oil; it tasted wonderful. Nothing like the olives I was used to which came in brine and were salty and unpleasant.

The last time I had been gainfully employed in a kitchen had been a few years ago. Jack had just moved in with me, and we had been about to celebrate our first anniversary as a couple when our hotel booking for a Fine Olde Traditional Christmas Dinner – Jack's idea, because he'd been going through a phase when being English and kitsch appealed to him – had been cancelled at the last minute. I foolishly assured him, and four of our friends who were going to be sharing the experience, that I could deal with it.

I spent several hours in our beautifully equipped but under-used kitchen on Christmas Day, only managing a lot of cursing, a burn on one hand and a cut on the other. Then later too: a ruined saucepan, a sink full of dirty cutlery and crockery, a minor fire when I left a tea towel over the gas hob and eventually a turkey that was rather curiously half-burned and yet in places slightly raw.

Jack's fantasy of spending the afternoon holding court at the head of the dining table, knocking back an expensive selection of wines, and everyone praising our domestic contentment, went – like the tea towel – up in smoke. Instead, it had been replaced by the two of us having our first proper row (muttered but quite nasty) in the kitchen. Meantime, our guests got spectacularly drunk and dined on smoked salmon, roast potatoes and cheese followed by a box of Bendicks Mints and a tub of Twiglets – the only things I couldn't have ruined.

'One day we'll look back at this and laugh,' Jack had said, as we'd poured his sister into a taxi that night.

I was still waiting.

* * *

'Jack thinks I should start up my own consultancy,' I said.

We had finished lunch the following day, and Zoe and I were outside on the veranda on some very comfortable chairs that looked as though they had been made out of old firewood, having coffee.

It was so quiet that I could hear the faint noise of Paulo doing some high-speed vegetable chopping in the kitchen, ready for the evening meals. No traffic hum, sirens blaring or other people. It was very strange and nothing like what I was used to. Sometimes the quiet could sound quite loud.

'And do you want to do that?' Zoe asked. 'I mean, who cares what Jack wants now especially if you've split up. It's what you want that matters.'

I stretched out my legs, crossed my ankles and admired the red polish on my toenails.

'Oh god, I don't know, Zoe. I never thought about it before. I've been such a corporate animal for decades, that the idea of being out there on my own feels rather scary.'

'And what about Jack?'

I shrugged. 'We had a row. But he still went off with a couple of friends for a long weekend in Scotland. Allegedly golfing, but, somehow, I doubt it. More like whisky tasting. He goes every year; it's been arranged for ages; I know he certainly wouldn't cancel just because I'm in the pits.'

Zoe huffed a bit with indignation.

'Well, personally, I would have expected Jack would have – you know... Been a bit more supportive. Not just clear off on a jaunt with the lads. I hope before he went he bought you some Bollinger and cheered you up by telling you how marvellous you are?'

'Well, no, he didn't,' I said, rather uncomfortable because that's what I'd been hoping he would do.

'And he helped find you a flight?'

'He didn't know I was going. I left him a note on the fridge to tell him to pack up all his stuff and leave.'

There was a long pause and then Zoe spluttered with laughter.

'Good riddance, I say,' she chuckled. 'Doesn't that tell you something, Clover? That you can be with someone for six years and yet take such a decision without even involving him?'

'I suppose so; I wasn't really thinking straight.'

Zoe reached over and hugged me. 'Well, his loss is our gain. It's lovely to have you here and you can stay as long as you like.'

'Are you sure?' I felt another twinge of doubt.

Zoe gave me an old-fashioned look. 'When did I ever say something I didn't mean?'

'Well, there was that time at the university disco when—'

Zoe rocked with laughter. 'You asked if you looked okay in that green satin dress and I said yes. And then—'

'Rich McKenzie told me I looked like a gherkin!'

We laughed at the memory until I felt tears come, but for a good reason this time.

Zoe wiped her eyes with a tissue. 'What an arse he was. Who cared what he thought? Let's have a glass of Barolo. And you can tell me what you thought of Gio.'

'What I thought of Gio?'

Zoe chuckled and stood up. 'Absolutely. Remember him? The gorgeous man who lives just up the mountain? Artistic, kind, handsome, single? You don't find many like that lying around. You don't think I really had a migraine, do you? I'll go and get that wine, shall I?'

8

'You're honestly telling me you're trying to set me up with Gio Agnello?' I said. 'You can't be serious? I'm not properly out of my relationship with Jack. I'm certainly not looking for another one.'

Zoe laughed and put two glasses of red wine down on the table in front of us.

'Why not?' she said. 'He's a gentleman. He has a lovely character, he's thoughtful and kind. And he's gorgeous. Which part don't you like?'

I tutted. 'I'm not interested.'

'If Jack really cared for you, he would have cancelled his stupid boys' trip and taken you somewhere instead. I bet you wouldn't have swanned off if he had been in the middle of a crisis.'

She was absolutely right about everything. Perhaps she could see things clearer than I could.

'No, I wouldn't—'

'Well, there you go then. I met Jack a handful of times and every time I thought he wasn't nearly good enough for you. He hardly spoke to me except to tell me how successful he was and how he was the same weight as he was at Cambridge when he rowed in the boat race. He showed absolutely no interest in me. He just waited for you and me to stop talking so he could carry on boring us with market rates and buy-outs. I think being away from him will be good for you. I mean, of course I'm sad – if you are – that you've been made redundant. But personally, I'm also really happy to have you here.'

'I'm happy to be here. But that's no reason to try and set me up with a new man before I've even got rid of the last one. And Gio didn't talk to me much by the end of the trip.'

'Gio is just a bit reserved at first. You can get to know him better when he comes round for dinner next weekend.'

'Oh god! Does he know your cunning plan? I'm going to be crippled with embarrassment now!' I said. 'Thank you so much!'

'My pleasure. Drink your wine. It's my favourite. We know the family who produce it. Perhaps we can take a trip to their vineyard while you are here.'

I took a sip. It was really good; I could taste raspberry, cinnamon, almost chocolate.

'This is wonderful,' I said, holding my glass up to the light.

And then I splashed some of it onto myself. I looked down at the stain with resignation.

'Told you it was. I'm right about lots of things,' Zoe said, 'including Gio. He's lovely. You'll see.'

* * *

I went back to my room when we had finished our chat and the excellent wine; perhaps I needed a nap. Or a very early night. I'd often felt that recently; perhaps it was my age, but of course it wasn't the sort of thing to do when I was at work.

There, in our glass-walled offices with everyone able to see everyone else, we had to be constantly firing on all cylinders. Anyone with their head down on their desk would have immediately attracted a crowd of sneering watchers. And if I complained of being tired with Jack, he would say I needed to go to the doctor to have my blood sugar levels checked.

But here, things were very different. I could go into my own room, shut the door and nod off if I felt like it.

In the event, I opened up my new laptop and logged onto the Wi-Fi again (which was surprisingly good).

I checked my emails, played a few levels of *Cookie Jam* and then sat by the window and looked out at the view. That surely was something I would never get used to: just sitting, doing nothing.

The side view from my incredibly expensive apartment in London was partly of the road below, which was usually jammed with cars, and partly of the buildings opposite and their impenetrable blinds. But of course, there was also a view of the Thames from the front, which added a premium to the cost of the place.

The view from my office had been pretty bleak: other buildings and windows, the faint outlines of other people, heads down at their desks. Yes, it was nice to be able to point out famous landmarks to clients, and it had given our firm a good standing to be in the heart of the city with all the other important people, but sometimes it didn't make up for the sheer awfulness of actually getting there and back every day. Tube delays, taxis, road closures. It wasn't unknown for a journey of a mile to take an hour.

I wondered how far I could get in an hour from here. Maybe even as far as the Swiss border or France. Perhaps I should have looked at a map.

A mad idea struck me. What would happen if I just hired a car and started driving, turning left or right when the fancy took me? Driving away from everything, just stopping for fuel and food, and staying at random places along the way. What if I entirely escaped from my life? Just ran away from everyone who knew me. Where might I end up?

I felt a moment of sheer panic. I closed my eyes and took a deep breath.

Instead of researching the route to Stuttgart or Barcelona, I went to explore the little kitchen area and found English tea bags and real coffee in the cupboard plus fresh milk in the fridge. So I made myself a cup of tea and sat back on the pillows on the bed to drink it. It was time to think.

* * *

What a wonderful thing tea was. It was not the first time I'd thought that. It was the British way of dealing with each and every crisis. Unexpected pregnancy, health scare, burglary, financial disaster, Martian invasion: put the kettle on and open up the custard creams. I wondered if the Italians did biscuits, apart from Garibaldis of course which were not my biscuit of choice. Nor those rock-hard things that come with coffee and were like a ship's hard tack of yesteryear. Without the weevils.

After a while I got up and finished emptying my cases, putting my clothes away in the huge but rather wobbly wardrobe. I seemed to have packed a lot of warm sweaters, dresses and skirts that would need tights and proper shoes to go with them. Maybe I hadn't thought this through very well. But where would I buy more casual clothes? Well, there must have been shops somewhere. After all, Italy was famous for its fashion.

I wandered around, looking at the little china ornaments on the dressing table, the pictures on the walls. There were a couple of lovely landscapes: the lake, the trees, the distant mountains.

And then I saw it. A pencil sketch hanging next to the bed. I peered closer, and, yes, there was my name at the bottom.

I tried to remember when I had found the time to do that. And then I got it: many years ago, it was the view from my room on a business trip to Venice. Just a funny little street, lined with tightly packed houses, ironwork balconies and flowery window boxes, bright in the sunshine. There had been a canal spanned by a stone bridge. It had been of no great importance probably, but it had been so beautiful, so casually perfect that I had felt the need to draw it. I'd turned it into a birthday card for Zoe; how wonderful that she had kept it and framed it.

I stood and looked at the sketch for a few moments, remembering suddenly how I had felt that day, making marks on paper. And it had been nothing to do with work. Happy, positive, in control of my life. Drawing was like that; it captured the time and the place far better than a hastily taken photograph. Why had I stopped drawing? Perhaps I hadn't found the time. Maybe I should try again? I certainly would have the time now.

Despite the slightly ramshackle décor, the barn was such a beautiful space with room for a big living area, a kitchen at the end and beyond that a large bedroom and bathroom. Coupled with the fabulous views from every window it was lovely, the perfect place for a break from the city and from other people. I was so fortunate to be here, I needed to remember that. After all I was a lot luckier than some people my age. I had my health, although my knees were getting a bit creaky, money in the bank and my flat.

Okay, I didn't have a job at the moment, but I had the courage to bounce back from this, didn't I? A lot of people were much worse off than I was. I just needed to focus, find my next challenge, my new path. I wasn't ready to give up and sink back into bewildered retirement. My brain was as active as it had ever been, my desire for the next challenge was as strong as ever. I just needed to figure out what it was.

I supposed starting up my own consultancy was a possibility. The trouble was it just didn't give me that buzz of excitement I was looking for. It just sounded exhausting. And the prospect of all those fishing phone calls I would have to make was awful. And word spread fast, people would know of my sudden downfall. And other companies might feel the same way about employing a woman of my age, but of course they would never be able to say so.

I wondered what had happened back in London at the monthly XS senior managers' meeting. The first one I had missed since – well, ever.

I could imagine it so clearly: the executives filing into that glass-walled room; the pale wood table; the bottles of designer water; horrible, stewed coffee from a complicated machine; muffins that no one ate; a pot full of XS pencils. Would they have mentioned me? My unexpected departure? Sad voices and regretful smiles from those treacherous bastards?

I could just imagine someone opening up my XS laptop, my beautiful spreadsheets, my files and notes, and poring over the information about the Olafsen deal – intel I had slaved and sweated over. Late nights and hours and hours of negotiating with stroppy Norwegian executives who expected guarantees for things that were impossible to promise. I could still feel their expectation that someone – in other words, I – would always be there to answer their questions, no matter the hour or the day. I still winced at the thought of wrangling over costs, the deadlock over something as ridiculous as printing, postage or the details of the hotel they were expected to stay in when they came over to London with their thin, blonde wives for yet another pointless meeting.

And to what end? Why had I got swept up in all this for so many years. It all seemed so futile.

Perhaps I didn't miss it as much as I thought?

It was only four thirty; I hadn't been here twenty-four hours yet. I had so much time ahead of me, perhaps even time to have a shower before dinner. But what should I wear? I certainly needed to change: I'd clumsily stained another shirt, and my jeans were feeling hot. I stood up and tried to look at my rear view in the wardrobe mirror. Perhaps, if nothing else, Jack had been right about this pair: they looked okay from the front, but from the back, those jeans were doing me no favours.

9

I had a shower and dried off on the daisy-trimmed towels and then, wrapped in a soft white robe, made another cup of tea, and went back to my chair by the window.

There were seventeen new emails which had arrived since I last looked, all of them spam. There was nothing from work of course, nothing from any of my old work colleagues. Nothing from Nina. I supposed they didn't know my new email address. It was the strangest thing. I felt annoyed, insulted even. That I should have given so much of my life to that company, for what?

I sent a brief cheery email to Ben, telling him my new mobile number, what had happened and where I was. Making light of it all, not wanting to worry him I supposed.

Maybe I should email Jack, who at that moment was probably teeing off at the golf course, or more likely it was raining, and he was in the bar with his cronies, guffawing and being pleased with themselves. In all fairness I should tell him I had left the country. That there was still no food in the fridge and only half a bottle of gin. And remind him that we were over, that I wanted him to take all his stuff away, back to his own flat. Suddenly I couldn't be bothered.

I should ring my mother to let her know I had arrived safely. After all I had forgotten to tell her I had a new phone number.

* * *

'And you're sure you are safe there?' she said.

'Of course I am.'

'Was the flight on time. It never is. All those strikes and delays one reads about.'

'It was, we were only five minutes late landing in Bergamo.'

'Well, that's a relief. My proper doctor popped in this morning. He's been away on holiday. He's been to somewhere called Barbuda. I'd never heard of the place; it certainly hasn't been mentioned on Pointless. He says the locum I saw was wrong to put me on that medication, because my blood pressure is fine.'

'That's good to hear. How was the music recital?'

'Alright, if you like that sort of thing. Which personally— Have you decided what to do? About work?'

'No, I'm just having a few days off, and not thinking about it.'

'That's a mistake. You will be yesterday's woman in an instant. Written off like me, as a pensioner.'

'I suppose I am,' I said.

'Never admit it,' Mum said fiercely. 'You lose a lot of kudos. I call myself part of the Silent Generation. Or, if pushed: a village elder. And if anyone asks me how old I am, I tell them my doctor has the right to know that information and they are not my doctor.'

I laughed. 'Good answer.'

'Some of the people here are definitely younger than I am, and they seem ancient. And some of the older ones probably need carbon dating. It's very tiresome. Always droning on about various ailments and medications. Surely there is more to life than this?'

'So, was that all she said?' Zoe asked later.

'I would have expected nothing less.' I said, 'I know she means well, but she says she's spending too long in the company of old people. She never used to be so glum; she was always so keen to meet my friends, for example. After Dad died, she said she would throw herself under a bus rather than go into sheltered accommodation. But then Winchester House is not a typical place. It's more like a village, and all that goes with it.'

'It can be so difficult. Paulo's mother came to live with us when she wasn't safe on her own. It worked really well, and she was no trouble. Apart from the poker nights.'

'Poker nights?'

'Oh yes, she had a little band of reprobates who came round to play poker two or three times a week. She kept it up until she was ninety. You wouldn't believe the language! And once there was a full-blown fight in the car park: some nonsense about card counting although how any of them could count cards, when one was registered blind and two needed cataract operations, I don't know.'

I laughed. 'They sound a lot of fun, actually.'

'Oh, they were. But then one after the other some of them died, until it was just Nonna left, and her youngest brother, Franco, and he was the baby of the group. He still lives just down the hill, and he comes in most days, just for a drink and a chat. Three of them stole Paulo's car once and went off for a spree. The police brought them back. They said they wanted to try tequila.'

'My mother has these extravagant tea parties, with fancy tea leaves that she buys in from abroad,' I said, when I had stopped laughing. 'Do you know, I think she's just bored out of her mind.'

'Makes you think, doesn't it?' Zoe said. 'I know how I would rather end my days.'

* * *

Later that night, I was sitting in my dressing gown, brushing out my hair and wondering if I needed a trim and some more high-lights to disguise the grey when there was a knock on my door.

'Come in!'

'Are you okay?' It was Zoe. 'Just wondered if you needed anything?'

'No, I'm fine,' I said. 'I'm just having a think.'

'You're not miserable, are you?'

'No, honestly, I'm not. I'm just trying to get my head round things. But thank you for a lovely day, it was just what I needed.'

'Paulo thought you might like to come and help in the kitchen tomorrow, unless you have something planned? The boy who usually helps him has gone off again; he's not all that reliable and I think there is a girlfriend somewhere. The only thing he shows real enthusiasm for is computer games, which for a young man that age is tragic.'

'I don't know how much use I would be,' I said, hedging.

'I'm sure you can prepare vegetables, stir things... It's nothing complicated. I do as much as I can, but this week I need to do the accounts and all sorts of boring stuff in the office that I have been putting off. Italian bureaucracy is infamous.'

'Well, of course I would like to help...'

She grinned. 'Great, I'll tell Paulo. He will be so pleased. He loves bossing people about in the kitchen. I'm sure you can scrape carrots and chop onions as well as the next person.'

'But...'

What did I want to say...? Weren't there machines to do that? Any vegetables I had encountered recently had been prepared by someone else. Or had come already-chopped in plastic bags from the supermarket.

'Anyway,' Zoe said while coming over to hug me, 'sleep well, and I'll see you bright and early in the morning.'

'How bright? And how early?'

She laughed. 'We are usually up and about at eight. Or sometimes nine if it has been a late night.'

Surely, she was joking. This was not a concept I was familiar with. Six o'clock was the time I sometimes left home for the journey into work in a vain attempt to miss the worst of the traffic. Which was optimistic in London.

'Great,' I said. 'I'll see you then.'

'And don't wear anything smart!'

I wandered about for a while after she left, tidying up, leaving my stained shirts to soak in the bathroom sink. Which was probably a bad idea as with most of my clothes of course, they needed to be dry cleaned.

I got into bed, leaving the curtains open so I could enjoy the view when I woke up.

Jack would be home at some point. Surely, he would wonder where I was. He would be optimistically looking for food and failing to find any. Perhaps he would stir himself and go to the corner shop where overpriced vegetables came in eco-friendly paper carriers and exotic olives were sold in china dishes. And then he would look around the flat, irritated at not being afforded a satisfactory welcome despite having been told to clear off.

He would want to talk to me about his triumphs on his golfing weekend with Alasdair, who had a laugh like a braying donkey, and Raj, who used too much cologne and thought he was irresistible.

More than likely Jack would have bought me a present to cheer me up and try and get round me. A cashmere sweater in the wrong size or a bottle of overpriced whisky which he would end up drinking. He would never realise that all I had wanted was to be able to talk to him, for him to listen and be sympathetic and outraged on my behalf, not tell me what I should do and who I should speak to. Was that what people called mansplaining?

Perhaps eventually he would remember our argument and start packing.

On balance, scraping carrots and chopping onions might be a preferable way to spend my time.

Against all my expectations I had a wonderful sleep that night and woke at half past ten.

Half past ten? This was unheard of.

I propped myself up on my pillows and thought about what I would usually be doing if I was still in London. Instead, I was lying in bed, looking out at the magnificent view of the lake. And somehow, I couldn't be sorry. Perhaps this break in my routine was a chance to regroup, get my wagons into a circle, before I plunged back into work.

Work.

Oh god! I was supposed to be helping Paulo in the kitchen... What had Zoe said, breakfast at eight? Had she been joking?

I got out of bed and thought about having a shower, but I was already late. I was never late.

I dragged on a pair of linen trousers and a clean shirt, jammed my feet into my sandals and dragged a brush through my hair.

I glanced at myself in the mirror; I looked a wreck. Pale and uninteresting.

I needed some make-up. I didn't have time. Not even for my trademark red lipstick. Oh really, what did it matter? And why did women wear make-up anyway? For men? For other women? For themselves?

Tripping over the uneven flagstone courtyard, I hurried to the kitchen door which was open. I edged around a cross-looking cat, curled up in a cardboard box. Paulo was inside chopping something, onions by the look of it.

'I'm so sorry I'm late,' I said, gasping, hanging onto the door frame.

The odour of garlic and herbs smacked up my nose like smelling salts.

Paulo turned to me with a broad smile.

'*Mi'amica*! Good day to you, my friend!'

'I'm so sorry, I was supposed to be here ages ago, and, I don't know how, I just overslept.'

Paulo wiped his knife on a tea towel. '*Per favore, calmati*! Calm yourself. It is quite okay.'

'But I was supposed to be helping.'

'Oh, certainly you can help, if you really don't mind.' He gestured towards the stone sink. 'There is always washing-up to do. Emilio, my – shall we call him – sous-chef, hasn't arrived. Yet again.'

'I don't mind at all,' I said, looking around at the mountain on the worktop to get through. Cutlery, several huge saucepans and any number of dishes and glasses.

I was used to brokering deals between international companies, chairing meetings and reporting back to shareholders but washing up was something I was definitely not used to doing. Back home I seldom cooked and when I did, there was a state-of-the-art machine purring away efficiently to deal with the aftermath.

'Where's the dishwasher?' I asked.

Paulo grinned and added a dirty saucepan to the pile. 'Standing in front of the sink in some very pretty sandals that I fear will be spoiled.'

It took me a moment to realise he meant me.

* * *

I didn't think I had washed so many dishes for years.

Once I got into the swing of things it was actually quite therapeutic. But then it was – for me – a novelty. Like occasionally taking a dog for a walk when you don't own one, or helping a friend clear out their fridge when your own is pristine and practically empty.

Paulo had been concocting some hearty stew for the evening meals, starting off with chunks of something that looked like a bag of dog treats. Apparently, they were chunks of ox tails. Forgetting the associations that were brought to mind, the smell in the kitchen as he stirred the huge vat on the stove was divine. The cat had wandered in, enticed by the aroma, and was sitting in a very inconvenient place between the stove and the table. Every time Paulo moved, it looked up at him with hopeful, amber eyes.

I went back to the sink, my sandals slipping on the wet, stone floor. Paulo had been right about those. I was already soaking wet from the neck down to the knees. Perhaps I shouldn't have worn those new trousers, or that shirt. Well, Zoe had warned me.

'What are you making?' I asked.

'*Guazzetto*, beef, slow-cooked for this evening. There is a recipe, but I like to add what I have. It's not just the ingredients, it's the time that makes it so good. You'll see.'

He handed me another dirty plate and bowl with an apologetic grin.

Back to the washing-up.

In my own kitchen it would have been hard to tell if anyone lived there or not, everything was hidden away in cupboards. Jack and I were minimalist, I supposed. Although having been to his flat a few times, I suspected he was rather more careless about tidying up and putting things away. At my place he was the sort of man who found toast crumbs rather offensive. How ridiculous.

Here, everything was on display. Pans hanging from a rail on one wall, crockery slotted into wooden plate racks, jugs and glasses on open shelves. In the middle of the room was a huge table with a metal top which was covered in bowls and dishes. In one corner was a cupboard, the doors open to show numberless jars and cans and about ten wooden chopping boards. This was not a place to store food or open takeaway cartons; it was a working kitchen. It was rather sexy.

There was a yelp of alarm behind me. 'Paulo! What are you making her do?' It was Zoe, spectacles on top of her head, a sheaf of paperwork in one hand.

Paulo looked around vaguely. 'She offered to help.'

'Yes, but...'

'It's fine,' I said. 'I'm enjoying myself.'

And funnily enough, I was. Even though I was boiling hot and soaking wet; my hands had taken on the texture of old prunes and my feet were cold.

'I meant scraping carrots or chopping onions,' Zoe said.

Paulo looked confused. 'But...'

'I was late on my first day,' I admitted, wiping my hot face with a damp tea towel. 'I overslept.'

'Well, that old reprobate Uncle Franco is in the bar,' Zoe said to Paulo, 'asking for lunch. You'd better go and talk to him.'

Paulo nodded, dried his hands and wandered off, stepping over the cat which meowed resentfully in protest.

Zoe shook her head at me. 'I think you had better go and change into some dry clothes, before Paulo starts giving you more of the lunchtime plates as well. And then come and have something to eat. You haven't had breakfast, have you?'

'I don't usually...'

I rescued my watch from the stone windowsill, it was one thirty. Where had the time gone? And I was starving.

I went back to my room to change and caught sight of myself. It was not the sort of reflection I was used to seeing. My hair was loosely tied back, a damp birds' nest. No lipstick, no mascara. There was a shred of carrot on my cheek, a tomato skin in my hair, and yet there was something about me that was different. I looked relaxed. But more than that, I looked, what was the word... untroubled?

This was very surprising. The frown line between my eyebrows seemed to have faded too. Perhaps I wouldn't need Botox after all.

I scurried around my room looking for some clean clothes. My laundry pile was increasing, overflowing from the plastic bag I had been using. I pulled on my unflattering jeans and a clean T-shirt. The only other flat shoes I had brought with me were deck shoes.

I took another quick look. Yes, that would have to do. Anyway, no one would be looking at me; no one would know me. No one would expect anything from me. It was a terrifically liberating feeling.

10

Of course, the first person I saw in the trattoria, sitting at a table in the window with Paulo, was Gio. Suddenly I didn't feel quite so confident, which was ridiculous. I double-checked that there were no further food remnants on my face or in my hair. I reassured myself that, after all, I didn't really know him, and he didn't know me. I doubted either of us had a real opinion of the other.

Although I did have to admit he was looking very eye-catching. Why, at that precise moment, did I have to think that?

'Ah, *signora*,' he said, standing up, 'I just popped in for lunch and I hear Paulo has been putting you to work. He is a hard boss.'

'Well, not really,' I said, a bit flustered.

Paulo pulled out a chair for me to sit down.

The rest of the trattoria was empty apart from two elderly couples sitting near the window.

'Now then, you must meet one of the special members of my family. Uncle Franco, this is Zoe's cousin, Clover. You must tell her how wonderful it is to live here. She is finding it very different from London.'

An elderly man, quite distinguished-looking and white-haired, stood up rather stiffly and took my hand across the table.

'*Sono deliziato*. Delighted to meet you,' Franco said, with a gallant little bow. Paulo wandered off to get us some food.

'Franco lives just down the hill, a little way. He comes here most days,' Gio said.

'You must be the poker player I've heard about,' I said.

He grinned. 'Welcome, welcome, I hope you are enjoying your stay here.'

'It's a lovely place,' I said, tugging at my T-shirt and trying to pat my hair into some sort of order.

Why was I feeling so nervous? Two minutes previously I'd been absolutely fine.

'The food is good and the welcome is warm,' Franco said, 'but please, sit down, let me get you a drink.'

What I wanted was an extremely large glass of wine. If I'd had one I would probably down it very quickly which wasn't a good idea on an empty stomach.

'Just some sparkling water, please,' I said, pleased at my own restraint.

'*Certo*.' Franco stood up, rocked a little to get his balance and went off to the bar, returning a while later with my drink. Gio and I sat in slightly tense, but not un-smiling, silence.

Franco sat down opposite me with a grunt.

I'd begun to notice that: the inability older people had of doing anything without sound effects. Getting up, sitting down, reaching into a cupboard for something, lying down in bed, carrying a shopping bag: each had their own accompaniment. Was I doing that too and not realising it? I'd have to check...

I took a long unladylike swig of my sparkling water, enjoying the sting of the salty bubbles in my throat and also the feeling of relief as my throbbing feet relaxed under the rustic, wooden table. I gave a predictable sigh.

Paulo returned with bowls of soup, some bread and several wedges of cheese on a stone slab.

'*Minestra maritata*. You would call this "Italian wedding soup": a perfect marriage between tiny little meatballs, *acini de pepe* pasta and parmesan. And these cheeses are from a place not far from here.'

I picked up a spoon; the bowl in front of me smelled wonderful, nothing like the soup I was used to which came in plastic pots from the delicatessen.

'So, you have had a hard morning?' Franco asked a few minutes later with a twinkle in his blue eyes. 'That young man who is supposed to be working here is gone. Someone said he has left the town.'

'Emilio? Has he?' Paulo said. 'I hadn't heard. No one tells me anything.'

'Well, it was nothing I couldn't handle,' I said. 'In fact, I quite enjoyed myself. Even if I did get very wet. I think I need to refine my technique. Particularly when it comes to rinsing the plates.'

'*Sin che si vive, s'impara sempre,*' Franco said. 'As long as you live, you learn.'

'A holiday is a good time to do new things. And what else will you do while you are here?' Gio asked suddenly, his eyes full of humour.

I took a breath, ready to say something clever about getting my mojo back, roughing out a plan to get my career in order. And then suddenly I couldn't think of anything. I also couldn't be bothered to put on a brave face. The prospect of work was becoming more unattractive by the hour. How odd that I could get used to the idea of freedom in such a short time.

I was not an aspiring Hollywood starlet pretending I was

working in a diner just waiting for my big break. I was a woman who had been cut off in my prime. Well, perhaps a few years after my prime, if I was being honest, but certainly a prime of some sort.

'I don't know,' I admitted. 'Perhaps I haven't thought this through properly.'

I always thought things through properly, at least I always had in the past. This new, bohemian way of living was very odd.

'That's the best sort of holiday,' Gio said, 'otherwise it is just work in a different place.'

The next day, Monday morning, I woke at seven o'clock. I knew now I didn't have to rush to get into the kitchen, so I sat in the armchair by the window with my morning tea. Looking out of the window at the view. The early morning light was pearly and opalescent, mist rising off the lake. I could see sheep, grazing peacefully on the hill side. I wondered who owned them and how people here made a living from them.

On the other side of the valley, I could see cars and lorries, making their way towards the towns. People going to work, following their routines. I realised that for the first time in decades, I no longer had work or any sort of routine. And despite myself I felt reasonably comfortable with the idea.

I fumbled in my dressing gown pocket for my phone and turned it on.

There were several messages on it, all from Jack. Ah, of course he would be back from his golfing trip now, back in civilisation. Probably with tales of how much he had enjoyed himself, the meals they had eaten, the brilliant way he had got out of a bunker. Ignoring the fact that I'd told him to leave.

I could just imagine him, crashing noisily through the door to my apartment, weighed down with his cases, some carrier bags of gifts for me, for his PA at work, for himself. Sniffing the air, hoping for lasagne. I started to go through the texts.

I'm back. Are you out somewhere? I've bought a really great new club. It's a TaylorMade. P7TW. The same as Tiger Woods. The weather was rubbish, but we got one round in. Raj was furious. He was playing like a girl. He got more desperate as it went on and eventually threw his putter into the bushes. We were in stitches.

Where are you? It's nearly six thirty. I'm starving. Shall I order something in? What time will you be back?

It's after seven. Look, I know you've been upset, but I'm back now. Let's just forget about the other night. I thought we might have a night in, have a good chat about everything.

Where are you? Has something happened? Please ring me, your phone is off and it keeps telling me to leave a message. You know I hate doing that.

If you don't ring me in the next ten minutes, I'm going to ring your mother.

The prospect of Jack ringing my mother was most unusual.

I've just spoken to Eleanor, and she says you have gone to Italy to see Zoe. Has she got dementia do you think? RING ME! Urgent!

What the hell are you playing at? Have you really gone to Italy? I'm sure Eleanor was just rambling on like she does. I could hear the television on in the background. Perhaps she was watching Montalbano or the Medicis and got confused.

Are you trying to make a point?

I stifled a snort of laughter. I had told him I wanted to get away, that I needed a break and, more importantly, that he should leave. He evidently hadn't taken me seriously.

It was nearly eight o'clock. Even allowing for the time difference Jack would be at work, at his desk with the view over the river. Tapping away at his computer, being important.

I finished my tea and then I rang him.

* * *

'What do you think you're playing at?' he said irritably. 'I have been worried sick. I thought you might have had an accident or something.'

'No, I'm fine. I told you I needed to get away, so I just went.'

'Well, when are you back? At the weekend? You took my suits to the cleaners, and I can't find the tickets. There's no food in the flat, the milk has gone off and there's a funny smell in the fridge.'

There was a moment's deep silence which I made no effort to fill. And then he sighed.

'Braithwaite has been on the prowl; I have a meeting with him and the other clowns from HR this afternoon. Some nonsense about – well, never mind. I mean, what are you doing?'

'I've been washing up,' I said, sipping my tea.

I thought about going back into the kitchen later on and felt an unexpected thrill of pleasure. I was looking forward to it in a way I didn't ever think I had with work. How peculiar.

Jack gave an exasperated groan. 'I'll ring you later. I've got seven sorts of shit circling my head at the moment.'

'That's a very unpleasant image,' I said coldly.

'Yes, well. As long as you're okay. Not planning to do anything silly. Eleanor said you were in a state and trying to be brave about things.'

'I might be scraping some carrots later,' I said airily, 'or chopping onions. I'm not sure.'

I wondered what Paulo would be making for the evening. The *guazzetto* had been delicious.

'Oh for... Look, I'll ring you when I get a moment, keep your phone on this time. Do you know where the stubs for the dry cleaning are?'

'No. And I hope you aren't still in my flat. I told you to leave,' I said.

'I think you're having some sort of breakdown,' he said. 'It's not surprising. After everything. I expect you are feeling untethered. Unnecessary. Without any real purpose. It's very common in women your age.'

'Thank you for the mansplanation about how I'm feeling. When I do get back, I want you to have moved out. Do you understand me?'

I waited for a moment, and he didn't answer. And then I realised he'd hung up.

11

And so, I spent another reasonably enjoyable morning in the kitchen tidying up and preparing vegetables. Although after about an hour I did wonder how many people Paulo was catering for. Ten? Twenty? Fifty? Who was going to eat all this anyway? I'd not seen the trattoria with more than a dozen people in it at any one time and that was including us. Zoe had said trade was poor, but she was hoping it would pick up. There didn't seem any sign of that yet.

Mid-morning, I took some coffee into the office where Zoe was wrestling with paperwork and accounts and cursing the computer which she said was almost an antique. Certainly, the printer made a lot of angry clunking noises when anything was expected of it, eventually spitting out paper onto the floor because the tray was broken.

'Perhaps you could buy a new one?' I suggested.

Zoe gave me a look. 'We manage perfectly well with this one.'

'I could buy one for you. To thank you for having me here.'

Zoe laughed. 'Don't be daft. How is the new job going?'

I felt a gulp of panic. Then I realised what she meant. 'It's fine.

I've finished the washing up and done some vegetables. Paulo must be expecting a coach party in or something. He's preparing far too much food.'

Zoe shrugged. 'He always does. Anything we don't use he sends out to the convent in the village. They distribute it to anyone who needs it.'

'Oh. I see.'

So was this area a poor one? I didn't know. It didn't seem so, although suddenly I remembered the empty houses in the town. The closed shops. That beautiful villa – its walls dry and crumbling. The weeds choking the ironwork railings. And young people? Where were they? I realised I hadn't seen any since I had been here, even the young man who was supposed to be working in the kitchen had gone. How oblivious I'd been.

'It must be hard, working like this,' I said.

Zoe looked up. 'You mean without many customers?'

'Well... yes.'

'We've had a hard couple of years, but we'll manage,' she said. 'We are hoping it will pick up with the better weather. In the summer months I bet you won't be able to get a table here. And Paulo spent the winter renovating the other barn – he's very good with things like that and he has friends who are builders – so we will be able to rent it out. It's nearly finished.'

It was on the tip of my tongue to ask why people would come here since, despite the wonderful scenery, there didn't seem much to attract tourists.

Zoe seemed to sense my question. 'There are wonderful cave paintings and drawings further up the valley. You should go and see them one day. Thousands of people come every year to see them.'

'Really?'

Zoe laughed. 'Absolutely. You should hike up there and see when the last of the snow has gone.'

Hike.

Not an activity I had ever considered.

'Yes, I might,' I said haltingly.

'Perhaps you might need to get some walking boots. Or you could borrow mine.'

'I'm beginning to think I should have brought some different clothes,' I admitted. 'Mine seem a bit formal for life here.'

'Yes, you are by far the best-dressed sous-chef we have ever had. I'll take you out one day soon and we will find something. I know a couple of really good places.'

I had a comforting image of myself in Milan, walking around the Galleria Vittorio Emanuele II, admiring those magnificent mosaic floors and glass-domed ceilings. I'd been there many years ago with Casper. Perhaps I would pop into the glorious Duomo to admire The Last Supper, or into La Scala. Though opera had always been Jack's thing rather than mine. He would be so annoyed to think I had seen it without him, that it was almost worth going.

'I'd love that,' I said. 'Let's go soon.'

* * *

For the rest of the week, I fell into a sort of routine. I helped Paulo in the kitchen every morning and had a siesta in the afternoon on my comfortable bed. I gave Zoe a hand with the paperwork when she had problems. I had always been a whizz with a spreadsheet, and I created a couple of new ones for her. Incomings and outgoings. Even I could see that the latter was far more than the former. Surely that couldn't continue, or they would be bankrupt...

'Wait until Easter – the spring. Things will pick up,' she said.

'Where do you advertise? To attract people?'

'Word of mouth usually. It's worked up until now.'

But the world had changed in the last few years. Places closing down, being inaccessible. People travelling far less. Surely they needed to do something more than spread the word? I wondered what I could do to help them.

* * *

The following Monday it was the finest of spring mornings, nothing like March in London when it always seemed to be too cold and wet to do much. I felt very intrepid, and since I had remembered to pack my Italian phrase book: I decided to walk into the nearby town.

There were a few shops, a bakery, which judging by the sign in the window seemed to open when it felt like it, a cute hardware store, with a display outside of wicker baskets stacked up in a wheelbarrow, and a small supermarket.

Now this could be fun. Supermarkets in London were places I tended to avoid, but here, everything was an adventure. I grabbed a basket and walked confidently in, humming to the strains of 'Volare' which was playing over the loudspeakers.

Fruit and vegetables were first, gorgeous-looking produce of impressive colour and quality. I found a paper bag and reached for some glorious tomatoes. Immediately a woman next to me hissed her disapproval and tapped my arm.

'*Hai bisogno di un guanto.*'

I looked blank.

'*Un guanto.* Glove,' the woman repeated, tugging at my sleeve.

Weird, it wasn't that cold.

She pulled a disposable glove from a box and shook it at me. 'Don't touch. Glove,' she said.

Ah. '*Grazie*,' I said, feeling rather cosmopolitan.

She huffed a bit at me and went off with her trolley.

First problem solved.

I'd always thought foreign supermarkets were interesting. It told you a lot about the locals. In this case it seemed that they liked a vast selection of pasta, proper coffee, dozens of varieties of olive oil and fruit juices. The place was well-stocked, and the aisles were narrow so they could really pack the produce in.

Everything looked so exciting, and I had my basket filled in no time. I put in *confetture* – obviously jam – and then found something called *crema di maroni alla vaniglia*. I pulled out my phrase book and my glasses, much to the annoyance of the Glove Woman who leaned across me and grabbed a huge jar of the stuff. Perhaps I should have some too if she was prepared to get funny about it.

I thumbed through my phrase book. Something to do with vanilla.

'It's a vanilla chestnut cream,' a voice said in my ear, 'very delicious.'

I spun round, knocking a whole row of pasta off the shelf behind me with my elbow.

'I'm sorry; I seem to startle you a great deal,' Gio said, laughing.

'Just a bit,' I said.

He bent to help me pick up the packages of pasta and we put them back into some sort of order before one of the assistants came and hustled me out of the way so she could do it properly.

'Can I help you with anything else? If you like sweet things, you should try Pan di Stelle. Italians love those, dunked in coffee.'

Gio went and pulled a package off the shelf and put them in my basket.

He frowned a little at the tiny jar of instant coffee in my basket, the only one I could find.

'*Santo cielo*. Good heavens. Not that coffee,' he said, pointing. 'If you will forgive my interference, try this one.'

He held out a packet of ground coffee from his basket. 'Coffee is too important to Italians; we take it very seriously.'

'Well, thank you,' I said, a bit flustered, 'I'll give it a try.'

I didn't like to say I was used to 'bean-to-cup' coffee at home thanks to the machine Jack had bought. I'd never actually used it without a lot of fussing and supervision from Jack. When he presented me with a latte or an espresso, he did so bursting with pride, as though he had invented and built the machine. Here I just had a metal contraption in my little kitchenette, and I wasn't sure how to use it.

'You have a Moka pot?' Gio asked.

Possibly. 'I think so,' I said.

'I will show you, it's very easy.'

I stocked up on a few other things: some gorgeous apples, milk and some rustic-looking bread. We paid for our purchases, and I followed him out onto the pavement with four very heavy bags and my handbag, which also weighed a ton.

In my supermarket-fired excitement, I hadn't thought about that. I'd only come out for a walk and now I had what felt like three hundredweight of shopping. *And* I'd had to pay for the bags because I hadn't brought any with me. That had earned me a stern look from the woman on the check-out.

Gio turned and looked at me, and then he reached out to help.

'Come,' he said. 'Let me take those. But, *momento*, you don't have a car, do you? How were you going to get all these things back up the hill?'

'Very slowly,' I said, realising he was right, 'perhaps in relays?'

He laughed and shook his head.

My basket had been so heavy I had resorted to pushing it along the floor towards the till with my foot. At least I'd had the good sense not to pick a trolley and fill that to the brim. In London I would have stuck out my hand for a taxi, but here there was no such opportunity.

He looked at my footwear, the canvas deck shoes, which were still splattered with the remains of some tomato sauce from yesterday's kitchen adventures.

'Then come, I will give you a lift,' he said, kindly, 'and then I will show you how to make proper Italian coffee.'

Despite myself I felt a silly flutter of delight. Which was pathetic.

'That's if you are not busy?' he added.

'I'm not busy at all,' I said.

His car was parked just around the corner but getting there took some time and several stops because people kept starting up conversations with him. First an elderly woman with a black felt hat pinned firmly over her brow, then a couple of middle-aged women with straw shopping baskets. I was sure they looked at my flimsy, unecological carriers with scorn.

Their conversation was brisk and far beyond my grasp of Italian, except for the odd word. Apart from things like *il tempo*, which I knew meant the weather, and *la neve*, which meant snow.

I looked up to the hills, wondering what it was like here when the roads were shut and the snow line on the mountains came down to include this town and the church and the supermarket. I was slightly uncomfortable, not able to engage in the conversation, but at the same time not able to wander off with my bags. So, I was sort of there, but not there.

The women gave me sideways looks.

'*La donna inglese*,' said one.

Well, I knew what that meant. The English woman.

I smiled and nodded rather manically, to show I was indeed there, and perhaps persuade them I knew what was going on.

The other said something I didn't understand, and they both laughed.

'Buon giorno,' I said, shifting my bags, which by then were cutting into my hands like instruments of torture.

They smiled and nodded pleasantly enough. I was sure they were wondering what on earth I was doing. And probably why Gio was with me.

* * *

Eventually we reached his truck, and Gio stored my shopping in the back, wedged in with a lot of muddy coats, a cardboard box and a rolled-up blanket.

'Sorry about the mess,' he said. 'I keep all my painting things in here; it saves time when I want to head out for the day *inaspettatamente* – unexpectedly.'

'It's fine,' I said, heaving myself up into the passenger seat, which seemed very high. 'And where do you like to go on an unexpected trip?'

'It depends on the weather.'

He started up the truck which gave a throaty roar, and drove off, giving a wave to another woman who had stopped to hail him. He rolled the window down and they had a brief chat about something while she darted me suspicious and slightly unfriendly looks.

'You know just about everyone,' I said after we set off again.

Well, all the middle-aged women anyway.

'I should do: I have lived here for most of my life,' he said. 'The lady in the black hat is my aunt and the two ladies with the shopping baskets are distant cousins. That last one was a friend of my wife.'

Ah yes, his wife.

I struggled to think of some way of extracting information out of him without seeming weird, but the moment passed, and I couldn't think of anything sensible to say.

Gio flicked a quick look at his watch.

'We can drop off your shopping, and then why don't you come to my house where I will make you coffee? *Proper* coffee.'

I had a moment's hesitation, a little frisson of something... Trepidation?

Zoe said he was a catch. I didn't want a catch, but on the other hand, he did seem pleasant company.

'That would be lovely,' I said, rather surprised and pleased with myself.

12

Back at the trattoria, Gio helped me in with my shopping and stood in the doorway to the barn while I put it all away.

'I remember this place when Nonna lived here,' he said, 'Paulo's mother. She was a wonderful woman. Always interested in everything, always talking. Franco took her death very hard. After all, she was his last surviving sister. They were great friends, despite the age gap between them and all the arguments.'

'They argued a lot?'

'Oh, *certo*, they did. I think it's what kept them both going. Franco said if there were an Italian Olympic arguing team, Nonna would have been the captain. I think it's what brothers and sister do.'

'I don't have either,' I said, 'so perhaps I missed out.'

'Ah. *Una figlia unica* – an only child. I can't imagine that. I was one of four,' he said.

'And do they all live around here?'

'Only Elisabetta, who is in Milan. Marco lives in Switzerland, Tomasso in France. But we meet up as often as we can. We write; we phone each other; we are a very close family.'

'That must be nice,' I said. I realised I sounded wistful, and I was clutching my loaf of rustic bread to my chest rather dramatically. I put it away in the breadbasket, brushed off the seeds and flour which had been deposited all over the front of my jumper, and turned with a bright smile on my face.

'Right,' I said, 'I'm ready if that offer of coffee still stands?'

'Everything okay?' It was Zoe, standing in the open doorway, an expression of acute interest on her face.

'I went shopping,' I said, 'and Gio gave me a lift back.'

I was blushing; I could feel it.

She didn't move, just stood trying to look innocently inquisitive, some might say nosey.

'So I see. Jolly good,' she remarked. 'I'm glad to see you again, Gio. Come for dinner soon.'

'I'd love to. We are going for coffee,' Gio said, blissfully unaware of the undercurrent between me and my cousin. 'I'm going to show Clover how to use a Moka pot.'

'How lovely,' Zoe said with a smile. 'I could have showed you in about five seconds – it's really easy.'

She gave me a meaningful look, her eyebrows twitching slightly. I decided to ignore her.

'Well, I won't hold you up,' Zoe said, 'unless there's anything you need? Milk or biscuits or – you know – advice?'

'No, I can't think of anything,' I replied sweetly.

Gio left to make his way to the truck.

'Can't use a Moka pot?' Zoe muttered as I passed her. 'Don't make me laugh.'

'I *can't*,' I hissed back.

'Have fun and tell me all about it when you get back. You minx.'

'It's just coffee,' I said, innocently.

'Yeah. Sure it is,' she said.

* * *

Leaving the trattoria, Gio drove us further up the hillside along narrow twisting roads. I wound down the window and the air was clear and fresh; the view stretched out for miles. Mountains, trees and wildflowers which were beginning to show sparks of colour on the rocky verges. We passed a few houses here and there, and of course the lake far below us, the glimpses of it not so frequent now.

After about ten minutes, he pulled off the road onto a dirt track which led to a large house, painted pale ochre with a stone slab roof.

I opened the door of the truck and slithered inelegantly down; well, it was really high up. Then one of my shoes fell off and rolled under the truck. I scrabbled about for a moment until I found it and my hair came unpinned on one side and fell over my face. All of a sudden, I felt very disorganised and foolish, though I didn't think Gio had noticed. Or perhaps he had and was being tactful.

The air here was colder, the wind fresher, and I drew in a deep, invigorating lungful and then coughed. Perhaps my city lungs weren't used to the lack of hydrocarbons and particulate matter.

He collected his shopping from the back of the truck.

'Come in,' he said, beckoning me with one hand.

Trees crowded around the building, as though they had been carved out to make way for the house. There was a covered veranda stretching along the front, with views of the craggy slopes and just a glimpse of the lake far below us.

He opened the door and led me inside. Well, this was an adventure and no mistake. Just over two weeks ago I had been in London: fumes from traffic; fast food outlets; people everywhere, crowding the pavements; everyone impatient and busy. And now I was in a place which Jack would have dismissed as the back of beyond.

'It's a long way to anywhere, isn't it?' I said.

Gio thought about this. 'I suppose so, but it's close to everything I want.'

I rather liked it. The feeling in the house was not just quiet – it was peaceful and welcoming too. As though the house had been ready, patiently waiting for us to arrive.

A few stone steps led down into the living room, which was large and furnished with sofas and a couple of big leather chairs next to an enormous fireplace. The spring light flooded in through the huge windows and a black cat was asleep on the rug, enjoying the sunshine. It raised its head as we came in and fixed me with a look which I would not have described as friendly.

Then it saw Gio, raised itself into an extravagant stretch and flashed its teeth at me, before coming to wind itself around his feet.

'*Buffo, come stai*?' he said bending down to ruffle the cat's ears. 'My cat has obviously had a hard morning.'

'I can tell,' I said.

'*Andiamo*. Come into the kitchen.'

The cat gave four meows in quick succession. I wondered what 'meow' was in Italian. Did cats have one language or many? Would English cats understand Italian cats? Or would there be a language barrier?

I liked cats and I held my fingers out and waggled them in the accepted manner. I even made *pss-pss-pss* noises which usually worked. The cat ignored me and stalked off after Gio, its tail held high. Perhaps I wasn't speaking cat Italian. Maybe I had said something offensive to him without knowing it. I followed.

The kitchen was lovely. With a high ceiling, white walls, huge, polished beams, a wooden table and chairs, and a deep nook that had obviously once been a fireplace but now contained a rather sexy red range cooker.

Gio went to the other side of the breakfast bar, flicked the kettle on and then reached into a cupboard and brought out a metal gadget.

'Here,' he said, 'the famous Moka pot. Ground coffee – not too fine. Fill up this little basket, but don't press it down.'

I watched his fingers, deftly smoothing the coffee. There was a little smudge of blue paint on the back of his hand. I wondered what he had been painting.

Unknown to him, on my side of the breakfast bar, the cat was sniffing my shoes.

He held out the base towards me so I could see inside. '*Aspetto*. You see, it's as clean as new. Some people think it should be allowed to build up old coffee stains, but I don't agree. I think it makes the coffee bitter. Now—'

He filled up the base with boiling water. And screwed up the top. Then he lifted the lid from the range cooker and put the pot onto the plate.

I shifted slightly and tried to look interested, despite the cat now trying to sharpen its claws on my trouser leg.

'I hope you don't think I am being *vanaglorioso* – a show off,' he said with a grin. 'I just like coffee made this way.'

'No, not at all,' I said, leaning forward in a display of curiosity, resting my elbows on the counter and disguising the fact that I was trying to dislodge the cat by shaking my leg.

The coffee started to brew, spewing out into the upper part, bringing with it a delicious aroma and then some rather rude gurgling sounds.

I looked down and realised the cat had attached its fangs to my trousers and was giving me a very purposeful look. I shook my leg again, hoping to remove it. The cat was having none of it. I could hear a faint growling noise.

'There,' Gio said, pleased. 'How easy was that?'

He passed me a mugful and I sipped it. It was delicious.

'What do you think?'

'Lovely,' I said, trying to ignore what was going on behind me. 'I'll have to try when I get home.'

Suddenly, furious at being ignored, the cat made a scrabbling lunge and managed to dig most of its claws into my bottom. I gave a startled squeak and – as had been the case quite frequently where food and I were involved – slopped my drink all over myself. I gave another yelp because of course the coffee was hot.

Gio and I stared at each other for a second. He must have thought I was bonkers.

The cat, although scrawny, was obviously athletic, because a second later it scrabbled up the back of my jacket and came to rest practically on top of my head. I froze, wondering how such a small animal could be quite so heavy.

'*Buffo! Gatto cattivo!* Bad cat, what are you doing?' Gio exclaimed, reaching out to dislodge the animal.

'It's fine,' I said weakly as Gio disentangled the cat's claws from my hair. There was a bit of grumbling from the cat and some wincing from me. How many claws did that cat have anyway, five hundred?

'I do apologise, I don't know what's got into him,' Gio said at last, having dumped the cat on the floor, where it immediately started to lick its paws, as if to say, *Good job.*

'Just being friendly I expect,' I said, dabbing at my coffee-stained shirt with some paper towels and pushing my hair out of my eyes. I really would have to do some washing; I was running out of clean clothes.

'I'm so sorry,' Gio said again, his face creased with concern. 'Is there anything I can do to help?'

Well, not unless you want to dab at my bosom with a damp cloth. Which might be interesting.

'No, honestly, no harm done,' I said.

'Well, if you're sure,' he said. 'Shall I make you some more coffee?'

'That would be lovely,' I said, smiling cheerfully.

Buffo and I exchanged a look.

I'm bigger than you are, cat, and I've got opposable thumbs.

We went and sat at the kitchen table: Gio on one side, me on the other. Buffo watched us, blinking slowly and probably planning his next attack.

'*Allora*, tell me, what brings you here, Clover?' Gio said after we had finished discussing the coffee.

'Well, Zoe is my cousin; we've known each other for most of our lives. And I...'

What should I say? Perhaps honesty was the best policy.

'...I used to work in London. I had been with the same firm for over twenty years and then out of the blue I was made redundant. I needed to get away, give myself time to think.'

He drew in a sharp breath. 'That must have been difficult. Very difficult.'

'It was. Work was all I'd known for so long; I couldn't quite understand what I was going to do next. Sounds silly, doesn't it?'

'No, not at all. Everyone needs to know they are valued and needed. Whether it's work or family or – well, anything really. But you told me you have a son. In Canada. You could go and see him?'

'I probably will,' I said. 'I'd like that. I was supposed to go last year, and the year before, but a breakout of a very inconsiderate virus caused travel problems, I'm sure you remember. Then I wasn't very well – luckily not Covid– and I had too much work on. Oh, mostly just daft excuses by the end. I should have gone.'

The truth was, Jack hadn't wanted to go, and pathetically I'd allowed him to influence my decision.

'*Forse*, perhaps you can go now.'

'Yes, I could but...'

But what about my career? My future? Shouldn't I be doing something about that?

'In my line of work,' I continued, 'it's very easy to fall out of the loop. For people to forget about you.'

'And your husband? What does he say?'

I fidgeted a bit. 'I'm divorced. I have been since Ben was a toddler. I have a partner. Well, I did. We are going our separate ways now.'

'And did he have any advice?'

Well, not much actually, except 'what doesn't kill you makes you stronger'.

'No, not really,' I replied. 'He thinks I should start up my own consultancy.'

Gio finished his coffee and put the mug down on the table between us.

'And do you want to do that?' he asked.

'No, no, I don't,' I said.

I was a bit surprised at myself; I'd said that without any thought or reluctance. And I knew in that moment it was true. I definitely *didn't* want to do that. The prospect of it had been like a lure, dragging me back into my old life. Even in the time I had been here – surrounded by the beauty of the lake and the mountains and the slower pace of life; the uncomplicated kindness of my cousin – I knew that something inside me was changing. How odd. I hadn't really noticed until that moment. How could the influence of a long, busy working life just fade? Was it to do with my age?

I suddenly thought about Jack. I hadn't really considered how he felt about all this. Had he found it more satisfactory to be in a relationship with a director, someone who called the shots at work and who had some impressive job title, rather than someone who was retired?

'Retired' always seemed such a depressing word. This person is not just tired, they are re-tired. To leave, to give up, to back off, to admit defeat. This woman is so extra super tired, that she can now be safely ignored. Would Jack and I have had anything to talk about except his work, now that I didn't have any? Would we have turned into the sort of couple who stayed together for the sake of appearances, or because we were too lazy to face a big change?

Well, retirement didn't fit my mood at all. The one thing I did realise was that I might not be in the finance game any longer, but my brain was just as nimble. I was going to do *something else*.

I realised that there had been a long silence. Gio was still sitting opposite me, not pushing me to say something, just waiting for me to come out of my thoughts.

'Sorry,' I said, 'I was miles away.'

He smiled. 'It's fine, you need time to think. Of course, you do. You have a lot of life left, a lot to give, plans to make and ideas to consider.'

I did, didn't I? How interesting. Actually, how rather exciting.

* * *

We sat and talked for a while, with him asking about my life in London, and me asking about his life in the hills. He seemed to live very simply. Painting things that took his attention, that pleased him. Sometimes a view, occasionally an animal or a person. A strangely-shaped stone or a flower in full bloom.

He was knowledgeable and interesting but in a gentle way. There was none of the showing off or point scoring I had come to expect from Jack. Or from my ex-husband either, if I could remember that far back. I realised it had been a very long time since I'd had a simple chat with someone without it turning into an argument or one of us making a heated point about something.

I was there for far longer than I'd thought I'd be. I realised because the coffee stain on the front of my shirt had dried. And Buffo had retreated to his patch of sunlight again for another cat nap.

What a life cats lead. Perhaps I might have taken a leaf out of his book. Eat when the fancy took me, learn how to sleep properly again, sit in the sun, look at the view and think sage thoughts. But perhaps not bring in dead mice or try and climb up people's trouser legs. Obviously.

* * *

At last, Gio looked at his watch and so did I. Only to realise I had forgotten to put it on that morning. Something else that was most unlike me. I had a fitness tracker too which I realised I must have left at home. Was I doing as many steps here as I had in London? Or fewer? Probably more.

'I'm hungry. What about a late lunch?' he asked. 'Very late, in fact. Would you like that?'

'I should be going,' I said hastily.

I shuffled forward to get off my chair.

'Why?' he asked, smiling.

I didn't know. It was just something to say – to cover up the feeling that I had probably long outstayed my welcome. That we had been doing nothing of much importance for hours. Just talking and drinking coffee, and then sitting and looking out of the window at the view.

'Because I'm sure you have better things to do?' I said.

'I can't think of anything better than this,' he said, and shrugged. 'Talking, drinking good coffee, getting to know you.'

That rang a bell... It was a song, wasn't it? From *The King and I*. Getting to know all about you. For a moment I was mentally rewinding the film, Deborah Kerr and all those children.

I realised he was watching me again, waiting for me to say something.

Did I have anything better to do? Wasn't this the sort of thing people were supposed to do on holiday? Relax, get to know local people, new places, new experiences?

'No,' I said at last, sitting back again, 'nor can I.'

13

And so, we had lunch.

It would in fact be nearly four o'clock by the time we sat down to eat.

Gio went to look in the fridge, accompanied by Buffo who was equally as interested. So much so that when Gio closed the fridge door, the cat narrowly escaped having his head trapped and gave an annoyed little yowl.

'I have bread, provolone piccante cheese, salami, tomatoes. Will that do?'

'Excellent,' I said. 'Can I help?'

'No, indeed, you sit and watch that view. Tell me if anything changes.'

So, I went back to my chair and did exactly that.

Outside, the light was beginning to fade. The sun had dipped down behind the hills, and the lake looked dark. A flock of birds flew across far below me. I could see their backs, the tops of their wings. Ducks or possibly geese?

That was something I'd always liked to do. To view things from an unusual perspective. Perhaps that was what I needed to do now – to look at my life and my future differently? Just for a moment London seemed a very long way away and I shuddered.

'You're not cold I hope?' he said.

He put a wooden platter of cheese and meat on the coffee table between our chairs and handed me a plate.

'I can get you a rug if you are?'

Oh, yes, that would be a great look, sitting huddled under a blanket.

'No, absolutely not. I'm fine – really,' I said.

He went back to fetch a basket of bread, a dish of tomatoes and a great creamy swirl of butter in a pottery dish. I was suddenly extremely hungry.

'I was just thinking that London seems a very long way away,' I admitted. 'It made me...'

What did it make me? Worried? Fearful? Uncomfortable?

'...it made me feel a bit odd,' I said at last.

'When will you go back?' he asked, holding out the basket of bread towards me.

I took a wedge and plastered some butter onto it. I didn't think I had eaten proper butter for a very long time. It was wonderful. Salty and rich – a perfect accompaniment to the peppery salami and the sweet tomatoes.

I finished my mouthful.

'I don't know,' I said at last.

And that made me feel even odder.

What was happening back at my apartment? Was Jack still there, wandering around with a confused expression, looking in the empty fridge in the hopes that something might magically appear? Or was he putting all his fitness gear and expensive grooming products into boxes? Had he, as I had suggested, packed up his dozens of Turnbull and Asser shirts and gone back to his own place?

'Then let's enjoy your time here. Let's not think of anything other than today, this moment, this meal,' Gio said. 'And let's have a glass of wine to celebrate all the good things in the world. We spend too much time worrying about the bad things, don't you think?'

I took another bite of my bread and considered this.

Bad things.

Politicians, work deadlines, reality television, traffic, tax inspectors, the price of petrol, people's irrational anger or their obsession with celebrities, football. They were some of the bad things in my opinion.

'Yes,' I said at last, 'I think you're right.'

He went back into the kitchen and returned with two glasses of red wine which he placed on the table between us. Then there was a crash and the sound of something breaking in the kitchen which sent him hurrying back, muttering, '*Buffo, è un tale ladro.*'

I assumed the cat must have been stealing something.

I carried on eating, vaguely aware of the sound of Gio sweeping up broken china.

After a few minutes he came to sit back down.

'I should know better than to leave salami unattended. Buffo cannot be trusted. He is well-named: Buffo, the Clown. Anyway, I hope you like red wine; this is nothing special, just something made locally.'

I took a sip, it was perfect. I raised my glass in his direction.

'Excellent,' I said. '*Eccellente.*'

Well, this was nice.

* * *

He drove me back to the trattoria about an hour later, through the dark evening towards the lights of the town. He even came around the truck to open my car door and help me down. His hand was warm and slightly rough against mine. He held it for a moment and then dropped a kiss on the back of it.

Good heavens, it was a very long time since anyone had done that.

'I have enjoyed your company, thank you,' he said.

'And I have enjoyed yours,' I replied.

It was true, I had. But looking at things dispassionately, we hadn't really done anything. Just shared some snacks, talked about food, watched the evening darken outside, drunk rough, red wine and kept Buffo away from the salami. A task which had not always been successful. Several times a black paw had poked hopefully over the edge of the table, making me laugh.

'Perhaps another time,' he said, 'I could show you something wonderful.'

Yes, I bet you jolly well could, I thought, *with all your hand-kissing and coffee-making and charm.*

'Let me know when you are free. We could plan an outing together.'

Well, actually, I was free most days, but it would have seemed a bit desperate if I'd said that.

'Well, wherever you think would be fun,' I said. 'After all, I don't know this area.'

'*Allora, buona notte*,' he said.

'Good night.'

Well, I veritably skipped back to my room as he reversed his truck out of the car park.

Five seconds later Zoe was banging on my door. 'Where *have* you been? That was Gio wasn't it?'

'Yes, it was. I've just been – you know – having a late lunch, talking.'

'Yes, right,' she said, then shut the door behind her and sat down on the sofa. 'Tell me everything.'

'You know already. I told you: I walked down to the village, I bought too much shopping, he brought me back and then took me to his place to show me how to make coffee.'

Zoe looked sceptical. 'You know how to make coffee. It's six thirty, surely it didn't take all this time? Or was he picking, roasting and grinding the beans first?'

'We were just chatting,' I said. 'No more than that. Although we did have a glass of wine and his cat leapt onto my head.'

'You look extremely pleased with yourself. Well, sadly I know something that may wipe that smile off your face.'

'What?'

'Jack rang.'

For a moment I was puzzled. My mind went completely blank. 'Jack?'

'He was trying to get in touch, you weren't answering your phone.'

Oh, him.

I went over to the bedside table where my mobile had been charging all day. Six missed calls from Jack, and two voicemails. The lightness of my mood faltered a bit, and I felt rather uneasy.

'What's the matter with him?'

'He says he's got an emergency on his hands, and he needs to talk to you.'

I was feeling very relaxed and mellow, for the first time in ages. I didn't want anything to spoil that.

'No—' I began. But the decision was taken out of my hands because at that moment my mobile started to ring, buzzing with such intensity that it almost rattled its way off the bedside table.

'I suppose I'd better answer it,' I said, 'or he'll just ring back.'

'Where the heck have you been?' Jack said without preamble.

'Just out,' I said. 'Have you finished packing your things?'

He tutted and ignored my question. 'I hope Zoe passed on my message?'

'Yes, she did. What's the matter?'

'I am upset. I'm furiously upset. I'm bloody upset-to-my-back-teeth upset.'

He sounded as though he was on the verge of tears which was most unlike him. Maybe my leaving and my ultimatum had made some impact after all.

I sent Zoe a despairing look.

'I'll leave you to it,' Zoe mouthed at me, and left, closing the door quietly behind her.

I flopped into a chair. 'What now?'

'I really need you to come back – it's urgent,' Jack said.

Not a chance. 'Why?' I asked. I didn't feel in the mood to give anything but the briefest of replies.

'Bloody Braithwaite, that's what's happened.'

Not me then, not our failed relationship, not his having to move back to his own place. Not upset about that.

I dug around in my memory banks. 'The HR chap?' I asked.

'I'm suspended.'

'From what?' I said, holding back a chuckle.

He scoffed with annoyance. 'Not that sort of suspended. I've been suspended from work.'

'Why?'

'I told you Braithwaite was on the prowl looking to pick someone off. It was like when the hyenas' group around the back of a herd of wildebeest, before they swoop in and snatch one of the stragglers.'

'I wouldn't have called you a straggler, Jack.'

'Ordinarily no, I'm not, but there's been some sort of complaint – a mix up. It's all too ridiculous but you know how these things go. Some little trollop in the office makes an accusation and before you know it there's a full-scale enquiry.'

My blood chilled a little. So, this really wasn't about us at all.

'What sort of accusation?'

'Harassment, sexual harassment. As if I would do... and certainly not her... Anyway, Braithwaite took enormous pleasure in summoning me to his office, which is much bigger than mine I might add – which is ridiculous because heaven knows what he does all day, other than shuffle papers and accuse hardworking people like me on trumped up charges. The world's gone mad. What happened to office banter? And her skirt *was* too tight, but then of course if you mention it you get accused of calling someone fat, and then heaven help you, you're a fattist, who hates all women. And it's a very short step to being labelled a misogynist, sexist, arrogant and part of the male, pale and stale problem.'

'Well, are you a misogynist?' I said.

'Of course I'm not. I love all women equally. Whatever their age, sexual orientation, race, religion, dietary requirements, political affiliation or allergies. But you the most, Clover, obviously. Bugger, there's someone ringing the doorbell. I'll have to go. It's probably Alasdair.'

'Well, keep your chin up,' I said, feeling unconcerned about where his chin might be.

Jack snorted. 'Put your chin up these days and someone is bound to punch it.'

'And if you haven't moved out already, which I hope you have, don't take any of my stuff.'

14

Zoe was back a few seconds later; it was almost as though she had been waiting outside my door, listening for the conversation to stop. Which was quite probable. Except she was holding an open bottle of wine and two glasses and had a box of breadsticks wedged under one elbow. So she must have gone somewhere.

'So?' she said without preamble.

'Which topic are you most interested in?'

She poured out the wine and handed me a glass. Then she kicked off her shoes and settled herself on the sofa with her feet up. She opened the breadsticks, took two and handed the box over.

'Finish telling me about Gio. All I know so far is you met in the village, had wine and a late lunch and he brought you back. What else happened?'

I could feel my cheeks flushing, which was ridiculous. Nothing at all had happened. Just two people talking.

'We just chatted about boring stuff. The weather, football, where to get the best deals on car insurance, junk mail, Formula 1.'

Zoe frowned. 'You didn't?'

'No, of course we didn't. We just talked about life, food we liked, places we had been...'

'Did he make a pass at you?'

'No, he didn't. I'm sure he's too much of a gentleman to do that. He did kiss my hand and tell me he'd enjoyed my company though.'

Zoe sipped her wine and sighed. 'How marvellous. Did you like it?'

'I suppose...'

Actually, yes.

'Ignore me. I'm just living vicariously. Paulo and I have been married for so long I can't remember what it's like to be in the first throes of a new romance.'

'Zoe, this isn't a new romance.'

She flapped a hand at me. 'Sure, if you say so. And what did Jack want?'

'Jack has been suspended from work. He has been accused of sexual harassment. He made an unfortunate remark about some woman's skirt being too tight.'

Zoe's eyes were round with horror, and then she spluttered with shocked laughter.

'Oh my god. Will they sack him?'

'There's going to be an investigation; that's all I know. So, it's no good asking me any more questions.'

We sat in thoughtful silence for a few minutes, drinking our wine and munching on the breadsticks.

'He'll just say it was office banter,' Zoe said.

Hmm, that's what he had said.

'Here, have some more wine,' she offered. 'Tell me what you think of Gio.'

'He's very pleasant.'

Zoe laughed. 'Don't be ridiculous. Uncle Franco is pleasant. The woman in the bakery is pleasant. Gio's an absolute fox. If you can't see that, you're crazy.'

'Okay, he's handsome, good company, charming and polite.'

'That's more like it. When are you seeing him again?'

'You mean on a *date*? Zoe, how old are you?'

'The same as you. Sixty. Nearly sixty-one. This is the most exciting thing that has happened for ages. So, you are seeing him again?'

'He said when I had a free day, he would show me something wonderful.'

Zoe clasped her hands together in excitement which was a pity because she was still holding a full wine glass and the contents splattered all over her lap.

I passed her a bunch of tissues and she scrubbed at the new red wine stain on her apron.

'Perhaps he is going to invite you back to his house again, and the place will be lit by a thousand candles, and there will be a fabulous meal and champagne and those little Baratti & Milano Gianduiotti – the ones in the blue wrappers. I may just die of jealousy.'

'I doubt that,' I said. 'He was talking about some cave paintings.'

Zoe looked disappointed. 'Oh, those... Still, if that's what sets you on fire, I suppose it's better than nothing. Perhaps he will take a picnic, in a cute wicker basket. And proper wine glasses, not the plastic mugs Paulo always packs. And a fabulous bottle of Barolo, and juicy peaches that taste of sunshine. And a rug. You must wear something gorgeous.' Her eyes lit up. 'We need to go shopping! I know just the place to take you. Tomorrow. I'll drive of course although I have been thinking of putting you onto my car insurance. That way you could get out a bit if the mood took you. Be ready at nine-thirty, or we will miss out.'

* * *

At nine-thirty the following morning, I was ready and surprisingly excited. It was weeks since I had been to a fashion boutique and even I, not a particularly die-hard shopper unless there was a very good reason, had been missing it.

I remembered the anticipation as I'd pushed the door open; the polite buzz to alert the assistants of my presence. The divine scent of new clothes and possibilities. Looking through the racks of dresses and shirts, the lovely subtle click of the wooden coat hangers. Perusing the artfully displayed shoes and handbags. The respectful and considerate assistants, eager to help.

I nudged the laundry bag of my food-splattered clothes a little further under the bed. I would deal with them later, after I had refurbished my wardrobe with some chic, Italian fashions.

Zoe knocked on my door and came in.

'Ready?'

'Absolutely,' I said.

* * *

We moved all the junk (empty pop bottles, bundles of paperwork, a straw basket filled with carrier bags and three pairs of sunglasses) from the passenger seat of her car and I hopped in.

'I'm looking forward to this. How long till we get there?' I asked.

'Oh, it's not far, and we will be early so there shouldn't be a problem parking,' she said happily, as she turned the car out of the driveway and into the lane.

'Who is helping Paulo out in the kitchen?' I asked.

'Emilio is back, feeling very sorry for himself. The girlfriend dumped him, and, as much as he might like just messing around on the internet, he realised he does actually need a job. There aren't that many going around here.'

'So, I've been sacked? That's twice in a month. It has to be some sort of record!'

Zoe laughed. 'I'm sure you could be a freelance consultant if you wanted to?'

'And that's the second time someone has suggested that too.'

* * *

We drove down the hill towards the lake, and everything looked lovely. The air was clear; the water sparkling. We joined the main road and turned right towards the signs that spoke enticingly of Milan and Bergamo and shops. The tree-lined avenue was a thing of beauty: cut into the land between the cliffs and the lake. And then, after only a few minutes, we turned off into a car park which was filled with little gazebos and dozens of people.

'Told you it wasn't far – we're here,' Zoe said brightly.

'This isn't Milan?' I said, confused.

'Of course it isn't; it's better,' Zoe said. 'You'll love it. Look, there's a brilliant parking place, next to the coffee stall. Let's get a cappuccino to revive us before we start. And there's usually a cannoli truck too – just delicious.'

We got out of the car, and I pulled my coat on against the cold wind which was blowing off the lake.

A devastatingly handsome young man served us with coffee in cardboard cups and next to him an equally attractive chap sold us bubbly, crunchy pastry shells which he filled with sweetened ricotta and chopped pistachios and covered with powdered sugar.

'Oh my god, this is so good,' I said, through a mouthful of exquisite calories. 'Why have I never had these before?'

'They are only worth having freshly made, and they have to have Masala wine in them: that's what makes them so great. And so sweet.'

I brushed the explosion of sugar off my face and drank my coffee. I didn't think in all my years anything had tasted that good.

'Is this the right thing to do before we go shopping?' I asked.

'It's the only thing,' Zoe said firmly. 'We need to keep our strength up.'

We moved on into the main area with all those gazebos.

'But this looks like a market?' I said, a bit confused.

'Darn right, and it's the best one for miles.'

My thoughts of delicately perfumed boutiques and accommodating saleswomen faded.

'Over here,' Zoe said, beckoning me. 'I'll show you the place I always go to.'

We passed pop-up stalls filled with fantastic-looking food. Olives in huge china bowls, massive rounds and chunks of cheese, pots of herbs and the most beautiful bread in wicker baskets. Focaccia crusted with rosemary and sea salt, ciabatta dusted with flour, round, sweetened breads studded with candied oranges, little buns thick with powdered sugar and lemon peel.

There were stalls selling handmade pottery, huge, cured hams, fresh pasta, marzipan fruits, slabs of nougat and chunks of almond brittle that made my teeth ache just looking at them. The aromas of the place were wonderful.

But Zoe was on a mission and wouldn't let me linger, and then I realised where we were going. In front of us were racks of clothes under canvas. Really? This definitely wasn't what I had been expecting. There were cotton dresses in vibrant colours, woollen scarves in every shade, silk shirts (at least they looked like silk), strange, fleecy garments with wolves printed on the back, an entire stall filled with very convincing Gucci handbags. Some rather unimpressive racks of women's blouses and dresses. Loose threads trailing. I'd never wear any of this stuff. My heart sank.

The next stall was filled with men's shirts, crisply folded in cellophane bags. Hundreds of pairs of socks. Trousers hung neatly over hangers.

Why was it that men's clothes were so much better made than women's? And cheaper? The myriad pieces that made up a man's shirt, and all of them neat and well finished. I once read that a dress shirt had twenty-six pieces. Why did men get the trousers with pockets deep enough for wallets, phones, loose change and car keys? The pockets on women's trousers were barely big enough for a tissue. Dresses with pockets were a rarity. Why was this? Was it some fiendish co-operation with the handbag manufacturers?

'Here,' Zoe said at last, smiling broadly.

A statuesque blonde woman, dressed in a fringed jacket and leather trousers, swept Zoe up into a hug and they chatted away for a few minutes in rapid Italian, until they both turned towards me. The blonde had a definite glint in her eye that made me slightly uneasy.

'Donatella used to work in one of the big fashion houses in Milan. She still has a lot of contacts. She gets the best things at a fraction of the price.'

What did that mean?

It meant bargains.

And she had a changing room. With a patio heater.

Good enough.

Donatella and Zoe had a spirited discussion for a few minutes and then we were off. By then I had given up on my original ideas and just did as I was told. Although the Italian fashion seemed to be rather more colourful than I was used to. And they seemed to like frills and what looked like real fur, which I didn't approve of.

Anyway, we spent a happy couple of hours trying on all sorts of things: summer dresses which I supposed I might need eventually, long cashmere-ish cardigans, even some suede trousers which seemed a possibility until I saw my rear view. (I really didn't have the bottom for them, even though Donatella seemed enthusiastic.) A gorgeous leather jacket which would have cost three times the price in London.

'Do you think I'm a bit old for a biker jacket?' I asked doubtfully.

'*Sei stupenda, cara,*' Donatella said, catching my drift. Stupendous, darling. *Hmm.*

I preened a little and looked into the mirror again. I did look okay, not exactly Olivia Newton-John, but passable.

'Absolutely not, you look fantastic,' Zoe agreed. 'You need some jeans that fit you though. Definitely not the ones you are wearing – something flattering.' She started flicking through the racks.

Hmm, perhaps these jeans ought to go after all, I thought. I'd had my doubts about them for a while.

I went back behind the curtain and started to take them off again, eager and ready for whatever Zoe picked for me, forgetting – as I nearly always did – to take my shoes off first. I then hurriedly tried to pull my jeans back up, lost my balance and fell over, dragging the privacy curtain off its hooks and nearly bringing the whole stall down around my ears. Several startled by passers caught a view of me struggling on the floor, and more embarrassingly of my knickers.

Like a true professional, Donatella braced herself against the poles holding up the sides and with Herculean effort kept it upright.

'No harm done,' she cried unconvincingly. 'Everything fine.'

I grabbed a metal clothes rack to haul myself to my feet and the side of it slipped down. All the coat hangers skidded to my end of the rail and whacked me on the head. Then I was covered in sweaters. With the skill of an Olympic gymnast, Donatella stuck out one foot to stop everything falling on the floor. It was most impressive.

'And some white trainers to wear with this dress,' Zoe said, oblivious to my clumsiness, coming back in and bringing with her a black, spotted, crepe dress and a denim jacket.

'I'm definitely too old for a denim jacket,' I said, panting slightly as I got to my feet, 'and I did maxi dresses the first-time round.'

Donatella looked up from her task of retightening the guy ropes and gave me a brave smile.

'*È di moda* – it's fashion!'

'Don't annoy her. She knows what she's talking about,' Zoe said warningly.

'Well, I thought I had *some* idea,' I said.

'Yes, if you're Ms Harrington/boss woman/boardroom person. But now you look like Clover Harrington: super-cool mature lady. Who knows exactly what she wants and doesn't care what other people think.'

Could older women like me look cool and hip without feeling like they were chasing their lost youth in a pathetic mad dash?

I looked at my reflection, expecting to be disappointed, but somehow, I wasn't.

'Well...'

I hesitated, and we all knew that she who hesitates was lost.

Zoe gave Donatella two thumbs up and they both cheered.

'That settles it,' Zoe confirmed. 'You're getting everything.'

* * *

I watched as Donatella speedily packed up all the things I had
bought – perhaps she didn't want to risk any more potential disasters – and felt an unexpected thrill of excitement. Most of them
were garments I wouldn't have given a second look only a few
weeks ago. Which just showed what I'd been missing out on. This
had been fun, far more so than buying another dull, formal outfit.
And some spiky uncomfortable shoes.

I realised I was feeling quite different from my usual self. It
was a mixture of *well no one looks at women my age* and *sod it, I can
wear what I like.* I felt unexpectedly happy.

'And the next thing we need is to make you an appointment
with Florentina,' Zoe said, swiftly passing another couple of T-
shirts and three sweaters to Donatella.

'Who is Florentina?'

'My hairdresser.'

After Donatella had bagged up the items, she still had to
check the stability of the tent poles and adjust the racks of
sweaters which I had managed to almost demolish. And then she
magicked up a bottle of Prosecco from a chiller box. She opened it
with a flourish, dowsing my deck shoes, so perhaps there was
some justice in that. I had nearly destroyed her stall, after all.

'*Berremo al successo* – we drink to success,' she said with a
broad grin.

So, we did.

15

Florentina, the hairdresser, worked from home: a beautiful little house in the village, next door to the baker. One afternoon, a week after the shopping trip, I found myself sitting in her front room, a striped towel draped around my shoulders. I looked at Florentina's reflection in the mirror in front of me. She was combing out my wet hair, her expression inscrutable. Then she picked up her scissors and opened and shut them a few times.

Rather slowly, which gave her an air of menace.

Zoe was sitting on the sofa, leafing through an old copy of *Oggi*. There was a picture of some starlet on the front, mouth pursed, eyes rimmed with elaborate make-up, looking like she had gone five rounds with George Foreman. And evidently about to burst out of her dress; I had never dressed like that even in my youth. But perhaps that was the look these days, what would I know? The younger generation of celebrities all seemed so different from what I had known. Angrier, bolder, and so *many* of them. A never-ending stream of so-called stars thirsting for fame. How exhausting.

Florentina turned to have a rapid-fire chat with Zoe who

replied, nodding and smiling. Florentina turned back to meet my eye in the mirror. Her smile was almost wolfish.

'*Facciamolo*,' she said.

Let's go.

No messing about with head massages and magazines and offers of coffee with a little wrapped biscuit on the saucer here then.

I gave a weak smile and nodded. Florentina spun my chair away from the mirror with the flair of a circus performer and her scissors flashed and clacked around my head. Almost immediately great hunks of hair fell to the ground; some onto her ratty old dog who had unwisely lumbered out of his armchair and strolled over to watch the proceedings. I had the temerity to look down at the floor, panicking when I saw just how much she was cutting off, and Florentina repositioned my head very firmly.

I looked over to see Zoe had moved onto another magazine, the cover emblazoned with a picture of Madonna in bondage gear looking furious. Well, she can't have been comfortable: all those straps and buckles.

Minutes later Florentina picked up a hairdryer the size of a Magnum handgun and was busy burning my ears as she dried what was left of my hair. Florentina turned me back and the three of us stared at my reflection in the mirror.

Now that the heat from the drier had cooled, my head felt unusually chilly.

I looked down at the pile of my hair surrounding the chair. There seemed a great deal of it. I reached up to check that there was some left. There didn't seem to be much.

'Fantastic,' Zoe said, smiling. 'You look ten years younger. *Sembra dieci anni più giovane.*'

'*Concordo*,' Florentina said, flicking at my neck with a large paintbrush. 'Is true.'

'I look ten years different anyway,' I said faintly.

My original thought was to scream and clasp my hands to my head, but it wouldn't have been polite, and the two of them looked so pleased. But then I wondered if any woman at the hairdresser had ever said anything other than, '*Yes, lovely, thanks*' when given a view of the back of her neck.

Even in the days of rollers and demi-waves and unusual colours – when a woman's first impulse would be to shriek, cry and then wonder how long it would be before she would dare go without a beret – we were always so polite. We would maintain a rigid smile until it was safe to go home and weep in front of a mirror, marvelling that we had paid so much to be made to look like a smurf (blue hair) or a sheep (eighties perm).

Zoe paid because she said it had been her idea, and then the three of us nodded and smiled at each other a bit more. Then as we left, Florentina got out the Dyson and started hoovering her dog.

'I'm nearly bald,' I whimpered, tugging at my fringe.

'Nonsense, you look terrific. Very chic. Very Lily Collins.'

'Are you sure you don't mean Phil Collins?'

Zoe laughed. 'You wait – it will be so much easier to look after too.'

Yes, I could probably just rinse my head under the tap and shake it dry. I didn't think I'd had such a short haircut since primary school. Oh well, as my mother used to say, it would grow back. Hopefully. Unless my unpredictable, sixty-one-year-old hormone reserves failed me again and I was stuck like this forever.

* * *

Paulo, the perfect husband, said all the right things when he saw me.

'*Bellissima*, you look... *una ragazza elfo* – an elf... *Una fata*... just lovely!'

I wasn't sure about being called a *fata*, until Zoe reassured me it meant fairy.

I left them to tidy up my room, where I occasionally caught sneaking glances at myself in the mirror and started to get used to the idea. At least I got to the point where I didn't yelp in surprise seeing my reflection before I had to get ready for supper.

I wore some of my new clothes: a pair of black linen trousers (very comfortable), flat leather pumps (also very comfortable) and a soft pink sweater which I was determined not to splatter with food. I swept up the pile of hairpins and combs that I no longer needed and put them into the bin. Then I put on some of my trademark red lipstick for the first time in days, and then, after another look at my reflection, wiped it off. It didn't seem to suit me any more. How odd.

* * *

Uncle Franco was in the bar of course, sipping a glass of red wine and chatting to Zoe. I slunk in, feeling ridiculously self-conscious.

'Ah, now, this must be your cousin's beautiful, younger sister?' Franco said with a mischievous twinkle. He stood up, rather tottery, and pulled out a chair for me.

'You are very kind,' I said, 'but I think you are also a flirt.'

'I always was, and *dio piacendo* – god willing – I always will be,' he replied.

We sat and talked for a while, Franco teaching me a few words of Italian and telling me about his family, which had been vast by the sounds of things, and confusingly a lot of them seemed to have the same name. There were any numbers of relations called Isabella and Sophia, Leonardo and Giovanni.

'Gio was named for his *nonno* – his grandfather – and his uncle. And his *bisnonno* – great grandfather. And he has two cousins also called Gio. Gio *il maestro* – teacher – and Gio *il costruttore* – builder. Your Gio is Gio *il bello* – the handsome one.'

'I don't think he is actually my Gio,' I mumbled into my wine.

Franco chuckled and wagged one gnarled finger at me. '*Vedremo, vedremo.*'

I'd have to look that up later. Perhaps I needed a notebook.

Paulo brought me a bowl of pasta and Zoe came to sit beside me.

'*Orecchiette con 'nduja sugo*: spicy, creamy, delicious,' he said.

It certainly was. And very filling so perhaps I didn't need the flatbread that accompanied it, but I ate it anyway. Good job those new trousers had a drawstring waist.

Zoe nudged me with her elbow and muttered rather conspiratorially.

'Gio was in while we were at the hairdresser's. He was checking how you were, which is nice isn't it? He's coming round for dinner tomorrow too. And he was asking Paulo if you are free next week. Paulo said yes, of course.'

'I might not be,' I said, pretending outrage. 'I might be doing something really important, or interesting, somewhere else.'

'Don't be daft!'

I briefly wondered what Gio would think of my hair. Not that it mattered of course. I could be just as interesting, and my hand would still be worth kissing whatever my haircut.

'He says if you are, he will pick you up at ten o'clock. On Saturday morning. Unless you tell him otherwise.'

'Where are we going?'

Zoe leaned in with a mischievous smile and took a piece of my flatbread.

'Who knows? Perhaps into Milan to see the cathedral, or along the side of the lake to look at the water. There are some wonderful churches and restaurants and trattorias. Very romantic.'

'I don't need romance,' I protested, 'just something interesting and stimulating.'

'In which case you could just sit and look at Gio all day.'

I nudged her with my elbow. 'I mean intellectually stimulating.'

'I expect he is that too,' Zoe said, all wide-eyed innocence.

I felt rather silly and giddy for a moment.

I wondered what Jack was doing. Was he at that moment slumped in front of his television with a bottle of overpriced beer?

He'd once caught me watching Eastenders, and thought it was a documentary about inner city social decline, until Peggy Mitchell had clobbered someone with her handbag and shouted, 'Get outta my pub!'

Jack had looked at me with infinite weariness and gone off to play Mahler very loudly in the study.

16

The following morning Emilio was back in the kitchen, trying to tell me about some internet game he had been playing. Which sounded little more than shooting people and blowing up buildings.

'Doesn't it get a bit tedious?' I asked.

Emilio looked surprised and his eyes lit up with unusual enthusiasm.

'Never!' he replied. 'And I am writing games. New games. I could make money with them. The internet is my life.'

Yes, I supposed for his generation it probably was. I wondered what he would have thought of my teen years when information had to be found in the library, in books.

I spent a busy hour dusting all the liqueur bottles behind the bar and polishing the glasses at the back of the shelf, which obviously hadn't been used for a long time.

Then, back in my room, and against my better judgement, I googled XS – *Finance with Heart* – to see if I had been mentioned.

Nothing. Not one word. It was incredibly insulting.

Surely my departure merited some sort of announcement?

Perhaps I hadn't been quite as important as I had thought… It was as though I'd just disappeared without a trace. Or been beamed up by aliens.

But I did have a nice chatty email from Ben. He was well; he was still with Brianna: a sleek, blonde, tennis-playing goddess I had met the last time they'd visited from Canada. They had been skiing in Whistler. He liked the idea that I was having a holiday. I replied saying I would come and visit him soon, and that I was looking forward to seeing them both again. It was beginning to feel exciting, to think that once I had got my head around everything, I might have some unimagined freedom.

That evening, anticipating another delicious dinner, and knowing that Gio was going to be there too, I changed into a rather smart, pale blue linen dress, cashmere wrap, and heels. Zoe and I sat out on the veranda, each with a glass of chilled Prosecco. Paulo was busy clattering around in the kitchen and a few customers were drinking in the bar.

Below us the dusky light across the lake was wonderful as the sun had set behind the mountains. There was a shimmering, silken quality to it, and with the utter quiet of the evening it was magical. The lights in the little town on the opposite side of the lake were twinkling in the dark.

'So, what else did Auntie Eleanor say when she found out about the redundancy?' Zoe asked.

'She said I had broken her heart and she wasn't going to tell anyone,' I said, 'and she used to have a smaller waist than Princess Margaret.'

'Then you don't need to mention it to her again, do you?' Zoe said. 'Just relax and enjoy yourself. Take some time off. Chill.

What did Baloo say in *The Jungle Book*? Fall apart in my backyard.'

I thought about that: actually relaxing into this lifestyle, getting rid of the last traces of resentment that still filled the edges of my mind. It was done now; I couldn't go back to the way things had been. And in a funny kind of way, I was beginning to see the possibilities that lay ahead of me. And they were rather interesting. Perhaps the future was not the scary place I had imagined. Maybe there were even unexpected advantages to this freedom that I hadn't considered yet.

'What is Paulo cooking for us tonight?' I asked.

'Risotto Milanese. He hasn't done that for a while. He adds wild mushrooms too. It's delicious,' Zoe said. 'Ah, cometh the hour, cometh the man! Now, best behaviour, Clover.'

A familiar truck pulled into the car park, stopping with a crunch of gravel.

Gio stepped out and paused briefly to look at the view, his back turned towards us. He had long legs, and a rather muscular frame. I could feel a flush rising up my neck and I prayed I wasn't actually blushing.

'D'you know, I might have to go and change. This outfit is a bit hot,' I said, tugging at my pashmina.

'That might explain why you're decidedly pink about the gills,' Zoe said. 'See, I told you he was attractive.'

'It's the Prosecco,' I said firmly. 'Do you think I could have a glass of red instead, this is giving me heartburn.'

'Of course,' she said sweetly. 'I'll go and get it.'

We watched as Gio walked across the car park towards us. He smiled when he saw us and raised a hand in greeting.

He certainly was eye-catching.

Even my inner turmoil couldn't stop me seeing that.

He greeted us both, pecking Zoe on the cheek as she returned with my wine and bowing over my hand rather gallantly. He had changed into dark blue chinos and a pale chambray shirt and if I hadn't stopped myself, I could have got quite silly about him.

I am just getting out of a relationship, I reminded myself. I was not available to Mr Temptation or anyone else for that matter.

'How nice to see you again; you look very elegant,' he said.

'You too,' I replied rather breathlessly. Perhaps I wouldn't bother changing.

What an incredibly daft thing to say.

'Have you had a good day?'

'Absolutely,' I said. 'Really good.'

I left it at that. He didn't need a full-blown account of my shopping trip or what level I had got to on *Candy Crush*.

'*Eccellente* – that's great,' he said. He rocked back on his heels a little. 'I hope you are enjoying your stay here.'

'I really am. It's so peaceful after London,' I said.

'London is a place like no other,' he agreed, nodding thoughtfully.

'You've been there? Did you like it?'

He sat down opposite me. 'Several times, and it wasn't the place for me to be honest.'

I bristled slightly. 'Why? What was wrong with it?'

'Nothing at all, but I found it too crowded, too busy. For me.'

'Well, it is a capital city,' I said, protectively. 'A lot of marvellous things go on there. There are museums and theatres and everything you could possibly want or need.'

'Except simple tranquillity,' he said, holding both hands out to the view below us.

'Well—'

Actually, he was probably right. I had slept better since I had been here than I had for a very long time. No car alarms going off, no police car sirens, no shouting in the streets below my window.

'You don't have to agree with me,' he said with a broad smile. 'We don't need to persuade each other we are wrong. We just disagree, and that's fine.'

This didn't sit well with me; I was used to a group of friends and colleagues who were prepared to sit up late into the night arguing about political leaders, the best car or restaurant or route between Virginia Water and Cambridge.

'Well, yes, of course,' I said. It felt rather good actually. Not to have to discuss it.

Gio excused himself at that point and went in to get himself a drink and chat with Paulo. Zoe gave me a sideways look.

'See? Isn't he handsome?' she said.

'Is he?' I said airily. 'I suppose so.'

She laughed. 'You're retired, not dead. If I didn't love Paulo so much, I'd be interested. And he's available. I mean he's single. His wife died some years ago. Now he lives alone, with some stray cat that saw an opportunity. It was all very sad, but it didn't stop the local ladies from zooming in to try and comfort him. No man has ever been given so many lasagnes.'

Which reminded me; Jack had wanted lasagne hadn't he?

I'd tried to make it twice during my culinary career. It was not an easy, throw-it-together, stick-it-in-the-oven dish as Jack assumed. It meant a lot of tedious ingredient purchases, chopping, weighing, stirring, tweaking and a massive amount of washing up. And both times it had turned out like portions of tomato-flavoured tyre tread.

'And did they?' I said at last.

'Did they what?'

'Comfort him.'

Zoe shrugged. 'No idea, but I'm interested that you are interested.'

'I'm not.'

'Yes, you are. Every woman around here under ninety-five is interested in him. He's—'

'Yes, I know, he's lovely. You said that already. I'm not attracted to superficial charm though, thanks very much.'

'Your dating history says different,' Zoe said annoyingly. 'And, *I was going to say*, he's a brilliant artist too. Some of the pictures in your room are by him. He used to teach and paint in his spare time, then when he retired, he started selling his paintings in one of the galleries in Milan. He does very well too. His work is much sought after; he's incredibly talented. There's a mega-rich man, a conte no less, who has a house on one of the islands, a summer palazzo. And he bought several of Gio's canvases and then his wife the Contessa commissioned him to do a massive picture of their house and the scenery. And then of course all their friends wanted one too.'

'He's right about this view,' I said, with a wave of my hand.

'It's gorgeous, isn't it? I never get fed up with it.'

'And in the winter?'

'We get snowed in. I suppose we could do something to make us more attractive to the winter sports trade like we used to, but these days we just prefer to hunker down and enjoy it.'

'You could go on holiday?' I said. 'Somewhere warm.'

'We could, but we don't want to; we are happy here, remember?'

'Happy as a dog in the sun.'

'*Felice come un cane al sole,*' said a deep voice behind me.

I leapt in shock and my red wine did a similar dive out of my glass and all over my lap.

I sat, appalled, watching the stain soak into the pale fabric for a moment.

With an alarmed squeak, Zoe threw her Prosecco after it, and we exchanged a horrified glance before we both started laughing.

'*Mi dispiace tanto.* I'm so sorry,' Gio said, handing me a clean white handkerchief. 'Did I make you jump? Yet again?'

I dabbed ineffectually at myself, and then stood up. Honestly, now I'd ruined at least three outfits with my sloppy eating habits.

Zoe watched me, one hand over her mouth, as I plucked at the wet fabric. I had a terrible urge to giggle in a way that would be embarrassing, and possibly never stop.

'I'd better go and change,' I said, my voice very tight with the effort of not laughing.

'I'm so sorry. I think that was my fault. I just came out to tell you that the meal is nearly ready,' Gio said.

'Then I'd better be quick,' I said.

I hurried away, gulping down a snort of laughter. It was a long time since I had felt so light-hearted, so silly, so free to enjoy myself.

* * *

'I wonder sometimes how two people can take the same ingredients and produce such different results,' I said, putting down my cutlery with a happy sigh. 'That was absolutely delicious, Paulo.'

Paulo grinned. 'Well, *grazie mille*, but it's just practice.'

'I could practice for years and not produce anything that good,' I said. 'Perhaps it's a natural talent?'

'Oh, no, it's been years of trying and working,' Paulo said. 'I love cooking for other people. I wish I could do more of it. I started cooking when I was seventeen and my mother died. I could either learn to make the sort of food she'd made me or live on expensive rubbish and... umm, how do you say it? *Alimenti trasformati* – processed food. Well, I think it was worth it, and here we are.'

Zoe blew him a kiss across the table. 'I know which I prefer,' she said, 'I'm spoiled.'

'Nonsense, I love cooking for you, for all my friends,' Paulo said. '*Mi scusi*, I must go in and put the coffee on. I have tiramisu if anyone is interested?'

'Perhaps in a while?' Zoe said. 'I'm so full at the moment.'

She reached across the table and emptied the last of the wine into Paulo's glass.

'I'll go and get another bottle, shall I?' she said. 'It's such a mild evening, I think we could stay out here.' She held up a warning finger to me. 'Now, be careful while I'm away. Don't miss your mouth.' She stood up, winked at me and went into the trattoria. 'What was she trying to do? Was this some sort of terrible matchmaking exercise?

'Zoe was telling me about your paintings,' I said at last. 'Someone who lives on an island who gave you a commission?'

'Ah yes, the contessa. She wanted a surprise anniversary present for her husband. It was a task I enjoyed a great deal. I had to visit her when he was away on business. I think it made some tongues wag. The local *pettegolezzi* – the gossips – were very interested.'

'I'm sure they were.'

'And her husband, the conte, he is a keen huntsman. There were those who thought he would see me off with his shotgun.'

'And did he?'

Gio laughed: a nice, cheerful sound in the still evening air.

'No, the contessa is very young and beautiful. Her husband is also young and handsome. *Sono così innamorati*; he idolises her. It was their first wedding anniversary. I was no threat to him I can assure you.'

I finished the last of my wine. 'And what is their house like?'

'It is a palazzo – more than a house. Built on the island you can see out there in the lake by his family centuries ago, as a summer residence. It's very picturesque.'

How marvellous to be a young and beautiful contessa with a palazzo and an adoring husband. I looked out over the lake and wondered what her life was like, presumably surrounded by servants and ancient family treasures. Renaissance paintings on the walls and marble statues at the head of a sweeping staircase. Perhaps she would drift about in elegant gowns, trailing a tiny hand on the ironwork bannisters, waiting for the handsome conte to return home with luscious presents for her. Gifts tied with ribbon, turquoise Tiffany boxes, shiny carrier bags with thick rope handles.

I was getting a bit overheated here; life wasn't like that. I didn't believe stuff like that.

I realised Gio was looking at me.

'So, you do watercolours?' I asked.

'Usually, but sometimes oils.'

'And you prefer to paint scenery or people?'

He looked thoughtful; his lower lip pushed out a little.

'I like to paint things that are worth capturing, that please my imagination, that make me think. Do you paint?'

'I used to enjoy sketching on a purely amateur level. These days I don't seem to have time.'

I went to sip my wine. And then realised the glass was empty so I looked a bit silly, draining the last meagre drop.

I hoped he didn't think I was an alcoholic. We exchanged a look.

'Zoe will be back in a minute,' he said reassuringly.

'Oh, I'm not desperate,' I said, putting my glass back on the table and pushing it away. And then grabbing at it with both hands because it nearly fell over.

He leaned back in his chair, the wood creaking.

'So, you are happy here?' he said.

I gave a careless little laugh. 'I told you: I needed a holiday, a break.'

He nodded slowly. 'You smile but your eyes are sad.'

I felt the sudden, terrible sting of fresh tears. It was such an insightful thing for him to say. He had noticed me, not just the face I presented to the world. I did a bit of throat-clearing and pretended to sneeze. I didn't need anyone feeling sorry for me, and certainly not him.

But for now, I realised, it was okay: I wasn't going to cry in front of him.

'I hope you will enjoy our trip out when we go,' Gio said after a few seconds.

'Where are we going?'

'Somewhere I love – a place that is special to me.'

'Then I'm sure I will,' I said.

I began to feel rather excited about it then, actually looking forward to doing something different, seeing something new and – yes, I had to admit it – spending the day with him.

17

Three days later, I was ready to go at nine o'clock, even though I knew Gio wouldn't be there until ten. He struck me as the sort of person who would be reasonably punctual, or even early, so I'd overcompensated.

I'd had a shower and fretted a bit about my hair which, when I'd first caught sight of it that morning, looked even more startling than it had on the first day. Then I'd realised that Zoe had been right: it didn't need much attention; it just dried into a very fetching shape with hardly any effort from me. And having had all the weight of my hair chopped off, it was starting to curl. I seemed to have cheekbones now too, and my eyes seemed brighter. I couldn't do anything about the grey hairs of course, but now that all my highlights had been cut away, they didn't seem that noticeable.

To waste a few minutes, and remembering the look of the *Oggi* cover girls, I dabbed on some eyeshadow, blending and fussing for that 'smokey-eyed' look. Then I realised that dark eyeshadow does unflattering things to more mature skin (wrinkles, crow's feet), and it looked as though I had been crying or was a raging insomniac. So, I washed it all off. I would just stick to mascara, and some lip colour. I pulled out my old signature lipstick, Rouge Amazone, looked at it thoughtfully for a moment and put it away again. Funny how once upon a time I had spent at least thirty minutes every morning putting on an expensive face-load of products, like some sort of mask, before I felt ready to greet the day.

Right now, my glossy acrylic nails were looking terrible. They needed either fillers or to be removed, and days spent in Paulo's kitchen with my hands in dishwater hadn't helped. Perhaps Zoe would know of a manicurist, or I could go on the internet to find one. Or perhaps I could just cut them and let them grow out? But how long would that take? My own nails hadn't seen daylight properly for a long time. I had been known for this: red lips and matching talons. A tiger boss lady. It all seemed a long time ago.

I opened my door, so I would hear when Gio arrived, and went to inspect my outfit in the mirror.

I was wearing my new jeans which seemed to fit rather well for a change, and a new white T-shirt. Perhaps I would wear the leather jacket too? Did I feel confident enough for the rock-chick look? I shrugged it on and admired myself in the wardrobe mirror.

Did I look cool or ridiculous? A sassy older lady? Or mutton dressed as lamb? I took it off again and pulled on one of my old jackets. Safer, blue linen. More appropriate for my age. Dull.

I might have been ordinary, less flexible than I used to be, a bit battered around the edges with one slightly dodgy knee... but no, whatever happened, I wasn't going to be dull.

I put the leather jacket on again and tousled my hair with my fingers. Very Audrey Hepburn in *Roman Holiday*. In a dim light through half-closed eyes perhaps. I snapped my fingers and posed in front of the mirror, smouldering my eyes and pouting.

'Cool, look at you, Clover. Get down and boogie,' I said aloud, feeling giddy.

I did a few half-forgotten, funky moves in front of the mirror. I used to like dancing. I was quite good at it too, I thought. When I'd been a student, I'd always been first on the dance floor, last to leave.

Funny how increasing years seemed to mean a decrease in the dancing one did. Perhaps it was the stiffening joints, or pure self-consciousness. An unwillingness to fling oneself into the music, the rhythm, the occasion. Only recently I had found myself dancing with Jack at some dreary function. Hanging onto each other, doing the pathetic side-to-side shuffle of the reticent grown-up. Not enjoying it at all.

I carried on twirling, jerking my thumbs, shrugging my shoulders to an unheard beat. *Earth Wind and Fire* perhaps, or *The Jackson 5*. Perhaps I would go to a disco when I got back to London. Although they weren't called that any more, they were *clubs*.

I would go to a club with some friends, and we would boogie. We would drink luminous cocktails, we would scream with laughter at nothing and we would fall out onto the pavement at two in the morning looking for chips. And if the young people sneered at us, we wouldn't care.

I thought about it. My closest friends were Isabel, who was a barrister with a controlling husband, and Lynne, who couldn't tolerate loud noises, flashing lights or carbohydrates. It seemed unlikely they would be up for such an adventure. The most we had done recently was to go out for a sedate lunch where we had all eaten salad and sipped mineral water.

It was then I realised that I hadn't told them about this trip to Italy either. Which was a bit sad.

But I could go to a club even if they didn't want to. I'd find someone else to go with.

'*Ha, ha, ha, ha, stayin' alive,*' I warbled. 'Not a dull old pensioner on the scrap heap after all, are you? *Whoo hoo*, Momma! You're one cool chick.'

'*Certo*, yes, you are,' said a voice.

I spun round, nearly falling over in the process as the soles of my new shoes had more traction on the rug than I'd been expecting.

Of course. Gio was standing in the open doorway, grinning.

I'd been a sensible adult for many years. How did I manage it these days: to behave so out of character, do such foolish things and get caught doing it? And by him of all people.

I gave a weak smile and made a big fuss about looking for my handbag. Which despite being rather expensive, didn't go at all with what I was wearing. It was the handbag of a businesswoman with pockets for my phone, work files and my keys, and even a small umbrella in a special slot. I didn't look or feel like that woman any more. After all I was technically unemployed, and, more importantly, I was on holiday. But could I consider myself to be on holiday when I didn't have a job? Perhaps I was retired after all, and to be honest, it felt pretty damn good. Mmm.

What would a cool, confident, older woman, who didn't want to lug around a handbag, do?

I made an executive decision. I moved a couple of bank cards into the empty slots in my phone case and just stuffed it into my pocket. I would embrace this new me and leave all the junk I had been lugging around behind. After all I wouldn't need any of it on this trip. Driving license, wallet, the keys to my flat, a notebook, several company-branded pens, a powder compact, a box of breath mints.

I'd left work with a nearly empty cardboard box and now I was ditching the handbag. That in itself seemed symbolic. Shedding pounds, one might have said.

'I'm ready,' I said.

'You look fabulous,' Gio said, 'and I meant to tell you when we last met, your hair is *meravigliosa* – wonderful.'

Well, that was a surprise. Jack never noticed that sort of thing. Once, about a year after we met, I had spent hours having eyelash extensions done and it had been a fortnight before he noticed. Even then, it was because a few of them had fallen out on the pillow and he thought I had some terrible disease.

'Thank you,' I said, biting back the words *you look pretty fabulous too.*

But he did. I thought there must be something about Italian men; perhaps they were born with inherent style. They looked great in sharp suits, but they also looked good in jeans. And a blue linen shirt with the cuffs rolled up and a red sweater knotted round the neck. Or at least Gio did.

We drove away from the trattoria, Zoe waving a tea towel from the veranda, and down towards the lake.

'I would suggest we get the ferry to the island. It only takes a few minutes. I think you will enjoy that,' Gio said. 'It's one of my favourite places.'

'Great,' I said, trying to sit still so my leather jacket didn't squeak against the leather seat of his truck and make embarrassing noises.

The ferry was a small blue and white boat with a few people already sitting inside away from the brisk wind which funnelled down the lake. But the air was crisp and clear, the snow-capped mountains in the distance sharp against the blue sky.

* * *

'This is such a special place,' Gio said as we got off the ferry. 'So peaceful, no cars allowed. But there are bikes and buses if you wanted to explore. Perhaps this time we will just take things easy.'

This time. That was thought-provoking. It suggested that there would be a next time.

We walked down a little paved street under the shade of trees which were coming into new leaf, past some mopeds and bicycles, past enticing-looking gardens and restaurants. Iron railings and steps leading up to houses, music playing from an open window, a dog sleeping in the sun. A cat curled up in an empty flowerpot. Everywhere was spotless. No litter, no splodges of discarded chewing gum on the ground.

Gio led me up some stone steps to the pathway which sloped up into the village. After a second, he turned to look at me, and reached out a hand.

'Careful,' he said, 'this next part is a little steep.'

I took hold of his hand, and we made our way to the top. There, we were rewarded by an even better view of the lake, the morning sunshine dazzling on the water as the sun rose higher above the surrounding mountains.

We stood side by side, with me puffing slightly and trying to hide the fact. Perhaps now I was unemployed/retired I would have more free time to go to the gym and work on my fitness levels. And actually, do more there than have a quick swim followed by a toasted teacake in the Cool-Down Juice Bar.

'I think there is a café just around the corner,' Gio said, 'unless it is too early for coffee?'

'It's never too early for coffee,' I said happily.

We walked along for a few minutes in companionable silence, a few Italian sparrows darting across the path in front of us, chirping and squabbling over twigs.

Gio was right, as we rounded the corner, the path opened out into a gorgeous little square complete with a statue of some saint and a stone horse trough which had been filled in and planted with flowers. There, to one side, under a green-and-white-striped awning, was a café.

'Let's sit outside,' he said, 'if it's not too cold for you?'

'Perfect,' I said. '*Perfetto.*'

I was smiling; I was happy and relaxed. I was enjoying myself.

It could have been the prospect of some of Italy's finest coffee and the possibility of a *sospiri* – the little lemon-glazed cakes I could see in the window. But added to that, I realised Gio was still holding my hand, and for some reason, that was making me feel very happy indeed.

* * *

We sat outside the café, drinking coffee that was rich and aromatic, and we had *sospiri* too, the tang of the lemon sponge a perfect accompaniment. We talked about the island and its history, and then he asked me about other places I had visited. And would I recommend them?

It was surprisingly hard to answer because all the holidays I had been on with Jack had been to expensive hotels with spas with every possible amenity. But we had hardly ever ventured out of them during our stay. Jack wasn't interested in the local culture, he just wanted luxury and swimming pools with swim up bars and elaborate food. Basically, for most of the time we could have been anywhere.

I remembered on a visit to Santorini I had persuaded him to visit the archaeological workings at Akrotiti, and he had shown all the enthusiasm of a teenage boy at a family dinner. He hadn't actually voiced his disapproval, but he had talked a lot about what he'd wanted to do the following day.

Gio was waiting patiently for my answer. 'There are so many places I would like to see. But—'

I stopped, it seemed pointless to start on about Jack and his 'surprise' holidays.

'Well, now you can, now that you don't have to worry about work,' Gio said, finishing his coffee. 'I thought you were going to see your son in Canada.'

'Yes, I will,' I said firmly. 'Perhaps in the autumn when the leaves are changing colour, but it seems a long time to wait.'

'Then go soon,' he said. 'There's nothing to stop you after all.'

I briefly thought about Jack being on a plane for twelve hours to Canada, a place of staggering beauty and endless possibilities, and I knew without a doubt that I would never have persuaded him to go. What did that say about our relationship? I was doing the right thing, ending it.

'No, there isn't, is there?' I said, imagining myself on one of the beautiful, pale-blue Air Canada jets, flying over endless forests and bright turquoise lakes hidden in the mountain ranges. 'And you, where would you like to go?'

He looked thoughtful. 'The Grand Canyon, Machu Picchu, Scotland.'

'Scotland?'

'Well, yes, I am a painter, as you know, and there is some beautiful scenery there. I went many years ago when my wife was still alive. I would like to go back.'

'Then you should,' I said.

I wondered for a moment about his wife: what she had been like, her character, her looks. Had he loved her very much? Did he still miss her?

A thought came to me from somewhere, that when one has loved, one can love again. As though love were a muscle which needed flexing. Had I been in love with Jack? Occasionally, at the beginning, I had thought so, but more recently I believed we had just stayed together out of habit. The realisation that he was at last out of my life made me feel slightly light-headed.

Gio gave a small smile and checked his watch.

'Come, I promised you something wonderful, didn't I? It is time we went.'

He paid the bill and we set off again, making our way around the statue of the saint, who now had a sparrow on his head, and towards a paved pathway leading gently uphill. Gio reached out and without comment, took my hand in his. Again. And the path wasn't even steep, so it wasn't as though I needed assistance.

It was a very long time since someone had done that. People, young people, didn't seem to hold hands much any more, which was a shame because it felt really lovely, to feel his hand holding mine. It felt friendly, affectionate, perhaps even protective. It felt right.

The little glow of happiness which I had been feeling all day warmed me. I liked him – there was no denying that. I sneaked a look at him. He was tall, handsome, kind and interesting. I liked his company and he seemed to like mine. What was this? A friendship? A blossoming holiday romance?

Would I let my unexpected freedom lure me into making an unwise decision, allow myself to feel more, do something else out of character? Clover Harrington, award-winning businesswoman, probably wouldn't... but Clover Harrington biker-chick probably would.

How awful. How potentially embarrassing.

But was it... really?

I had been in a six-year relationship with Jack, but we were not going to go the distance. Now, without the distraction of work, I could see myself and my life more clearly, and there was a lot about it I didn't like any longer.

And I *was* different, that was the thing. These last few weeks had made me see that. But it didn't mean my opinions mattered less than before, that my preferences could be ignored.

A realisation came to me as I walked through the little lanes, the sunshine filtering through the trees, birds splashing in a stone birdbath tucked away in a garden.

I didn't actually need anyone. Unexpectedly I had the freedom to do what I liked when *I* decided. To go where I pleased, eat what I wanted, think my own thoughts. Whatever I did next, it was up to me. How marvellous.

18

Slowly we made our way higher, through twisting little streets and past a church where a single bell was tolling the hour. Midday.

'Here we are,' Gio said, stopping in front of some high iron-work gates. 'We are on time.'

'On time for what?' I asked, intrigued.

'You'll see. I am trying to impress you.'

'Is this the place you told me about?'

'It is. Come.'

He opened the gates, and we walked through along a brick lined driveway towards a glorious villa at the end. A classic stone palazzo with windows shuttered against the late-morning sun.

An elderly man was watering the terracotta pots in front of the house, and he jerked his chin in greeting, not stopping his task.

Gio opened the front door and waved me inside.

'The contessa is not home; she is away in Switzerland visiting her family until the summer months. But I asked if I could show you around and she was very happy for me to do so. I thought you might like to see.'

I followed him inside and gasped. The hallway was the size of my flat, with marble floors and columns supporting an ornate ceiling which had been painted with clouds and cherubs. Door led off to huge rooms, where I could see some of the furniture shrouded in dustsheets. There was a lingering smell of lilies and old, cold books. There were statues and cabinets filled with small treasures: exquisite shells carved from alabaster; enamel boxes festooned with flowers; a tiny hunting dog made of bronze, perfect down to the last whisker.

The sculpture was the sort of thing I had only seen on antiques programmes where the dealer selects something worth a small fortune from a shoebox of oddments and says, '*Now this could be interesting.*' Nearly always the owner had bought it for 50p in a charity shop or at a car boot sale.

'What a wonderful place,' I said, speaking in a whisper, as though we were intruding.

The light was subdued; the tapestries and paintings were protected from the sun by the closed shutters.

I wondered again what it must be like to live here: the beautiful young woman with her adoring husband, casually spending their days walking past all this glory. Perhaps not even noticing the gilt-framed portraits on the walls.

I stood and stared up at one: a full-length painting of a young woman dressed in a green velvet riding habit, a feathered hat tipped over one eye. Wide dark eyes, a strong straight nose, a generous mouth. At her feet, a dog gazed up adoringly. Behind her, a romantic vista of mountains and swirling clouds.

'The conte's grandmother,' Gio said. 'She was thought a great beauty. And this was her husband.'

Another full-length portrait: a man in riding britches and glossy boots. His expression was stern. His eyes were dark and brilliant.

'He wasn't bad either,' I whispered.

We moved on, past a line of paintings of stern-looking men and some gloomy landscapes, to the next portrait. A pale, pretty face surrounded by a halo of blonde curls. She was dressed in blue, in a flowing chiffon evening dress that matched her eyes.

'And this is Eva, the present contessa,' Gio said.

'She's gorgeous,' I murmured. 'What a life she must lead.'

'But I wanted to show you this,' Gio said.

He took my hand and pulled me into another room, one that was smaller and more intimate, away from all that glory.

'This is the family sitting room, where they spend most of their time. And this' – Gio waved a hand at a huge landscape on one wall – 'is the painting I did for her. I told you about it, do you remember?'

'Wow,' I said.

The work showed a view which I guessed was from a terrace overlooking the lake. Stone arches framing the view of distant mountains and cliffs on the other side, flowers spilling out of marble urns. A riot of colour. Sitting to one side on a stone bench was a woman I recognised as the contessa, dressed in white, her sunhat in her hand.

'Do you like it?'

'Of course, I do. it's fantastic.'

Gio smiled, pleased at my reaction. 'I told you I was trying to impress you. And look. Here in this corner. Do you see the lamb? It is *il mio machio di fabbrica* – my trademark. For my surname, Agnello, the lamb.'

I stepped closer to see the brush marks: the little details of birds flying across the azure sky, a boat out on the water churning up a white wake and there, in a corner, a lamb, its fleece white against the green of the grass.

'How long did it take you?' I asked.

'Five or six weeks to get the basics done and then several weeks adjusting and adding. So, you see this is what I do. This is what I love.'

'Amazing. It's such a talent, to be able to do this. The contessa is a lucky woman, to have a home like this, a life like this. It all seems perfect to me.'

He came to stand next to me. 'And yet she is lonely and often sad.'

'Good heavens, why?'

'I have painted a moment in time, remember. This is not her life. She has known sadness, as have we all. No children, a husband who is away very often on business; she is new to this sort of life. I think sometimes she must struggle.'

'And yet she lives here; she has opportunities. She could go anywhere, do anything if she is unhappy.'

'But she loves her husband.'

'Love makes us do funny things,' I said.

'It does,' he agreed.

And there in the soft dim light, he turned towards me and kissed me.

Just once, and then I pulled back.

'I'm sorry,' he said. 'Are you going to slap my face?' He sounded quite serious.

'I've never slapped anyone's face.'

'That's good,' he said.

My knees gave a bit of a tremor.

They hadn't done that for years. And the last time they did, it was after I'd done a 5k run for charity. This felt very different.

Exciting, slightly naughty and daring. And unexpected. Although the hand-holding might have been a bit of a clue. It seemed to signify closeness, warmth... even trust. And I had liked it.

But should I have been holding hands, letting a man kiss me?

Well, why not? I was a free agent. I felt inside me a new determination to strike out of my set old ways, to allow myself to do something new, to take a chance on life, and more importantly, take a chance on myself. I didn't have to answer to anyone.

Gio checked his watch.

'*Allora*. I have shown off for long enough. You have seen my painting. Let's find lunch?'

'That would be lovely,' I said.

I kept on surprising myself. I was suddenly very hungry, and more than a little pleased. If a man like Gio wanted to spend time with me, to show me a place he loved, to kiss me, then I was up for the challenge.

* * *

We found a little place by the water's edge where we shared a pizza as big as a bicycle wheel. Remembering my recent capability of spilling food down myself, I made sure to tuck my linen napkin into the neck of my white T-shirt which made him laugh.

'You are a mystery, Clover,' he said, shaking his head. 'One minute so formal, the next minute *pazza* – crazy.'

'I'm starting a new part of my life,' I said, hoping I didn't have a string of cheese on my face. 'I'm working it out as I go.'

'I'm happy for you,' he said. 'I had to do something similar. It's not easy, I know. But it's easier with friends.'

Was that what he was? A friend? I felt he was something more than that. Or he could be. The slight awkwardness between us, after that kiss, had gone.

He topped up our wine glasses from the little carafe we were sharing, and while he did so I took the opportunity to look at him properly.

A kind face, still handsome although the features had, perhaps, like mine, been blurred with time. Silver through the thick dark hair, a firm chin, brown eyes that crinkled when he laughed. Was this the face of a friend, or could it be something more? His hand on the wine carafe was lined, the veins slightly prominent. Nails neatly cut.

'You're very quiet all of a sudden,' he said, looking up and catching my gaze.

I could feel myself blushing, caught out.

'I'm just thinking,' I said.

'Are you thinking, *What am I doing with this man?* Who takes me on boat trips and kisses me in the gloom of an empty villa?'

'Pretty much,' I admitted.

He laughed. 'I am thinking similar thoughts, Clover. What am I doing?'

'Let's just enjoy our lunch, and think about that later,' I said.

'Good idea,' he said, and took another slice of pizza. 'We both need to think. Don't we. But... later.'

We. We were a *we*. Were we? I didn't think so. I wasn't ready for that. But I did find him good company and attractive. Rather sexy actually. Was it possible to be just friends with a man like that?

* * *

We took the ferry back to the edge of the lake and found his truck in the car park. And then he drove me back to the trattoria. We sat in his truck for a moment, the evening cool and dark around us.

'Do you want to come in? I asked. 'Coffee? I know how to make it now.'

'If you're sure,' he said.

He reached across and put his hand over mine. I felt myself tremble.

Sure about what?

Now I wasn't sure if I was inviting him in for coffee or something else entirely. Why was I so edgy? Why did I feel such a mixture of excitement and nerves?

He followed me into the barn, and I messed about for a bit in the kitchen, looking for the coffee maker, finding mugs, wondering if I had any biscuits and what underwear was I wearing... Should I even have been thinking that? No, I shouldn't.

I handed him a mug and our eyes met. *Flipping heck*, I was nervous, and yet at the same time I knew that I – what was the word – *desired* him. Good heavens. I think he was feeling much the same, which was very satisfying. It was a long time since I had felt desired.

He put his coffee mug on the table and came towards me. He was going to kiss me again, I knew he was, and I wanted him to. And then who knew what would happen this time. Had I locked the door? Perhaps we would just fall gracefully onto the bed together and he would...

There was a sudden loud knocking, and I could hear Zoe calling my name. I realised I had been holding my breath.

I went to open the door.

Zoe was there, an apron over her cotton dress, her expression anguished.

'Sorry about this, Clover – I did think of ringing, but I know reception is patchy, and anyway I wanted you to have a nice day out before...'

She gave me an apologetic look and stepped to one side.

My mother, perfectly coiffed and co-ordinated, came into the room and swept me up and down with one of her glances.

I gaped. I could feel the blood draining from my face, and I felt a bit woozy for a second. Of all the things I had imagined happening that evening, this was probably the last.

Mum's mouth pursed in a very familiar way that spoke of disappointment.

'Jeans? And a leather jacket? Have I taught you nothing? And what on earth have you done to your hair? You're having a breakdown, aren't you? I got here just in time; I can feel it. A mother always knows.'

I took a step back and grabbed hold of a chair for support. 'Mum. What are you...?'

She followed me in.

'Where have you *been*, Clover?' she began. 'I've been sitting in that bar for an hour and a half. I was talking to a very charming man so I can't grumble, but I didn't think you would actually be out enjoying yourself. I thought you would be here licking your wounds and fretting. I'm sure I sent you a message to let you know I was on my way. I suddenly had *the feeling* – you know I am a bit psychic sometimes: I knew that your cousin Deborah was going to have twins – and I just dropped everything. I'm missing the Easter Bonnet Masterclass for this. Some young man from the local technical college who thinks he is Phillip Treacey. Of course, he isn't, and he tends to be a bit heavy with the feathers and the sequins. I said to Janice, I shall look like Shirley Bassey on tour if his Christmas crackers were anything to go by.'

'I didn't get a message. I had no idea you were coming. I thought the doctor said you shouldn't travel?'

Mum waved one hand dismissively. 'I'm sure I told you – he was just a locum. When Doctor Smith-Wilkinson returned from Barbuda, he said I was as fit as a woman half my age and the change would do me good. So here I am. And not a moment too soon by the look of you. You look as though you have had some sort of *crise de nerfs*.'

'I am fine, Mum. Honestly. I'm having a great time here. Really there is nothing to worry about.'

'Really?' Mum said, arching one eyebrow inquisitively at Gio.

'I'm sorry. This is Gio Agnello. A friend of Zoe and Paulo's.'

'Is he indeed? Well, I'm delighted to meet you Mr Agnello.' She held out the back of one hand towards him, and Gio took it and bowed over it very politely. 'I hope you have been looking after my daughter. She has been through a terrible time.'

'I have, *signora*.'

'Good. Well, I won't keep you,' Mum said pointedly.

Gio gave me a funny little half-smile. '*Buona serata*, Clover. *Signora*. Have a good evening.'

'You too,' I said, watching with some disappointment as he left. Zoe went too, closing the door behind her with great care.

Mum sat down in the most comfortable chair and crossed her legs which, even at her age, were very elegant. Pity I hadn't inherited that particular gene.

Mum smoothed her hair so that her charm bracelet jangled, fussed a bit with the hem of her skirt and straightened the pearls she always wore.

'Now then, you must tell me *everything*. Jack has been very worried; I can assure you. Phoning me at all hours when he can't get in touch with you. I suppose the phone signal isn't very good over here. We are spoiled in England with technical things. We take it all for granted.'

'It's perfectly fine,' I said. 'It can be a bit patchy here because of the mountains.'

'I suppose so. They are a bit too big really, aren't they?'

'Perhaps we could get them lowered?' I said sarcastically.

'Don't be silly. Is that coffee I can smell? Do you have decaffeinated? No? Oh well, I won't bother. I said to Zoe I would be happy staying in here with you, but she insisted I go into the new rooms Paulo has been working on. She said it would be like a formal opening ceremony. Perhaps we should cut a ribbon? I've always wanted to do that.'

I sent up a silent prayer of thanks to my cousin. The prospect of sharing a bedroom with my mother was so awful it didn't bear thinking about.

'What an excellent idea. I'm sure you will be very comfortable,' I replied.

'Well, I have to say it's very refreshing to get out of England and away from all those old people in Winchester Hall. There are far too many Velcro slippers there for my liking. It's like watching a parade of guinea pigs shuffling about in the mornings. I told Doctor Smith-Wilkinson I was feeling distinctly jaded. I certainly never want another conversation with Janine about her bunions. And he said, well why not get away, Eleanor? For a little mini break. And I told him about you, and he positively beamed, almost ordered me onto the next plane. And if nothing else, it will get me away from Jack and his incessant calls. He can't be getting much work done, he's on the phone to me most of the time.'

'Oh dear, well I'm sorry about that.'

'Perhaps I am exaggerating a tiny bit. But he keeps moaning on about everything; did you know he had been suspended? Janine knows someone who has a sister who works in the same office. The gossip is probably all over London by now.'

'Yes, he did say something.'

Mum sniffed. 'Money laundering – that's my guess. His eyes are too close together. You can tell a lot about a man by his eyes.'

'I told him to move out,' I said.

'Good. I never did really take to him.'

Was Mum listening to me for once?

'All that nonsense about the boat race,' she continued. 'He never did talk about the fact that they *lost* to Oxford that year, did he? Anyway, here I am. Zoe said something about dinner in the trattoria once I am settled in. Do you think that's a good idea?'

'It's an excellent idea; Paulo is a wonderful chef.'

Mum pursed her mouth doubtfully. 'As long as there's not too much garlic. It gives me indigestion.'

I thought of the skeins of garlic hanging on the wall in Paulo's kitchen. Perhaps I wouldn't say anything.

'Well, you get settled,' I suggested, 'and I will see you later. Did Zoe say a time?'

'Do you know, at Winchester Hall they serve dinner at six? I think it's so people can see the end of *Pointless*, and then they all burst out of their rooms, and scurry down to the dining room in a herd. And of course, one has to scurry with them otherwise there is nothing left worth eating. What a scrum! Sometimes there is a log jam on the stairs if Betty McTavish is there before them. She really should use the lift; it would be better for everyone. Anyway, I've booked a table for seven-thirty. My treat.'

I wondered what Mum would be expecting – half an hour with cocktails before being escorted to her seat?

'That sounds ideal,' I said. 'I need to freshen up too.'

Mum swept a glance over me again. 'Well, yes, you can't go looking like that. People will think my daughter is a Hell's Angel. Perhaps a nice frock?'

'So, seven-thirty it is, Mum. And how long are you thinking of staying?'

'I might ask you the same question.'

I bustled around, hanging up a towel and looking in my wardrobe to decide what to wear. If nothing else, the activity would give me time to think and regroup my chaotic thoughts.

I looked around to see Mum poking about in the bookcase,

examining the china ornaments on the dressing table, peering out of the window at the dark evening. This was going to add a whole new dimension to my stay here, and I wasn't sure how that would be. I'd started to feel relaxed and carefree, and now my mother was here, I feared a lot of that might change. I wasn't sure I liked the thought.

19

I encouraged Mum to go off and freshen up in her own room. I showered, dried my hair in five minutes – still quite a novelty - and applied some moisturiser. It looked as though I was getting a bit of a tan. Then I put on some more of my new clothes.

I'd always thought there was something exciting about wearing something for the first time. For dinner I chose my new spotted maxi dress, the white trainers and the denim jacket. I scrutinised myself in the mirror and felt rather pleased with my reflection. I looked younger, rather chic. I'd become used to seeing myself in severe business suits and dresses, hair swept up into a tight French pleat, make-up perfect. Now I looked – well, rather cool.

* * *

My mother didn't agree.

She was sitting at the best table in the trattoria window, elegant as always in a tailored dress and court shoes. Rather surprisingly Uncle Franco was at her side, looking very dapper in pale slacks and a blazer.

Her face lit up when she saw me and then just as quickly fell. She fiddled for a moment with her pearls.

'Franco, perhaps you could get my daughter a glass of wine?'

'*Certo*, it will be my pleasure.'

Franco heaved himself up and limped over to the bar, although I noticed he had abandoned his usual walking stick.

Mum sighed, narrowed her eyes and turned her gaze onto me.

'What *are* you wearing now? Is this what Italian women wear? Or is this fancy-dress night and no one told me? You look like a throwback to the sixties. And a denim jacket? Really?'

I sat down and smiled back at her. 'I'm comfortable.'

'When did comfort have anything to do with fashion?' Mum hissed.

'Mum, I'm not at work now. I'm happy like this. Just be happy for me.'

She drew in a deep breath ready to continue, but then Franco returned and gave me my glass of red wine.

'*Perdona un vecchio* – forgive an old man – I am confused,' he said, sitting down with a grunt. 'This lady is your mother? And yet, surely not. She is too young, too glamorous.'

Mum, always a sucker for a compliment, lifted her chin.

'I *was* very young when I had Clover,' she said. 'I had a smaller waist than Princess Margaret when I married.'

Franco nodded. 'English ladies are so beautiful: complexions like *latte e rose* –milk and roses.'

'Well, I always have tried to protect my skin; the sun is so aging,' Mum said, sipping her gin. Her bad mood was obviously rapidly fading.

'I am the luckiest of men tonight,' Franco continued. 'Two beautiful ladies to talk to.'

I watched in some amazement as he and Mum started chatting away like old friends. I felt quite the gooseberry.

'So, what would you like to order?' It was Zoe, mischief in her eyes and a pencil and pad in her hands. 'Paulo recommends the *pappardelle di coniglio*; it's very good indeed.'

'*Deliziosa!* One of my favourites,' Franco said, kissing the tips of his fingers to emphasise the point. He turned to my mother. 'You must try it.'

'Well, then, if you recommend it, Franco, let's try that. No garlic in mine, thank you, Zoe,' Mum said.

Zoe widened her eyes at me and didn't say anything.

Mum turned back to Franco, and they continued their conversation, which from what I could tell consisted of a lot of compliments from Franco, and some half-hearted protestations from my mother.

Zoe and I exchanged another look, and she came to sit next to me.

'So, everything okay?' Zoe muttered as she pretended to scribble on her pad.

'Great – we had a lovely day. Sorry you had to deal with this; I honestly didn't know she was coming.'

'Don't be daft. It's fine. She said she was here to look after you and pressed a wad of cash into my hand for a room. I could hardly refuse. And how did it go with Gio?'

I could feel myself blushing and Zoe snorted with laughter.

Mum looked up with a bright smile. 'Perhaps we could have some sparkling water?'

Zoe nodded. 'Of course, I'll just go and get it.'

'I'll come and help,' I said and hurried after her, almost tripping on the folds of my maxi dress. I couldn't remember having difficulty walking in this type of garment the last time it was in fashion.

'So? Gio?' Zoe said as she found a bottle of Pellegrino and some glasses.

'We had a lovely day out; he took me to see the massive painting he had done in the villa on the island. We had coffee and then we had lunch. We shared a pizza. It was— '

'Cut through the crap. Did you get on?'

'Yes, I think we did.'

'You think?'

'Well, he kissed me.'

Zoe clutched the bottle to her chest, almost dropping it.

'Wow!' she exclaimed. 'And when I banged on your door, he was there too! Did I interrupt a particularly interesting moment?'

'Well, we will never know now. It was probably just as well. I'm not really ready for all this sort of thing.'

She grinned. 'I told you he was lovely.'

'Yes, he is actually, but don't let my mother hear you say that because she will jump to all sorts of conclusions.'

We both looked over to where Mum and Franco were deep in conversation, my mother fluffing out her hair in a very girlish way. Franco was talking with expansive hand gestures.

'What *are* they doing?' Zoe said. 'If I didn't know better, I would say they are flirting. Franco is *eighty-one*.'

'Well, Mum is seventy-nine.'

We stood and watched for a few more minutes while Franco gestured out of the window, and Mum looked to see what he was pointing at and gave a trilling laugh.

'Well, I never,' I said. 'I think you're right.'

Mum had always been an attractive woman, but at seventy-nine... Was this behaviour really – terrible word – appropriate?

* * *

We had an enjoyable evening and a delicious meal, and we were still sitting at the table at nine-thirty, the last to leave. I went out to the kitchen to help Zoe who was doing some clearing up. Paulo was scrubbing the metal top of the table while the cat gnawed noisily at something underneath.

I went back in to see Mum and Franco lingering over their coffee and liqueurs, still gossiping away, while outside the night was dark, the few lights from the village sparkling through the windows.

I joined them, listening with half my attention as they chatted about cars. To my certain knowledge, Mum knew nothing about them other than how to get in or out of one.

She leaned over towards me.

'Franco was an engineer. Very important. He worked for Maserati. Even I have heard of them.'

At last Franco stood up and bowed over her hand.

'Ah, *signora*,' he said, and then he nodded to me. 'Thank you both for a most enjoyable evening.'

'Well, thank you, Franco, for your company,' Mum said with a sweet smile.

'*Bene allora*, tomorrow,' he said, 'I will collect you at eleven o'clock?'

'Marvellous,' Mum said. 'I will look forward to it.

She watched him as he walked to the door; he was now quite sprightly compared with when I'd first met him. He turned and waved at Mum, and she gave him a little waggle of her fingers in return.

'Now this is more like it,' Mum said, turning back to me, her eyes bright from a few glasses of Pinot Grigio and a large glass of Tuaca. 'At Winchester Hall this is the witching hour – the place is deserted. Apart from the cleaners and a few of the slightly younger residents. Absolutely everyone is in bed. Peggy, who could bore for Europe about her son and recycling, and Sue, who is always trying to bitch about someone if she gets the opportunity. And Douglas and Judith, who are married and never let anyone forget it. As though anyone would try and make a move on either of them! Both dull as ditch water. And I never trust a man who wears a cravat unless he's at a wedding. They are always banging on about making up a four for bridge, and when we do, Douglas has to mess about with two pairs of glasses and muddles up spades and clubs.' She huffed. 'Anyway, this has been such a fun evening. I feel all the better for some stimulating company.'

'So, what's happening tomorrow at eleven o'clock?' I asked.

Mum gave a pleased little smirk. 'Franco is going to take me out for coffee and then a little drive, just down to the lake. He says he knows a lovely bistro where we can have lunch. He says we are in for a cold snap; it might even snow, so I have to wrap up warm.'

I was astonished. I think my mouth was gaping slightly.

'You've been here a day and you already have a date?'

'Apparently,' she said airily.

'I didn't know he had a car. I thought he walked here because he couldn't drive.'

Mum shrugged. 'He says he can, and I have no reason to doubt him.'

'Right. Fine,' I said, vowing to have a word with Zoe.

Having a car was one thing, being fit to drive it was another. Never mind the considerations of insurance and a current driving license.

'Now then, I need my beauty sleep,' she said, 'so I'm off to my lovely room. You were right about that. I was expecting some hovel with a tap and a tin bath and the wind whistling in through the window frames. It really is very nice in there, even better than your room. And such a lovely view. I don't know why you didn't suggest I come here years ago.'

'*What?* I did, Mum. And you said you didn't want to. That Zoe had given up her life to run a pub with a gigolo. And broken her mother's heart.'

Mum's eyebrows shot up. 'I'm sure I never said such a thing. Well, that pasta thing Paulo made was delicious. I couldn't taste any garlic at all. I wonder what was in it. Chicken?'

'Wild rabbit,' I said.

Mum went rather pale, put a hand to her throat and blinked hard.

'Really. Oh dear. I remember people eating rabbit after the war. I swore I'd never... and then there was that myxomatosis thing that put everyone off. Do you think Paulo shot it himself? Oh dear, I hope I won't throw up. I'll just tell myself it was chicken. Or what's that awful stuff? Tofu. Wild tofu. You can't get sick from that.'

I grinned and gave her a hug. 'You'll be fine. Now then, off to bed, sleep well and I will see you in the morning.'

Mum picked up her liqueur glass and drained the last few drops.

'Wild rabbit,' she said faintly. 'Oh well, when in Rome.'

* * *

The following day, Mum and I shared some *cornetti* and apricot jam in my room. She was obviously very excited, although she did her best to hide it, and hardly ate anything.

'I hope I look alright,' she said, patting at her hair. 'I mean it's nothing formal, is it. Just a drive in the car.'

She was wearing a pale blue twinset and a dark blue skirt.

'You look fine, Mum. Really great. You still have a good figure.'

'Well, I always thought I didn't have much education, so the least I could do was look after myself. You should see some of them in Winchester Hall! There is one woman whose only hobby seems to be cake. She's never without a box of Mr Kipling French Fancies in her handbag. And Daddy was always so particular about how I looked. I suppose these days I would be sneered at. Just a corporate wife, cosying up to all those dull businessmen and their snobby wives on his behalf.'

'Nonsense, you were always a great asset to him. He told me so. The last time I saw him. When he was in hospital.'

Mum looked shocked. 'Did he? He never told me. I wish he had. I would have liked a few compliments from time to time. And I think I deserved them, after all those dreary dinners and awards evenings. It's why I was always so determined you would achieve more. That you wouldn't be relegated to the same sort of role I was.'

I looked out of the window. 'Perhaps I have been,' I said at last. 'Perhaps women will always have to fight for the sort of things men take for granted.'

Mum came and stood behind me, putting both hands on my shoulders.

'You've done a huge amount over the years,' she said. 'You've played your part. I'm proud of you.'

This admission was a shock: I hadn't ever really seen things from her perspective. I felt quite emotional and weepy for a moment.

'Thanks, Mum. That means a lot,' I said at last, rather choked up.

'Now then, none of that. We still have a battle to win,' she said firmly, wandering back to look out of the window, 'persuading the rest of the world that women like us still count.'

'When I came here, I didn't know what on earth I was going to do. I felt almost like a non-person.'

'It would probably be very peaceful but I'm afraid they

wouldn't have you,' Mum said absently, moving the curtain to one side.

'Who wouldn't have me?' I asked, confused.

Mum shook her head sadly. 'No convent would take you as a nun – you're spoiled goods.'

I sighed. 'Not a nun-person, a *non*-person.'

She gave a little laugh. 'That's a relief, I couldn't see you as a nun anyway. Although it suited Audrey Hepburn. You and I still have things to do, bucket lists to empty, opinions that matter.'

She was right. We did. I too had goals which were more personal than what was in my personnel file.

'I hope you will be warm enough,' I said at last to cover the silence that had surfaced. 'It's not a very bright day. It might even rain.'

'I shall take a warm coat, don't fuss. And I have a headscarf. I'm not planning on doing much walking anyway.' Mum went to look at herself in the wardrobe mirror and tweaked at her cardigan. 'Oh well, it will have to do. So, what are you up to today?'

'I'm not sure, but I think I will go and see if Paulo needs any help.'

Mum tutted. 'Helping out in a pub kitchen at your age. That's a bit of a comedown, isn't it? Is there really no chance they want you back at work?'

'I haven't heard a word from them since the day I left.'

'Ungrateful lot,' Mum said and snorted. 'After all those years, all those late nights and weekends spent working. I hope they go bankrupt. And they all get warts.'

'Unlikely,' I said, laughing.

She wandered around the room for a bit, picking things up and examining them.

'So, this man you were with. Gio. Tell me all about him – is he someone I should be aware of?'

'He's just a friend of Paulo's, that's all.'

Mum went to peer out of the window. 'He's quite dashing though, in his own way. Franco said he's an artist.'

'Yes, he is. He did these two paintings.' I went to show her. 'You can see the lamb in each of them. That's his trademark.'

'Oh yes. That's nice. They are rather good, aren't they? Ah, there's a car pulling into the drive. I think it must be Franco. It looks like some sort of vintage. How wonderful!'

We both went to stand in the doorway. Outside the air was cold, and the wind whipped around us.

It was indeed Franco, driving a dark blue, vintage car with whitewall tyres that looked almost tank-like. He slowed to a dignified halt and got out to usher Mum into the passenger seat. She looked very pleased with herself.

'Have a lovely day,' she called.

'Take care of her, Franco, and see you later,' I said rather anxiously as he closed her door.

'*Certo* – of course,' Franco replied.

And then they were off, the wheels crunching heavily over the gravel, through the gates and out of sight. Well, I hadn't expected this at all.

I went off to the kitchen to see if there was anything needing doing. By now I'd started taking orders and serving food too, and I was quite enjoying it.

20

Just after ten thirty the following morning, Mum came into the trattoria kitchen where I was peeling and crushing cloves of garlic.

'Well, you're a dirty stop out?' I teased. 'What have you been up to? I went to check on you at nine thirty and you still weren't back.'

Mum raised her eyebrows. 'Nothing. Franco took me to such a lovely place for lunch. We had a splendid time.'

'That must be the longest lunch ever.'

'Oh well, you see... then we went onto have a drive around to the other side of the lake. That is such a comfortable car. He told me it is a Maserati Quattro-something-or-other. 1966. I remembered that because it's the year England won the World Cup. It has a wooden steering wheel and no end of horsepower. He did tell me, but I wasn't listening the whole time.'

'I hope he has a valid driving license and insurance?'

Mum laughed. 'Of course he does; he drives very well. I didn't have to cling onto the door handle once. Not like when Daddy was driving. I used to think my feet would go through the floor sometimes.'

'Well, I'm glad you had fun. And then what did you do?'

Mum tutted a bit. 'Honestly, I feel as though you are the parent, and I am the child. And I can't get used to your short hair. You look like you should be playing Tinkerbell in *Peter Pan*. Well, then we went back to his house for dinner and some friends of his dropped in. It was quite a party. He made some very nice pasta thing with vegetables and no garlic. Not spaghetti, thank heavens, because I have never been very adept with all that twirling. He's taking me out again – we thought perhaps a trip to see some churches. When the weather is a bit better. He doesn't want me to get cold; he's very attentive. So refreshing. Not like Daddy who didn't notice when I had flu, or shingles for that matter. I honestly think I could have been lying on the floor unconscious and he would just have stepped over me.'

'Well, I'm glad you enjoyed yourself,' I said, returning to my garlic chopping. Whatever I had thought about having Mum here, it definitely hadn't been this. I supposed I'd hoped, for a second, she'd be fussing over me in one of her rare mother-hen moments.

She had never been very convincing at that though, so perhaps it was just as well it wasn't happening. When I was younger, if I was out of bed and had eaten something I was well enough to go to school. I went when I was incubating chicken pox once and had to be sent home in a taxi.

'Franco is going to pop in for lunch later: he wants to introduce me to some more of his friends. And what about that nephew of his? Gio? Franco was telling me all sorts of interesting things about the family. How his parents used to argue all the time, and the split between him and his wife. I can't remember her name.'

My interest went up tenfold. 'What did he tell you?'

'She went off with some chap from Genoa years ago, turning her back on the children, and then came back when she was ill.

Apparently, Gio looked after her until she died, which under the circumstances was very noble I thought.'

'Yes, indeed,' I said.

Something else I hadn't expected. I supposed I had assumed that theirs was a lifelong love match only blighted by her demise. Perhaps there was more to this story than I had realised. And maybe it explained Gio's comment about having to think things through.

'So, what shall we do this afternoon?' Mum said, settling herself in a chair. 'Let's be honest, there's not much to do here, is there? And what is Paulo making with all that? Garlic surprise?'

'A slow-cooked shin of beef. It has a lovely red wine sauce. You'll eat it tonight. We could go for a walk into the town later if the weather clears. There are a few little shops – you could meet the local people, get a feeling for the place.'

Evidently this didn't match up to Mum's expectations. She pulled a face.

'Hmm. Lovely. It's a bit cold for that. You should hire a car. Perhaps Zoe would lend you hers? I'll ask. I'm sure she won't mind. We could go to Milan.'

Before I could answer that under no circumstances was I going to risk all those tunnels on my own with only my mother for navigational assistance, sleet started lashing down against the windows.

I pulled a sad face. 'Perhaps when the weather clears up.'

'Well, what are we going to do? I can't just sit here all the time with you.'

I felt a moment's panic. Winchester Hall might not cover all the bases as far as Mum was concerned but at least they kept her occupied.

'I'm going to be busy here for a while,' I said. 'You could

always find a nice book to read. There are a few in my room, in the bookcase.'

Ignoring Mum's grumbles that she *hadn't read a nice book since 1997*, I scraped all the chopped garlic into a bowl and washed my hands.

'I'm going to take some coffee and find someone a bit more interesting to talk to,' Mum said, filling her mug, and then she wandered off into the dining room.

I poured some coffee for Zoe and found her in the back room she used as an office, surrounded by piles of paperwork.

She looked up as I knocked. 'Just the woman I wanted to see. Gio rang, wondering if you were free.'

'In theory, yes,' I said. 'Though in practice, no, because my mother is looking for entertainment. Franco is popping round for lunch later with some of his friends, but other than that she's getting a bit restless, and I don't think the town has enough to occupy her. She's talking about driving to Milan and I don't think my nerves would stand it.'

'Well, let's wait until she's met up with Franco; I'm sure he will divert her. You can always help me with this filing. I'm weeks behind. And I'm getting to the point where I can't find anything.'

We spent an hour or so together, with Zoe sorting papers into piles and me putting them into the right place in the filing cabinet. And then, after a long wait while her computer loaded up, I opened the spreadsheet I had created for her and added the most recent figures. It still wasn't looking good.

'Have you thought of having a tasting menu evening?' I asked. 'That sort of thing is really popular in London. I could spread the word on the local internet sites if you help me with the Italian.'

Zoe looked thoughtful. 'We did think about it once, but it never came to anything. Paulo might go for that. But he's not very enthusiastic at the moment.'

'Well, why not have a word with him and see what he thinks. You've got friends with a vineyard, haven't you? We could ask them too; they could suggest complementary wine for each course.'

'Yes, actually, that's not a bad idea. There's a local cheese maker too – he might join in. Anything to boost trade. Everyone needs a helping hand at the moment.'

Mum wandered in with a paperback in her hand, and then when Zoe asked her if she wanted to help, drifted off again, muttering about finding some more coffee.

Zoe and I worked on for a while, with Zoe muttering to herself, and me wondering why they ordered such uneconomical quantities of food when they had storage for more.

'It's midday,' Zoe announced suddenly. 'It's gone very quiet out there. Let's take a break, and see if Paulo is free for a chat.'

* * *

In the bar we found a cheerful scene.

Mum, sitting up very straight in her chair, was next to Franco, and a couple of elderly friends were sitting on the other side of the window table. They were all enjoying coffee and a plate of biscuits.

'Well, I've never played but I'll give it a try,' I heard Mum say with a laugh. 'Ah, there you are, dear. Franco is here. And here are some of his friends: this is Stefano, who is a retired builder; and this is Alberto, who worked for the government. Alberto's wife is joining us soon; she worked in entertainment. I'm not sure exactly what.'

I nodded and smiled at the newcomers, and they nodded and smiled back very pleasantly. Stefano, in a waxed jacket, was rather chunky with a gleaming bald head and Alberto sported a flat cap and a beige anorak. There was a pack of cards in the middle of the table.

'What are you up to?' I asked.

'We're going to play something called Texas Hold 'Em Poker,' Mum said. 'I've never played before. I think it might be rather fun, don't you? You could join us if you like.'

I remembered Jack having poker nights occasionally before I had banished him to his own flat because of the noise and the amount of whisky consumed. It nearly always ended with an argument and the table overturned.

'I'll leave it for now, thanks,' I said. 'Don't bet the farm, will you?'

'I haven't got a farm,' Mum said, confused.

'We always used to play, and then after Nonna died, we lost heart. It's just for fun, and forfeits,' Franco said reassuringly, 'not for money.'

'Good,' I said suspiciously.

* * *

It was a long time since I had enjoyed forty winks in the afternoon. Was this the way to go, or was I falling into the trap of behaving like an old person?

No one batted an eye at young people snoozing on the bus or lying on a rug in the park at lunchtime. But if I had settled down for a nap by the Serpentine, people would have probably called social services. It was the same with sitting down. No one saw anything wrong with the younger generation sitting on the pavement to wait for a bus, but if older people did it, they were sneered at as though they were vagrants.

I remembered years ago reading something about horses: young ones lay down to sleep, but unless they felt absolutely safe, older ones didn't. If they did, there was usually something wrong. Perhaps older horses took longer to get up again. I knew the feeling.

I was woken up by Mum, barging in with a handful of poker chips which she deposited on the bedside cabinet.

'I'm rather good at this game, you know,' she said proudly. 'Franco says I'm a natural. He wants to start up the poker club here again. We've had such a laugh. He says I'm a miracle worker. And Alberto's wife Maria is charming. She used to be a dancer – I think that's what she said. *Ballerina esotico.* On cruise ships. Anyway, I'm quite exhausted from all the chatter. I'm picking up some Italian too. Stephano taught me some words to use when I get back home: *verme.* That sounds like a sort of pasta, doesn't it? And *stronzo.* I'm sure that's a sort of beer but maybe not. I shall sound quite cosmopolitan to the old fossils in Winchester Hall.'

'Perhaps you should get him to translate before you start calling Janine a *stronzo*,' I said.

21

In the following week I barely saw Mum at all. She settled into a routine of sorts. A very late breakfast with me, usually coffee and the Pan di Stelle *biscotti* for which she had developed quite a liking. Franco called for her every day about lunchtime in his massive vintage car and took her out for a 'little drive', as she described it. On most days they went to see churches and museums and cafes and wine bars up and down the length of the lake. In the afternoon she took a nap, to prepare herself for an evening with the poker players.

I, meanwhile, was mostly always front of house in the trattoria, taking orders and generally helping out. I was enjoying myself immensely, and it was certainly a good way to learn Italian.

The one thing I did notice though, was the absence of new customers. It seemed to be the same people. A retired couple called Enrico and Eva who lived in the town and were partial to desserts. Three elderly friends, Catalina, Giulia and Ludovica, all around seventy, who liked the lunchtime specials of soup and cheese. And occasionally the staff from the supermarket came in to celebrate a birthday. It wasn't exactly a strong client base.

'I can't remember when I last enjoyed myself more,' Mum said late one morning as she dunked a Pan di Stelle *biscotto* into her coffee. 'You really should join us one evening. I have a good mind to start a poker club when I get home.'

'Oh, you are planning to go home then?' I said.

Mum looked surprised. 'Of course I am. I just mean to shake things up a bit when I get back. There's nothing wrong with that, is there?'

'I thought you had come here to – you know – look after me?'

Mum went over to the window, looking out for Franco's car no doubt.

'Well, you seem perfectly fine as far as I can tell. Can I borrow that blue scarf? You're working in the trattoria; Zoe told me you are planning a tasting evening, which sounds fun. She takes you out in her car, and you have an admirer. Although I haven't seen him for a few days. Has he cooled off?'

'You seem to think my life is all sorted. And it's not.'

'Well, in the words of the immortal Kenneth Wolstenholme at the end of the World Cup final in 1966: it is now. Gio's truck has just pulled up outside. Looking for you no doubt.'

I went to peer over her shoulder; we must have resembled a couple of meerkats looking for predators.

Zoe hammered on the door and came dashing in, a tea towel over one shoulder.

'Gio is here!' she said, and then she darted away again, slamming the door behind her.

'Right then, perhaps I'll see you later,' Mum said with an arch of one eyebrow.

'Shouldn't you be giving me sage, maternal advice, smoothing my hair and telling me mother knows best?'

Mum snorted. 'When did you need my advice, or take it for that matter? And you've hardly got enough hair left to smooth.

You're sixty-one. I assume if you can't look after yourself by now you never will. Anyway, I haven't got time for that and let's be honest, you seem to be doing quite well on your own. There's something rather attractive about these Italian men, isn't there? I imagine when the Romans invaded Britain, they were very popular with the girls. Far more stylish and attractive than the muddy Anglo-Saxons. Hmm. Have a good day.'

She trotted off back to her lair and a few seconds later Gio knocked on my door.

Honestly, I had come to Italy for some calm, some peace and quiet away from all the stress of everyday life and other people. It was getting like Piccadilly Circus. Well, perhaps not that bad, but pretty close.

'Hello,' I said. 'I wasn't expecting you. Everything okay?'

How did he manage to look more attractive every time I saw him?

He grinned. 'Fine, great. I understand from Franco that your mother is unexpectedly busy with the local card sharks. I thought as it's another cold day you might like to come and sit by my fire and have lunch.'

I sighed with pleasure. The prospect was very appealing.

'I think that would be lovely.'

* * *

We drove up into the hills, the way increasingly obscured by low cloud and banks of mist. Water drops hung on every branch; the road was dark and wet.

'The temperature is dropping. The forecast is for snow,' Gio said. 'Late for the time of year but it happens. The weather is definitely changing.'

I wiped the condensation off my window and peered out.

'I can't remember the last time we had snow at home, not proper snow when the roads get blocked. In England everything closes at the mere threat of snow.'

'Sometimes the ski resorts get none when they most need it.'

'Do you ski?'

He laughed. 'I used to but not now – for some reason falling over hurts more,' he said. 'These days I prefer to paint the scenery, not shed blood over it.'

At last, we turned off the road and down the slope leading to his house. There the cloud hung low, trapped between the branches of the trees. It was very quiet, no birdsong or traffic noise from the valley below. Walking to the door, I shivered, my breath steamy in the cold air.

But inside, the place was warm, snug and cosy. The fire was glowing with slow-burning logs. Buffo was asleep in front of the hearth, of course. I unwrapped my scarf and pulled off my gloves.

'This is lovely,' I said. 'I must say, you're very domesticated.'

'I have to be,' he said. 'If everywhere is a mess, there is no one else to blame.'

He went to make coffee, I sat down in a chair by the fireside, watching the cat for any sudden moves.

'So how do you spend your time?' I asked Gio on his return. 'My mother was complaining there is nothing much to do here.'

'I'm just back from two days in Milan, delivering some of my work to a gallery. But you know I paint, of course. I read. I write to friends and my children – proper letters. Yes, indeed, don't look so surprised. I cook, and I think. I enjoy my time. The same things you probably do when you are home.'

'Not quite the same,' I said.

I tried to think back. What exactly was it that I had done at home?

'I'll just go and fetch a few more logs for the fire,' he said.

What did I do? I rested my head back, listening to the pleasant sounds of someone else moving about, doing things, being in charge.

I was always busy doing something, but if I thought about it, there were few things I really enjoyed. Did I like the opera? Once in a while. Or impenetrable productions of obscure playwrights? No, not really. Galleries and exhibitions, where we met the same circle of people, all wanting to be seen as cultured and interesting?

Many times, I had wanted to have a nice hot bath, then put on my dressing gown with my feet up and spend the evening channel-hopping or reading, but as a couple that's not what we did. Looking at things from a distance, the relationship felt exhausting. Without Jack in my life, things would be very different when I went back. Better. More serene.

When I went back. How odd. How alien that sounded. How unappealing.

How could this be me? I was a London person, wasn't I? Someone used to the bustle of the city. Who, without really thinking about it, knew the shortcuts and dodges, the many little ways of negotiating all those people, all that traffic. And yet, here I was, sitting in a quiet chair, in front of the fire with a man who I hardly knew, and for the first time in a very long time I felt – what was the word – peaceful. How strange and unexpected.

I checked Buffo was not about to launch an unprovoked attack and closed my eyes. Then I opened them again and saw the cat sitting up and watching me. I was not sure that cats had many expressions, but this one certainly did, and I didn't think it was particularly friendly. I would test it.

I closed my eyes again, and this time when I opened them the cat was sitting a little closer, looking disinterestedly at something in the distance. The next time it was at my feet. A feline version of grandmother's footsteps. It blinked at me.

'There's a good cat,' I said. 'Nice Buffo. You're not going to – you know – leap up my legs again, are you?'

'Here we are,' Gio said, pushing open the door with his shoulder. He deposited some small bits of tree into the log basket and Buffo scarpered away in a flurry of startled paws. 'I see you're making friends?'

'Well, sort of,' I said.

'He's very friendly really,' Gio said, bending to ruffle the cat's ears as it crept back up to him. 'Right, the coffee should be ready. I'll get you some.'

For Buffo the lure of someone going into the kitchen was too great and he followed Gio, miaowing in Italian all the way. From my place by the fire, I could hear Gio chatting to the cat, also in Italian, and occasionally I heard a miaow in return. It was rather endearing actually. But a bit sad too, to think of Gio living here with only a cat to talk to most of the time.

'Here,' Gio said, putting a tray on the table and sitting down on the sofa next to me. 'Sorry for the wait; Buffo needed his third meal of the day. He really is the greediest of cats. But you look very peaceful.'

'I am,' I said. 'This is a very relaxing place to be. I can see why you like it here.'

He poured out the coffee and handed me a mug. 'I have lived here for nearly forty years. I have simple tastes and I have everything I need here: including company when I need it.'

'It's lovely.'

I wanted to ask about the wife deserting him and her illness, but I didn't have the nerve. I didn't want to bring her into the room anyway: she had probably been beautiful and wilful, and he had probably loved her very much.

'My wife always disliked living here,' he said, as though he had read my thoughts. 'She needed more excitement. It was only when she was ill that she returned.'

'And you looked after her?'

He nodded. 'Of course. Her partner abandoned her. She was still my wife, still the mother of my children.'

'That was very compassionate of you.'

Strange, that wasn't a word I had applied to many people.

'It was just the right thing to do,' he said, 'but it makes me think. What is happening with your previous partner back in London?'

'We broke up. Jack should have moved out of my flat by now.'

'And how are you coping? You have lost your job, your companion. Does that make you sad?'

I thought about it: was I sad? Work somehow seemed a far-off place; the end of my relationship with Jack was in many ways a relief. An unexpected freedom.

'No, funnily enough I'm not sad at all. I was devastated at the time about the redundancy, but perhaps I have changed. Maybe I can see a way through.'

'Of course. You can talk to me about it, tell me what happened if you want to?'

'About work?'

'Of course. I'm a good listener. These years on my own have taught me a great deal.'

'I don't think I want to talk about work,' I said at last. 'I've been doing a good job of keeping it from my mind. Not so long ago it was all I thought about. Now, I wonder what exactly I was doing. What difference I was making to anything.'

'I'm sure you were good at your job,' Gio said, putting his empty cup down on the table.

I rested my head back on the cushions.

'I was. But it all seems a bit meaningless now when I think back. All those years of planning and wrangling and pushing people. Spreadsheets and conference meetings. Deadlines and delays. Worry, disappointment, sleepless nights, urgent phone calls at all hours. No time for the one important thing in my life: Ben, my son. I always seemed to be fretting about who was going to pick him up from school, where he was, what he was doing. I missed so much of his childhood. And now he's grown up, and gone—'

I stopped, and to my absolute horror, I started to cry. The very last thing I had wanted or expected. And this wasn't just a few self-pitying tears to be wiped away casually with my sleeve, hoping he wouldn't notice. It was proper, full-on sobbing and wailing and gulping. And, knowing me, a red face and a runny nose. I was not a pretty sight when I cried.

Beside me, I heard Gio give a little noise of alarm and sympathy and I felt a handkerchief being pushed into my hand.

'*Così triste, cara*. Oh dear.'

I did a fair bit more sobbing and even a bit of snivelling. I could feel his sympathetic gaze, his hand on my shoulder. For some reason this made me cry even more.

It was a very long time since I had shown my vulnerability, even longer since a man had shown me simple kindness.

But even I couldn't cry for ever, and I was beginning to feel ridiculous. Any idle thought I had about the attraction between us must surely have been ruined by my behaviour. And I must have looked a sight.

At last I took his handkerchief and did a good, long honking blow into it. So attractive.

'*Va bene* – it's okay,' he said. 'I think you needed that, didn't you? A good cry?'

'Can a cry be good?' I said rather shakily.

He laughed kindly. '*Certo*. Of course. You have been through a difficult time. You are bound to be upset. You do miss your son, and you can't pretend otherwise.'

'I'm so sorry.'

I felt him put an arm around my shoulders and pull me in against him. He was wearing a dark green sweater which smelled of pine and warm wool. I rested my cheek against it and breathed a great, long shuddering sigh. For the second time, I felt he had actually noticed me. I wasn't someone's employee or boss. I wasn't a relation or friend. I was me, in my own right, with my own worries and feelings.

'*Mia amica* – my friend – you need not apologise. I have seen the sadness in your eyes from the very first, and all the times you have laughed with your friend and hidden your feelings from everyone. Even her. You have been brave, but eventually everyone needs to let go, let their thoughts out. Like grief – mourning for what is lost. And perhaps fear for what is to come?'

'Don't, you'll make me cry again,' I said, having another, less trumpeting blow into his handkerchief.

I closed my eyes and let my head rest against his chest. I could just hear his heart beating. At the back of my mind, I thought, *Yes, this is what Jack should have done.* Comforted me. Listened to me. But he hadn't. And he never would have.

Later, I wouldn't know how long we'd stayed like that. Perhaps an hour, perhaps less. He asked me about Ben, what he had been like as a child, what he was doing in Canada, how I was feeling. I could hear his voice rumbling in his chest. His arm around my shoulders was comforting and strong. Occasionally he kissed the top of my head. It was the most soothing thing in the world.

I was, for the first time, able to admit out loud that I was not just angry about what had happened, I *was* sad. And yes, I was anxious for the future and ashamed of being a terrible mother.

And a neglectful daughter. I had been distant from the two people who mattered most to me. My son and my mother. And for what?

At last he pulled away from me.

'You are being much too hard on yourself,' he said. 'Your mother seems very lively; your son has made his way in the world. I'm sure we would all do some things differently if we could. I will fetch you a brandy – I think you could do with one, don't you?'

'Yes, please,' I said. I looked away, conscious of my puffy eyes and runny nose. 'I must look terrible.'

He put a finger under my chin and tilted my face up to his. His smile was very kind.

'*Sei una donna molto bella*,' he said.

And then he kissed me.

And this time I kissed him back.

And he kissed me some more and I really liked everything about it. The softness of his sweater, the hardness of his body underneath it. The feel of his face against mine. The slight roughness of his stubble. His hands in my hair. The way he whispered things I didn't understand.

'*Mia cara amica, non ti preoccupare, sono qui.* I'm here. *Sono qui.*'

Don't worry. I'm here.

Some time later he went to get the brandy. It was only then I realised Buffo was sitting at my feet, looking up at me in quite a kind way (if that cat was capable of such a thing). But then he gave me a rusty miaow, as though asking what I was playing at. I reached down and he allowed me to stroke his sleek head for a moment before taking himself back to the fire.

'Here – Vecchia Romagna Riserva. I keep it for special occasions,' Gio said.

I took the glass. 'Is this a special occasion?'

'Oh, I think so,' he said, and leaned over to kiss me again. Just very briefly. 'See what you think.'

I wasn't a great fan of brandy as a rule, but this was delicious, rich and fruity with a slight spicy taste.

'Better?'

'Yes, much better. I'm sorry I made such a fuss.'

'You don't need to apologise for anything. I can tell you have had a lot to deal with. Now then, I am going to put another log on the fire, and then cook you dinner and pour you wine and kiss you in front of the fire while the night is dark and cold outside,' he said. 'And when we have done that, I would like to make love to you. What do you think?'

I looked up into his dark eyes and felt an unexpected and long dormant clench of lust and longing. Was this one of those moments when I would strike out, do something different?

'I think that's a wonderful idea,' I said, my voice a bit croaky.

Actually, forget about the dinner...

22

I woke the following morning knowing several things were different.

Firstly, me. My location. I was in a strange bedroom, under a crisp white duvet, with supremely comfortable pillows. And I wasn't alone.

Secondly, also me. I was feeling very *very* pleased with myself. We had done as Gio had suggested. Eaten an exceptionally tasty spaghetti carbonara, covered with shavings of black truffle, and some exquisite little side salads. We'd drunk wonderful red wine from his friend's vineyard, and another glass of very expensive Italian brandy, and then we had gone to bed. Simple as that.

When people did that on television, there was a great deal of shoving and crashing about and gasping and clothes being dragged off in a sensual way. And very noisy kissing, which was a bit off-putting in my opinion. The women always seemed to be pushed up against doors or wardrobes too, which couldn't be comfortable. A door handle in the small of one's back would really hurt. And in the morning, after hinting at hours of debauched passion, they always seemed to be half-dressed. Certainly with all their underwear on. Which wouldn't happen.

And yes, it wasn't like that at all. There was no covering up afterwards. No embarrassment, no awkwardness, and no messing about with *Should I–Shouldn't I* thoughts.

He had given me a cotton dressing gown that trailed around my ankles and a new toothbrush. And then we had got into bed, and we had reached for each other with mutual desire and hunger. Holding each other close in the darkness, touching and enjoying each other. And he had done as he'd said he would: he had made love to me, as no other man ever had. It had been marvellous. Perhaps this was what other people experienced all the time; I really had been missing out on something and not known. But now I did.

Then, the third thing happened, which was equally as unexpected, when he pulled back the curtains on the new day. It was still not properly light, but there was a glow about the dawn that seemed almost luminous.

'Ah,' he said, 'so it has snowed in the night. I thought it would.'

Even at my age, I could still be excited about snowfall. I scrambled out of bed, definitely not still in my underwear, put on my dressing gown and went to look. We stood side by side, he put an arm around me and we watched as the flakes outside fell onto the newly softened landscape. It was glorious, flawless, romantic. Every tree, every rock, each fold in the landscape I could pick out in the early morning light was covered in snow – lots of it.

'It's so beautiful,' I said, 'so perfect.'

He dropped a kiss on the top of my head. 'I will fetch you some coffee, and we can stay in bed and watch it fall.'

And so, that's what we did. After I had hurried into the bathroom, had a shower, brushed my teeth and made some sense of my hair which that morning really did look more Albert Einstein than Audrey Hepburn. Honestly.

After an hour or so he went to fetch *cornetti*, more coffee and some peach preserve which he said his great-aunt – she of the black felt hat – had made. And still the snow fell.

'I can try and get the truck out to the road, but I think we might be stranded here for a while,' he said.

He had one arm around me, pulling me close to him. My head nestled on his chest.

'Good,' I replied lazily.

He turned to grin down at me. 'I didn't think you would mind.'

'I don't. I could stay here all day, just watching the snow. And being...'

I stopped. What had I been about to say?

'...being here.'

I didn't want to think about the other people I had shared a bed with, but I did. Not that there were that many. I was sure I was below the average.

This felt different, as though it meant something more than the others. It felt like we were equals. Together because we both wanted it. Perhaps needed it.

'I'm sure we will find something to do with the day,' he said and leaned across to kiss me again.

In the end we didn't get out of bed all day. Something I had seldom done in my life except on the few occasions when I'd been ill. Well, we did brush the *cornetti* crumbs out of the sheets, and he found me a clean pillowcase when I spilled coffee on one of mine. But that was his fault really. He should have given me a warning that he was going to dive under the covers.

It didn't get properly light all day; there was a pinky-yellowish tinge in the sky and the snow didn't stop until late afternoon. Only a short trail of Buffo's reluctant footprints in the snow broke the pure white surface.

By then the light was fading again, and the evening grew dark as we went to the kitchen for more food. He assembled a selection of tasty things on a tray and lit the fire. He opened another bottle of wine, and we sat together in front of the flames, just enjoying each other's company, while Buffo sat in the hearth and watched us.

Gio passed me a glass of wine which glowed red in the firelight.

'You are wonderful. I knew when I first saw you that you would be special to me. And you looked so suspicious, so exhausted.'

'I was,' I admitted. 'I thought you were a kidnapper.'

'And see, you were right! I have kidnapped you. Brought you to my home and you cannot get back. For now.'

I didn't want to go anywhere. I was quite happy where I was.

We sat and talked, and sometimes we just watched the fire. I told him more about my life: about Ben and his partner, who I had only the briefest of information about. Gio told me about his life and children, and recently how he had withdrawn from so many things.

I began to see that we were both lonely, had both been damaged by other people. That strangely we were both in the same place in our lives, where we were looking for something different, for things to change.

I decided to stop trying to be happy and just be happy.

London seemed another world to me that evening. A place distant and dimly remembered and not really with any affection, which surprised me. I had always thought I'd enjoyed my life there. Busy and slightly hectic as it was, always on the edge of panic.

'I wonder how the poker players are getting on…'

Gio laughed. 'I have not seen Uncle Franco so bright and cheerful for years. Your mother must be having a good effect on him.'

'What a thought,' I said, 'but I think it is mutual. After my father died and the house became too big for her, she decided to move to a residential place. It obviously provides the care and company she needs, but too little excitement. I'm glad for them.'

Was I? Was I comfortable with my seventy-nine-year-old mother having an admirer? Perhaps he was just a friend she had made. I'd assumed they were simply laughing together and enjoying each other's company. No more than that, right?

So, hang on, it was okay for me to spend the day in bed with Gio but not for my mother to do something similar? Always assuming Franco *could*. Perhaps he could? And assuming that my mother wanted to. But would she?

That was a bit hypocritical of me. There was no age limit on anything really. Friendship, love, desire, need. There were all sorts on celebrity fathers in their sixties, seventies and eighties in the news. I'd done things and felt things I'd never expected recently, and I was sixty-one. At what age did a magic switch flick to the off position?

At least neither of us would have to worry about unwanted pregnancy. Maybe I didn't want to think about it too deeply after all.

* * *

And so we spent another night together. There was a wonderful feeling between us, not just the pleasure of our physical relationship, but also the companionship, the friendship. Could you be friends with a lover? I hadn't thought so before then.

As I lay awake in the darkness, I thought about this. I tried to put the facts into a mental spreadsheet which in the past was the way I'd sorted out problems.

Gio and I made each other laugh and we talked about everything. Our families, the world, music, travel, books, what we wanted to do with the years left to us. In those few days I had learned more about him than I had ever known about any man before.

On the other hand, we lived nearly a thousand miles apart. I'd checked on my phone app.

It brought it home to me that the time I had left was limited and precious. Time was a currency that I needed to spend wisely. I was not going to live forever after all.

Maybe one day I would decide to go into some sort of care, just as my mother had. I couldn't imagine it at all. And I felt a pang of regret and doubt. She had always been a sociable, gregarious woman, and she had made the best of her life at Winchester Hall, but had she really been happy there? I had assumed so, but now I wasn't sure.

She always seemed to have a lot to grumble about, criticisms of other residents and of the routine. I felt rather guilty. I should have made more of an effort to involve her in my life. I would in future; after all I would certainly have the time.

Which brought my thoughts back to what I was going to do next. Was I going to go back to London, to take up the threads of my old life? Did I want to turn into the sort of unconditionally supportive partner my mother had been to my father? Or was I going to try and forge a new path for myself?

If I changed my mind and decided to form my own consultancy, or look for another job, what would I need to do? Ring my contacts; write emails; arrange meetings for lunches where I would lay out my plans, my aims and objectives, my – god forsaken phrase – mission statement.

I turned over and snuggled into Gio's warm back. My resolve was firming up. No, I would not do those things. With my remaining years I would please myself, spend my time doing something for me. I would visit Ben in Canada – perhaps one day I would have grandchildren – and I would travel: see all the places I had wanted to explore before firstly my career and then Jack had taken over.

Which brought me to Jack.

I imagined him removing his belongings from my apartment. Leaving spaces where his artwork had hung, his books had been stacked; collecting up his music and his clothes. The apartment held memories. It would seem lopsided and odd to be there on my own. It sounded draining.

And then suddenly, from nowhere, a strange thought came to me. I didn't have to live there anyway. I didn't even need to live in London any more. I could go anywhere, do anything. Live where I pleased, with the things and the people I wanted around me.

I was so excited I almost woke Gio up to tell him, but then he gave a soft sigh and shifted in his dreams, and I just rested my cheek against his shoulder and went to sleep.

In the morning a thaw had set in. We could see through the kitchen window that all the snow had fallen off Gio's truck into rather depressing, slushy piles. That was the thing about snow: it was great to anticipate, exciting when it arrived, and disappointing and unattractive afterwards. Like every takeaway I'd ever eaten.

'I will be able to take you back to the trattoria this morning,' he said sadly, pouring from the Moka pot. 'I cannot keep you here any longer. My kidnapping has gone wrong.'

'I thought it was rather successful actually,' I said, grinning.

He smiled back and passed me a cup of the coffee. 'Perhaps you will return of your own free will next time?'

'I certainly will. But I do need to go back for some clean clothes, have a shower and let Zoe and my mother know I am okay and not lying in a ditch somewhere.'

He kissed me across the countertop. 'I hope you are okay. I certainly am.'

We shared a leisurely breakfast, and then I collected my things together and we drove back down the hill to the trattoria. They didn't seem to have had much snow at all and I felt lucky that I had been stuck amid such a glorious and unexpected scene.

I clambered down from the truck, waved Gio off and made my way to the barn.

* * *

As I passed the kitchen door, Paulo appeared, on his way to the dustbins with some cardboard. Zoe was close behind him.

'Ah! *Mi'amica!* You have returned!' Paulo said cheerfully.

Zoe leaned forward. 'Where have you been and what *have* you been doing?' she murmured.

I could feel myself blushing. 'Nothing.'

'A likely tale.'

'I just went over for lunch, and it snowed. And we were a bit stuck.'

Zoe raised an eyebrow. 'It didn't snow until very late last night, but it didn't settle here at all. So did you have fun?'

'I might have done,' I said, trying to sound casual.

'How marvellous. I knew I was right!' she said and punched me gently on the shoulder. 'Still got the old magic then? When are you seeing him again?'

'I don't know... He said he had some things to do, and he would see me soon,' I said, suddenly feeling a moment of teenage panic. 'Do you think he meant it?'

'Of course, don't be daft. I knew you two would get along, and the way he's been looking at you, it was only a matter of time before something happened.'

I was absurdly pleased by this. 'Really? What way? Did he say anything?'

'He passed Paulo a note during playtime.'

'Oh, very funny. Have you seen Mum today?'

Zoe called across to her husband. 'Paulo, have you seen Eleanor?'

Paulo looked up from stuffing some cardboard into the recycling and grinned at me.

'Not today. Perhaps she is staying with *her* friend.'

Oh god, what must they have thought of us?

'Now, give me a few minutes,' I said to Zoe, 'and I'll be right over. Let me know what I can do to help out. Isn't there a party of ten in at lunchtime?'

Zoe shook her head. 'They've cancelled because of the weather. And apparently a new wine bar has opened up in the next town. Ridiculously cheap, and with a flashy website to bring new customers in. It seems to be working. To be honest there isn't much for you to do today.'

She gave a shrug, but I could see she was upset.

I really did need to do something to help them. And soon.

* * *

I went into my room, showered and dressed in some fresh clothes. Then I went to the bar and polished all the tables. I even started polishing the chairs, which were looking a bit battered and scruffy. There needed to be some sort of update here to appeal to new clientele – even if the regulars didn't like it – otherwise they could be going out of business.

The idea of a tasting menu... That was something I could research. And if the trattoria needed a website... Well, I had enough skills to create one. I was sure of it.

And hang on a second! Emilio seemed to know a lot about technology. If he was clever enough to write computer games, he could certainly sort out a website. Perhaps I could press him to help me.

23

_____

That afternoon I put on a warm coat, found my sketch pad and box of pencils, and went out onto the veranda. Below, the lake looked dark and forbidding; opposite, the mountains were topped with snow, the crevices in the rock outlined in white. I made a few tentative pencil strokes, wondering if I still had any talent.

Time passed, and I realised that I hadn't thought about much at all. That was the beauty of sketching: it required a little concentration, but at the same time cleared the mind. And I was quite pleased with the result. Perhaps I would do this again. Maybe I would travel the world with a Moleskin journal embossed with my initials, making notes and little drawings. Like Picasso or Hemingway.

I would draw the rocky coast of Biarritz, the splendour of the Rockies, the Taj Mahal, and no one would nag at my shoulder and say we would be late for dinner or ask why I was doing that.

I paused, drawing my coat around me because the afternoon was getting chilly. I could see that it was possible to go to those places on my own. Yes, it might be a little unnerving to start with, but – well, why not? The world was not going to come to me.

I went back to my drawing, shading some of the peaks and crags of the cliffs overhanging the lake. And then I looked up to see Gio's truck coming into the driveway and my heart did a little, pleased leap.

He came over and sat down beside me, kissing my cheek.

'I must tell Paulo I am here. I have come to collect some food for the convent.'

He looked down at my sketchbook, moving my hand aside when I tried to cover it.

'But that is lovely,' he said. 'You have a talent for this.'

'Do you think so? I haven't done this for years.'

'Indeed, I do. We must go further up the mountain when the weather improves – the views there for drawing are wonderful. A bit of a walk but worth it.'

'I'd like that,' I said, forgetting all the disparaging things I had ever said or thought about walking.

'And I know a delightful place on the way where we could eat. It's owned by a distant cousin.'

'You seem to have a lot of cousins.'

'It's true. He is a character; I think you would like him. So, how has your day been? Have you been working hard?'

'I've been thinking about Zoe and Paulo. I want to do something to increase the number of customers they get here. I've been thinking about a website for the trattoria and also a taster evening. With local produce. You have friends with a vineyard, don't you? I think they do too. And you know someone who makes cheese. There must be other people around here who could help?'

He nodded. 'Yes, I am sure there are. And I think that is a very good plan. What can I do to help?'

'I'm going to ask Emilio to help with the new website. And if you could get in touch with some of the people you know, that would be a start.'

'What do Zoe and Paulo say about this?'

'I haven't mentioned it yet. I thought I would get a few facts straight first. Get my ducks in a row.'

He looked surprised. 'You have ducks?'

'No, I mean get my ideas straight.'

'Ah, *bene*. There is a wonderful recipe Paulo sometimes cooks, *ravioli di anatra e tartufo nero*. Duck and black-truffle ravioli. And Alberto could help us find the truffles. Now, what if I come back at seven thirty and collect you? We could go out for dinner at another place I know. Down by the lake. And talk about it some more.'

'Owned by a cousin?'

He laughed. 'No, not owned by a cousin. A friend.'

'I'd like that a lot,' I said.

'Then I will see you later,' he said and kissed my cheek.

I watched as he and Paulo loaded up the truck with some boxes, and then he waved and drove away. I waved back. What a nice man he was; what an unexpectedly healing place this had become for me. I was feeling suddenly filled with purpose and optimism.

I went back into the trattoria and found Emilio at the sink with a very sulky face, scrubbing a huge roasting pan.

'Emilio, I need to talk to you.'

* * *

I went into the bar at seven o'clock and there, talking to Paulo, was Gio. His face brightened as he caught sight of me.

'There you are, and you look lovely. Would you like a drink?'

'No, I'm fine. Let's go if you're ready – we have a lot to talk about.'

'*Assolutamente*,' he said and grabbed his car keys off the bar.

'Have a pleasant evening,' Paulo said with a wink. 'I will look after things here.'

'If you see my mother, can you tell her I want to catch up with her?'

'Of course, I will tell her. I'm sure she will be in later.'

We drove off from the trattoria and down towards the lake. The traffic was busier now, trucks and lorries speeding west to Bergamo and Milan, or east towards... somewhere else. I hadn't really got my bearings even after all this time. Perhaps they were going to Switzerland.

I remembered my feelings when I'd arrived here, of just wanting to escape from everything: to drive randomly into the distance, to find new places which would make me feel better about myself. Perhaps after all I had found that place already. It was a pleasant, warm thought.

I sneaked a look over at Gio, his profile lit by the dials on the dashboard and the occasional beam of headlights coming towards us. I realised this was making me feel happy too: being with him, doing something spontaneous and fun. I began to relax again.

'Where are we going?' I asked after a while.

We seemed to be passing right beside the water, the road occasionally going through rock arches. I could see steel struts above us, covered with netting, presumably to keep falling rocks off the road.

At last, we reached the lights of a large town and Gio swung the truck smoothly into a car park. I could see a glassed-in veranda overlooking the lake, the whole thing illuminated by strings of lights and candles on each table. It looked very inviting.

'This place is not owned by any cousin,' Gio said as we walked inside, 'but by good friends. You will see.'

'Gio! *Amico mio! Come stai?*'

We were warmly greeted by a tall, bearded man in a striped apron who then called just about everyone out from the kitchen to say hello. There was a great deal of manly hugging – aka a brief embrace with hard pats on the back – and cheek-kissing, and then everyone turned to stare at me. When Gio introduced me they hugged and kissed me too. I didn't think I had ever been made to feel so welcome in any restaurant. Even the other diners turned in their seats to see what all the fuss was about, and they all seemed delighted to see us too. A couple even waved their napkins at us. Perhaps this was what being a celebrity was like? It occurred to me that this place was full of people. What brought them here? I would find out.

Eventually we were led to a table in a corner overlooking the lake, which glittered darkly below us in the lights from the veranda. It seemed everyone wanted to serve us. I saw a bit of undignified shoving on the part of two young waitresses, before the elder of the two asserted her position and brought us menus, a basket of bread and a jug of iced water.

Tall, bearded man was back. 'Gio! My friend, it has been a long time!'

'Antonio, *è passato troppo tempo*. It has been too long!' Gio said.

They chatted away for a few minutes, and at one point I was obviously mentioned. *La donna inglese*. Antonio favoured me with a smile and bowed over my hand.

'*Piacere di conoscerti*. Pleased to meet you,' he said. 'I hope you will enjoy your evening.'

'*Grazie*, I'm sure I will,' I said.

I thought, not for the first time, how most of the people I had met spoke far better English than I did Italian. I really should have made more of an effort. Perhaps I would do that with my spare time: learn a new language. I had picked up a few words and phrases working in the trattoria, but I could do more.

'I recommend the *casoncelli alla Bergamasca*,' Gio said, after Antonio had left us a carafe of wine and gone back to the kitchen. 'Pasta stuffed with beef and herbs, with butter and sage sauce.'

'Sounds ideal,' I said, glad that I had resisted eating earlier on.

Gio placed our order, poured me a glass of red wine and reached over the table to take my hand.

'I have missed you today. I think Buffo missed you too.'

'Did he? That sounds unlikely. How marvellous.'

'I told you he would get used to you. He's quite friendly really.'

'I'm sure he is.'

Someone, a stout man who was with an older woman and two teenage boys, shouted across the room.

'Gio! *Come stai?*'

'*Sta bene*,' Gio replied. The two men raised their glasses to each other. 'That is my accountant, and the woman with him is his wife – she runs a shop in the next town. She sells craft things and artists' materials. They are old friends of mine,' he added.

'You know a lot of people; everyone seems to know you.'

'Well, I have lived here most of my life. I expect it is the same for you and all your friends in London.'

Well, no, actually. If I thought about it there were very few times I had been out and bumped into a friend. Obviously, there were plenty of people I knew, just to say hello to, socialise with and exchange idle pleasantries, but recently I'd not had the opportunity to make real friends. What was it people said about being in a crowded city and feeling alone at the same time? And I hadn't really seized the opportunity to make friends at the school gate when Ben was little. I'd left all that to the au pair.

Our waitress brought our meals over. A beautiful pottery bowl of pasta with a delicious topping of crispy pancetta, a generous sprinkling of parmesan and a fabulous, buttery aroma.

'It is one of Antonio's specialities,' Gio said. 'Wonderful.'

And it was too. Something about it was both simple and yet delicious.

'The food around here is brilliant,' I said after a few mouthfuls. 'I have been so spoiled. I hadn't expected that.'

'There is an Italian saying: *lascia che la vita ti soprenada.* Let life surprise you.'

'Well, it's certainly done that in the last few days,' I said.

We exchanged a rather meaningful glance, and he smiled.

'You have surprised me, Clover; I have surprised myself. Little did I know that day at the airport that this would happen.'

That what would happen? What exactly did he mean?

'Now, tell me what you have discovered,' he continued, 'in your research for the tasting evening?'

I took a long sip of my wine, enjoying the taste of it.

'Well,' I said at last, 'the first thing I did was speak to Emilio. He is more than capable of designing a website. Apparently, he has offered to do it before now, but Paulo said they didn't need one. I told him I would pay for his time – he was very happy about that.'

Gio tilted his head to one side enquiringly.

'But you need to speak to Paulo and Zoe first,' he said. 'To get their agreement?'

'I will. Paulo is such a great chef; his food is wonderful. We just need to tell people. Have you managed to speak to anyone about the taster night?'

'I have left messages with my friends at the vineyard. And with Luigi, who makes a fabulous ewe's milk cheese. I am sure they will get back to me very soon. And I have heard of a new place on the other side of the lake where they make chocolates. And of course, there is a bakery in the town where they make wonderful bread. Most of it goes to Bergamo. To the high-end delicatessens there.'

'Excellent,' I said, filled with energy and enthusiasm.

'You need to speak to Paulo and Zoe,' Gio repeated.

'I will. I promise.'

The waitress took away our plates and Antonio brought us some desserts in shallow porcelain bowls.

'Hazelnut panna cotta with chocolate ganache,' he said, standing and looking at his creations rather fondly.

I sampled a spoonful. It was fabulous.

'*È delizioso*,' I said. 'This country has everything. It's so beautiful, and the people are so friendly. *L'Italia è così bella*.'

Antonio clapped his hands with delight. 'You are learning Italian, *signora*. *Va bene*. And always remember what Giuseppe Verdi said, *Potresti avere l'universo se posso avere Italia*. You can have the universe if I can have Italy.'

At that moment, sitting there, in the candlelight, I felt that would be a fair swap.

* * *

And so, we finished our meals, drank coffee from little red cups, nibbled tiny amaretti biscuits wrapped in paper. The room was nearly empty by then; people had gone off to their lives and their homes.

'A final trick,' Gio said.

He rolled up our biscuit wrappers into cylinders and stood them on the dessert plates. And then he set fire to the tops. I watched, wondering if Antonio would mind, but he was just watching from behind the bar with a big grin on his face.

And then almost as they were extinguished, the wrappers flew up towards the ceiling.

'Make a wish,' Gio said.

And I did.

24

We went out into the cold, dark night and drove back up the steep road, past the turning for the trattoria and onto Gio's house. And it felt absolutely the right thing to do. There was no one else I wanted to be with at that moment, no one else whose company I enjoyed more. It was a comfortable feeling.

We went into the shadowy house, the warmth from the fire welcoming us and Buffo asleep on a chair. Gio didn't put the lights on; he just hung up my coat and took me in his arms.

'You're sure,' he said. 'Sure this is what you want to do?'

'Yes,' I said. 'I'm sure.'

'Then let's sit by the fire for a few minutes with a brandy, to take the chill of the evening away.'

And there in the warm darkness he kissed me, his face against mine, cold from the night air. Tomorrow I would think things through more clearly. This could be the start of it: the new beginning I needed and wanted.

* * *

I woke the following morning to a bright, cold day. What time was it? Nine o'clock. *When did I rediscover my ability to sleep?* I wondered. For so many years I had verged on being an insomniac: waking at odd hours, fretting about something, rehashing old board meetings and generally trying to see the big picture. Occasionally I had taken a swig of flu medication to help me nod off. Now it was as though I had reset my inner clock. I could allow myself to relax.

And yet, at the back of my mind there was something rumbling away, bubbling up to remind me. Ah, yes: Paulo and Zoe. I needed to sort that out today.

The bedroom door opened and Gio, showered and dressed, came in with my morning tea.

'*Buongiorno, bellissima,*' he said, kissing my forehead. 'Good morning, beautiful lady.'

'Good morning,' I said, stretching and sitting up in bed. 'You're spoiling me.'

'Not at all,' he said. 'You were sleeping so peacefully; I didn't want to disturb you. I am going out today, up into the hills. To paint, to think.'

'I must go back,' I said.

He nodded. 'I know.' He went to look out of the window.

'I'm going to speak to them,' I said. 'I promise.'

'You don't need to promise me anything,' he said. 'You don't owe me any promises.'

'Well, I want to,' I said. 'You're absolutely right: I can't just steam ahead thinking I know what's best like I used to.'

'I will take you back when you are ready,' he said. He paused, looking away, as though he wanted to say something important. In the end he just looked back at me, a little smile on his face. 'I must go and feed Buffo. He will be angry to be kept waiting for his second breakfast.'

I stretched out languidly, feeling rather sultry and happy. I even felt quite affectionate towards Buffo, though he had spent the previous evening savaging my scarf behind the sofa. I rolled over to look at the clock and fell out of bed with a thump and a small scream.

'Are you okay?' Gio called.

'Fine, absolutely,' I shouted back, scrambling up and getting back into bed.

After making an effort to calm down and rubbing a bruise on one elbow, I drank my tea, looking out at the view and thinking.

I imagined the event I'd been planning: the taverna full, everyone happy and a lot of people enjoying Paulo's wonderful food instead of just a few. Increased profits and footfall – that's what it was called. Zoe had liked the idea. But would they appreciate my secret preparations? Suddenly I wasn't sure.

I dressed and made my way to the kitchen where Gio was packing up a canvas satchel with paint brushes and supplies. I wished that I could go with him. Or maybe even just stay here, reading, thinking, maybe making a meal for his return. Which for someone like me, who was not a skilled cook, was an unexpected thought.

'Have a good day,' I said.

He smiled. 'You too.'

'I'll do my best. When will I see you again?'

'Soon.'

I wanted to stand once more in the comfort of his arms, but I didn't. I needed to get on with things. I followed him out to the truck and clambered up inside. Was there an elegant way to get into a truck? I hadn't found it yet.

He stored his canvas bag on the back seat, moving a cardboard box to one side and folding up a rug.

And then we left, following the road back down to the trattoria. At my suggestion he stopped at the gateway, and I got out. As I watched him driving away, I felt as though I was losing something. A little piece of security.

* * *

Zoe was in the bar, washing glasses. She turned round as I came in.

'Ah, at last! There's a letter for you. It came yesterday.'

'A letter? But no one knows I'm here.'

She held out a cream envelope and I took it. 'Well, someone does.'

I recognised that slogan, even though it was a rather irritating new one. XS – 'The Beating Heart of Finance'.

'What's this?' I said foolishly.

'Well, if you open it, you'll know.'

I hesitated for a moment. Memories of that day when I had been unceremoniously escorted out of the building, thinking that my life was ruined, that I had no future. How wrong I had been.

I opened the envelope and pulled out a letter. Heavy cream paper, embossed.

I looked down to the signature. Nick Crane, *C.O.O. Chief Operating Officer.*

Nick Crane? He hadn't lost his place in the company then; in fact, it looked as though he had been promoted. How absolutely typical.

Zoe peered over my shoulder. 'What does it say?

I read the letter and then re-read it, incredulous.

What?

'They want me to go back,' I said at last, 'on a consultancy basis. Six months to start with, probably longer.'

Zoe sniffed. 'So, all those clever men can't cope without you after all!'

I re-read the letter, wondering if I had misunderstood. But no, it was true.

They were having issues with the Olafsen deal; they needed my input – something about staff shortages, time pressures. Then a paragraph about how I had always been highly respected, that my knowledge of the industry would be so valuable. Then a little throwaway comment, that Mr Olafsen himself insisted I should be involved.

So that was it.

I remembered him: Sven Olafsen. Tall, rather handsome – in a Viking sort of way – and very short-tempered. I had spent many hours with him and his board, thrashing out some miniscule part of the deal, waiting for the inevitable moment when he would throw down his pen and storm out of the room, his assistant at his heels.

I passed the letter over to Zoe and she read it, twice. And then she looked up at me, doubt in her eyes.

'So?' Zoe said at last. 'They are suckering you into something. Do you want to work for them again?

I took a few moments to remember that cold day when Nick Crane had carried my banker's box downstairs for me. How bewildered and lost I had felt. And I tried to equate that with how I had felt since I had arrived here in Italy. And frankly there was no comparison.

Perhaps there was a magical, healing power in the clean air of the lake, the simple life I had been living. And, perhaps, I had allowed Gio to play some part in that. He'd helped me to understand that I didn't need a fancy job title, expense-account lunches or taxis everywhere to be happy. I had reconnected with my mother properly for the first time in ages. I was communicating with my son.

I tried to imagine the scenario if I went back into the XS offices, dressed once more in a formal suit and heels. Someone taking my laptop bag from me, doors being opened. There would be murmured welcomes from people who had not expected to see me again. Perhaps I would be taken to a large office with a view over the Thames. Someone, perhaps Nina, would bring me coffee; Nick Crane would pop in, rubbing his cold hands with pretend pleasure, and flash his veneers at me.

'Back where you belong – I knew they wouldn't manage without you. I told them at the time—'

Weasel.

And then I would be given back my work laptop and I would open it, looking at all those beautiful spreadsheets and columns I had created. Nick Crane would tell me what meetings had happened in my absence, the problems encountered, the complete inefficiency and stupidity of people other than himself. He would try and make me his ally – us against them – so that when I pulled off the deal, he would stand next to me and claim some of the credit. Yet again.

The whole thing sounded too horrible. No matter how much they offered to pay me, firstly, I wasn't that person any more and secondly, I didn't care.

I cared about my health, my son, my future. I wanted to wake every morning with a peaceful mind. I never again wanted recurring nightmares about meeting rooms and deadlines and the pot of XS pencils that all broke when I tried to use them. I didn't want to oversee the details of another conference in a big, soulless hotel, for people whose only concern was the prominence of the person they were seated next to at dinner.

At the back of my mind, an idea had been forming over the

last few days. One I didn't have properly sorted, but it wouldn't go away. I didn't want to waste any of the time left to me people-pleasing, conforming or making the best of it.

I was sixty-one, and I only had a limited amount of life left. It might be a few years, or it might be many. After all, my mother was still firing on all cylinders at nearly eighty. And, thinking about that, I wondered where she was. I hadn't seen her for days.

I took a deep breath. It was time to say out loud the things I had been thinking.

'I've been giving it a lot of thought, Zoe. No, I don't want to go down that path again. I've realised there is more to life than that. And things are going to change. To start with, I'm going to sell my flat,' I said. I felt oddly calm and yet there was an undercurrent of excitement. 'I'll put money on Jack not having moved out, but this will sort that once and for all. I'll have to go back and organise things, of course.'

'Really? Are you sure? What will you do?' Zoe said.

'I don't know. But I don't want to carry on doing the same stuff, pretending nothing has changed, living in London for no real reason. I can do better than that – I know I can. I want to do something else, something different. And maybe to start off with that's where you and Paulo come in. I want to have a chat later; I'd like to suggest something. A plan.'

* * *

Paulo looked doubtful. He leaned back against the table in his kitchen and folded his arms.

'A taster evening? Zoe mentioned that some time ago, but I didn't really think about it. What do you mean? I don't understand how this will benefit us. It just sounds like a lot of work and no guarantee that anyone will come.'

'That's what publicity is for. We spread the word all around this area. Towns, villages. Leaflets in all the stores. And, of course, the internet.'

Paulo rolled his eyes and flapped with his tea towel at the cat who had been trying to get into the rubbish bin.

'*Alora*, the internet. What time do I have to mess around on the internet?'

'You don't have to. You already have someone who can deal with that.'

'Who? Not me I can assure you,' Zoe huffed.

'Emilio,' I said.

Paulo scoffed. 'Emilio cannot be trusted to wash up a spoon without supervision. Sometimes I wonder why I bother employing him. All he talks about is – ah. I see. All he talks about is his computer and the internet. Is that what you mean?'

'Exactly,' I said, 'and I have spoken to him, and he is very keen to help. He can design a website, publicise the trattoria, get more people coming in. I would buy the hardware needed; you needed a new printer even before I arrived. A faster computer would be really useful too.'

'I hope he would be better at this website than drying glasses. He takes an age to do anything, and he is never happy. Never,' Paulo said.

'But if he was happy doing this, then you might be surprised what he can achieve.'

Zoe looked doubtful. 'All this is going to cost a fortune.'

'I am happy to pay for that,' I said.

Paulo looked offended. 'I am not a charity case, not yet anyway.'

'It's not charity. I want to repay you, both of you, for your kindness and your hospitality. Staying here at maybe one of the worst times in my life... well, it's made such a difference to me. I want to be useful again. I know I'm a hopeless cook, but I do know my way around a business opportunity. And I can help, believe me.'

Zoe was still unsure. 'How much would it cost anyway?'

I estimated quite a lot but for the moment I would keep that to myself.

'I would make a payment to Emilio once he sorts the website out, and for a small fee he can keep it updated every month with news and menu changes and things going on here. There are so many local producers in this area. Wine and bread and cheese. And organic fruit and vegetables. And meat and chocolate. People like that sort of thing; they want to think they are eating good food. And you produce good food, Paulo – there's no question of that. We just need to let people know about it, and the taster evening would be a good place to start,' I said.

I was almost breathless with my enthusiasm.

'And what if it doesn't work?' Paulo said, his lower lip stuck out with doubt.

'Then you will have lost nothing,' I said firmly, 'but it *will* work. All you need to do is sort out a menu. Cook something really fantastic. *Specialità della casa*. Gio will help too: he can design some posters and he has friends nearby who make wine and cheese, and other things too. And I can help Zoe with the ordering and the deliveries. I'll deal with the business side, and you can just enjoy the cooking.'

'Oh boy, that sounds like even more of your spreadsheets,' Zoe sighed.

'You'll learn to love them. Just think about it. What do you say?'

There was a long pause while Paulo looked out of the window and Zoe watched him.

'It's Easter next weekend,' he said. 'I am going to be busy with that.'

'Well, it would take me and Emilio some time, of course, to get everything up and running. So, it would be after that. Whenever you were ready.'

Another silence. At last Paulo drew in a deep breath. '*If* we did this – and I'm not saying we will, I'm just saying *if* – I would need black truffles. Lots of them.'

Zoe caught my eye and winked. And then she did a surreptitious thumbs up behind Paulo's back.

From the bar we heard a sudden shout of laughter.

Zoe grinned. 'Sounds like Eleanor's in the bar, playing poker. Again. Let's go and see.'

25

I followed Zoe back into the bar where, indeed, my mother was playing poker. She was sitting at what had become her usual table in the window, accompanied by Franco, Stefano, Alberto and his wife Maria, who was bright in a yellow sequinned dress.

'There you are!' Mum called over happily when she saw me. 'I was wondering where you had got to.'

I went over to kiss her cheek. 'I was wondering the same thing, Mum. You never seem to be here.'

Mum pulled a face. 'Well, talk about the pot calling the kettle black – you're not exactly visible here half the time. I've been thoroughly enjoying myself; I haven't had so much fun in ages. Franco has taken me all over the place. Milan, Bergamo. We are thinking of taking a trip to Venice too, aren't we?'

Franco looked up and nodded enthusiastically.

'*Certo*, we are. Perhaps after Easter, when the crowds are less.'

'You could come with us, if you're not too busy?'

This last comment was said with a certain emphasis.

'Could we have a chat, do you think?' I asked.

Mum looked at her cards, stuck out her lower lip and nodded. 'I was going to fold on this anyway.'

She picked up her glass of wine, followed me to the other side of the room and settled herself in a chair. I had to admit she looked very well: bright-eyed and happy.

'So, what's all this about?' she said.

'I'm thinking about you, that's all. One minute you are in a retirement village complaining about having high blood pressure and the next you are up all hours, playing poker and gadding about.'

She widened her eyes at me. 'Why shouldn't I gad about? I'm enjoying myself. Franco is excellent company; we have some laughs, and he is teaching me Italian. And the other day I had to pay a forfeit, and they made me sing. Franco played the music on his phone, and I had to sing 'That's Amore'. They were very appreciative. Anyway, it's better than the time Stefano lost and had to exchange his clothes with Maria, and I did his make-up. Isn't it annoying how a lot of men have better legs than women? And you have been gadding about too, come to think of it.'

'I'm just worried about you, that's all. I know you have found life at Winchester Hall a bit difficult since you moved in... I don't want you further upset by all this change. You know, unsettled. Are you thinking of going back soon? It might be for the best.'

Mum's eyes flashed angrily, and she took a deep breath.

'Don't you dare tell me what I should do. I'm nearly eighty and believe me I have gone through more advice about how a woman should behave than you've had hot dinners. The modest virgin bride; the adoring, subservient housefrau; the perfect wife and mother; the woman who probably had more intelligence than her husband but could never show it because society didn't value or expect it.'

'I know that Mum, but—'

'Do you know how long it is since a man kissed my hand? It's certainly over fifty years. Do you know how long it's been since a man told me I was beautiful? Probably over sixty years, as your father was not given to compliments or flattery. But still I had to defer to him; it was expected of me. He was the head of the household, the man of the house, the one in charge. Why do you think I was so delighted when you forged a career for yourself? Why do you think I was so hard on you when it came to exam results? Because I never had your chances, and if I had been born thirty years later, I might have. In my day, we weren't really expected to do much more than get married and keep house. And that's what I did. And what a dull, predictable life I led. Always being the supporter, never the champion.'

'Don't be cross with me – I'm happy you are enjoying your stay here. I really am. I just don't want to see you taken advantage of. Or hurt.'

Mum tossed her head.

'If, at my advanced old age, I take pleasure in some harmless flattery and flirting from an attractive man then I jolly well will,' she said. 'Heaven knows I am owed it. I don't want my day to start at six-thirty and finish after an early dinner. I like getting up late and going to bed late. I always did. Don't make the mistakes I made. Assuming that what life threw in your path was the only option. Because I have had a lot of time to think about it and it's not. I've been surrounded by a lot of old relics since I moved into Winchester Hall, and I suddenly realised I was fossilising too. And even though I'm nearly eighty, I'm not ready. Not ready at all.'

She paused and sat back in her chair, looking at me rather crossly.

'I'm not either,' I said.

'Good.' She reached forward and patted my hand.

'And if you think I'm being taken advantage of, think again. Franco didn't know what hit him the first night we spent together.'

'*Mum!*'

She looked rather pleased with herself. 'Well, honestly, Clover, you think your generation invented sex. Just because you had the pill and all that stuff. Let me assure you, you didn't. We might not be as – shall we say – athletic as we once were. Franco's knee has been giving him a bit of trouble. But there's a lot to be said for a good old-fashioned cuddle. I haven't had so much fun in decades; you know, your father was—'

I held up one hand. 'I really don't want to know.'

Mum patted her pearls. 'No, I don't suppose you do. Anyway, I'd better get back to the game.'

'You aren't playing for actual money, are you?'

Mum snorted. 'Of course not. I'm not that daft. I've already told you we play for forfeits. Last night Franco lost, and he had to... Well, let's just say it's a good job the local policeman is the son of Franco's friend. I was in stitches. I can't remember when I laughed so much. We never did find his other shoe.'

'I don't need to know. I don't want to be an accessory after the fact. Mum... Do you think we could spend a bit more time together, before we have to go home? I suppose I'm just thinking about the future. I'd like us to talk about it properly. Yours as well as mine.'

She stood up and put a hand on my shoulder. 'Of course we can. And if I have learned one thing from this trip, it's that futures don't make themselves. You have to create them.'

26

Mum was right when she said she liked to get up late. I didn't see her the next day until eleven o'clock. By then I had walked into town and bought some bread and – remembering the need to use a disposable glove – some gorgeous little tomatoes. And some cheese. Perhaps I would make us some lunch from all that. If she ever got out of bed.

When I got back, I went into the kitchen to help Paulo do some vegetable preparation. He was back to his usual, cheerful, pleasant self. How did he manage it? Didn't he ever have off days when he behaved like Gordon Ramsey in the kitchen? Shouting and cursing and throwing things about? Were he and Zoe really that compatible and if so, how?

'There you are.'

It was Zoe, coming in with a pile of freshly laundered tea towels which she dumped in a drawer.

'You're really happy, aren't you, Zoe?' I mused aloud. 'I mean, I've been here for a while now, and you and Paulo never seem to argue or roll your eyes at each other. I spent the last couple of years permanently on the edge of irritation with Jack. I think the gloss had worn off our relationship, and it was only the fact that both of us worked such long hours that kept us together. Because we were usually apart.'

Zoe shook her head. 'That's no way to live. And Paulo and I get on so well because we actually like each other. I mean, it doesn't hurt that he's so handsome and charming and' – here Paulo looked over delightedly and blew her a kiss– 'all the other stuff. We've made each other mad sometimes, but the great thing is, over the years, both of us have learned to say sorry to each other.'

I thought about this and realised it sounded very wise and sensible, but also odd coming from my free-spirited cousin. The girl who had left a trail of broken hearts in her wake during her teens, who had argued endlessly with boyfriends at university and vowed never to get married at all. And then, the summer we left university, she met Paulo on a beach in Sardinia, and that was that.

'I used to think losing my job would be the worst thing that could happen – but I'm beginning to think it's turned out to be the best.'

'I'm glad you feel that way, and even more glad you are not going to be drawn back into your old life.' She glanced at Paulo and lowered her voice. 'So, these ideas you have for the trattoria… I can't tell you how excited Paulo is about it, now he's had time to think. He was talking non-stop about it last night. It's a brilliant plan.'

'I'm so glad you think so,' I whispered. 'I didn't want you to think I was coming here and bossing you both around. I just think it would work – really I do,' I said. 'I want to do something positive for you, to thank you.'

Zoe went to pour us coffee from the pot on the heated ring and came to sit down at the table with me.

'And what else do you want?' she asked.

'I want to buy a proper house. With a view and some atmosphere. My apartment had a nice outlook, but I was hardly ever there to see it. And I never did meet my neighbours, except to nod and smile on the way out to work. And it had zero character. Yes, it was eco-friendly and easy to maintain, but it was bland. Uninspiring. I suddenly feel I want to knock down walls and discover old fireplaces. Use some other colour than pale grey for decorating. Buy some outrageous light fittings. Perhaps even a chandelier. ...now, there's a thought.'

I could feel my excitement and enthusiasm rising by the minute.

Zoe sipped her coffee and munched on a biscuit. She looked thoughtful.

'I have an idea. I'll have a chat with Uncle Franco and get back to you.'

'About what?'

'Oh, just wait and see. I'm not exactly sure yet,' she said with a small smile. 'So, now you have decided what you don't want and who you don't want to be with, where does Gio fit in to all this? I thought you two had a bit of a thing going on.'

'Oh, sort of, I think,' I said, hoping Zoe wouldn't see how my face changed when I thought of Gio. Because I was beginning to realise he was important to me. 'But this shouldn't involve him. I've only known him five minutes. He went off yesterday to focus on some painting. And that's fine. I'll tell you who *does* have a bit of a thing going on, and that's Mum and Franco. She told me enough to confirm it's *not* just a friendship where they discuss prescription regimes and how awful the younger generations are.' I gave Zoe a meaningful look.

Zoe burst out laughing. 'Really? How marvellous. There's hope for us all. Paulo, did you know about this?'

Paulo turned from the stove. '*So cosa*? Know what?'

'Eleanor and Uncle Franco. They are – you know – *hanno una relazione*. In a relationship.'

Paulo shrugged. '*Non c'è limite di tempo*. There is no time limit, is there? For anything.'

I supposed not.

'Ah, there you are, for once,' Mum said, posing in the doorway.

She didn't look anything like the mother who had arrived to visit me in her sensible twin sets and court shoes. She was wearing a bright pink dress and some flat shoes decorated with sparkles, and she had replaced her trademark pearls with a necklace of chunky glass stones.

She followed my gaze. 'These shoes are so comfortable, and practical too. Franco is slightly shorter than I am, so it works.'

'You look terrific,' I said, feeling almost dowdy in comparison.

Mum sat down at the table and Zoe passed her some coffee.

'I do like it here,' Mum said, 'and I've been trying to work out why. I think it's because no one expects anything of me, no one assumes anything. At Winchester Hall, there was a long and spirited discussion among the old crones when Janice came down to breakfast one morning wearing a bright orange cardigan. I thought she looked fine, but the perceived wisdom was it was *a bit much*. It turns out she's a bit colour blind and thought it was pale peach, but honestly, who cares.

'I like your new look,' I said. 'It suits you.'

'Italy suits me; the sunshine suits me,' she sighed, stroking her glass beads. 'I shall feel very hard done by when I go back. I mean, I was reading that the Italian healthcare system is one of the best in the world—'

Where was this train of thought taking her, I wondered?

'—and there is a big party here next weekend, for Easter? Franco has asked – no, *begged* – me to stay on a bit longer. So, I will be here. Will you?'

'I think I will,' I said, 'but it all depends. And what was last night's forfeit, dare I ask?'

'Alberto had to eat three dry biscuits without water and then whistle the Italian national anthem. And it's really long. So, what have you been up to? Any news?'

'I had a letter from XS – an offer to do some consultancy work.'

'I hope you turned that down,' Mum said. 'Do you know, I feel twenty years younger since I've been here. Perhaps there is something to be said about the Mediterranean diet after all. And of course, the occasional glass of wine doesn't hurt either.'

Occasional? *Hmm.*

'And Clover has had a fantastic idea,' Zoe added, 'for us to have a taster evening, with local produce. Paulo will need to find some truffles, to test out a recipe.'

'That sounds nice,' Mum said, 'and I love truffles. Perhaps I could pick some up in the sweet shop?'

'I think we need to ask Alberto and Ascari,' Zoe said.

* * *

Gio arrived at my door the following day.

'How did the painting go?' I asked.

'Very well,' he said, kissing me. 'Then I had a phone call from Paulo, and another from Alberto. It seems you have been shaking things up a little. Zoe is very excited about it all. Now, are you busy today?'

'Not at the moment,' I said.

'Good, then have you got time to come with me? Just a short trip. Your mother has been talking to Franco, and Stephano. And he has been talking to Zoe. Who checked with Alberto.'

'It seems everyone has been talking to everyone,' I said, a bit bemused.

'So, *vieni con me* – come. See what you think.'

I grabbed my denim jacket and followed him to his truck. 'Where are we going?'

'You will see – just keep an open mind, and think about it.'

'Think about what?'

Gio grinned. '*Abbi pazienza.* Have patience!'

We drove down to the town and past the little shops. The hardware store now had a display of gardening tools and pots in the window, with soft-toy bunnies peeping their heads out. The supermarket window was full of chocolate Easter eggs lavishly festooned with bunting, plastic flowers and a couple of religious statues.

We drove for about a mile and then Gio slowed down, turning the truck in through the open iron gates of the villa I had noticed when I first came here.

He stilled the engine and held up a huge, iron key.

'I got this from the agent in Brescia. Shall we see if it fits?'

I frowned at him, puzzled. 'What on earth are we doing here?'

We walked up the short, weed-raddled drive towards the villa. Ivy had crept up the walls and was partially blocking some of the upstairs windows. The paint on the external shutters was flaking after years under the hot Italian sun, and one shutter had fallen off completely, lying smashed in the garden.

Gio unlocked the front door, and it opened with a groan from the rusty hinges. Inside there was a tiled floor, thick with dust and dried leaves that had blown in. In front of us in the gloom I could see a staircase, carved and elaborate once, now shrouded in cobwebs and dirt.

We explored, the rooms empty and echoing to our footsteps. Gio took my hand.

'I have been looking at this place for a long time. I remember when it was a family home. It has been empty for perhaps over thirty years. It could be perfect,' he said, 'with time, imagination—'

'And a great deal of money,' I added.

'But think of the possibilities,' Gio said. 'It was beautiful then; it can be beautiful again.'

We walked through the house, where just a few random pieces of furniture were left behind. There were marble fireplaces, grates filled with soot and dried leaves. Everywhere there was the smell of grime and decay. I pulled back the edge of one of the heavy curtains, trying to see the view, and the fragile fabric shredded in my hand and fell to the floor in a cloud of dust.

'Who lived here?' I whispered (because the house seemed to encourage that).

'A man from Milan. He had it as a weekend cottage, and then his business failed, and no one wanted to buy the place. Some of his family still live not so far away, near Bergamo. You know this area has some problems despite the beauty of the landscape. The lack of jobs for young people means they move to the cities for work. And places like this are not wanted unless a rich person buys them for their holiday homes, and they bring little to the locality. There are so many places like this, even castles and old farms, where no one wants to buy them. I could save this one.'

'And then?'

'Ah, well, then...' He looked at me and grinned. 'The potential is endless.'

We entered a dining room, where a huge chandelier in the ceiling was shrouded in dusty cloths. It was amazing that it hadn't been removed by the family. I could just imagine this place filled with people, light and laughter. Perhaps with an extravagantly long table, and a sideboard with a polished silver candelabra. In the drawing room I could visualize comfortable sofas, chairs, lamps and curtains pulled back to frame the unparalleled view across the lake.

'It's too much, too big a project,' I said. 'I wouldn't have the first idea how to deal with the building work or the bureaucracy that went with it.'

Gio held up one hand in agreement. 'Nor me, but Stefano and Alberto do. They know everything there is to know about it. And they know the right people to ask.'

'The cost of this house and the cost of the building work... It would be enormous.'

'I think you might be surprised. This is not London. The Italian government is keen to see rural areas like this one attract more people. And I think the family would be open to any suggestions I might make.'

We went upstairs, the light green-tinged in patches from the ivy over the windows. Five huge bedrooms, and only one bathroom which was depressing with its huge iron bath, cracked sink and brass taps, green with age. Up another flight of wooden stairs, we found a gloomy attic, festooned with cobwebs hanging from the beams of the roof. In one corner there was a broken chair and a travelling trunk, open and empty except for a newspaper, dated August 1977.

'How sad it all is,' I said.

'But think of the possibilities,' Gio said.

We went back downstairs to the side of the building where there was a long, arched veranda, enclosed with grimy glass. The tiled floor was dirty and had a few pieces missing.

'This is the reason I have brought you here. To ask your opinion. I've had an idea for a while now. I have always thought this would make a wonderful art gallery. This region has many fine food producers, but there are also so many creative people who live around here. Potters, sculptors, artists and jewellers. I wonder if bringing them together under one roof to display their things might be a good idea. Like your idea of bringing together the local food producers. Perhaps someone with the ability to arrange these things could organise courses too. To teach and understand different mediums. You are right: we cannot wait for other people to solve our problems. We need to come up with our own ideas. Someone with your talent would be invaluable, I'm sure. If you were here.'

'It's a bit different from what I am used to doing,' I said doubtfully.

'But think of the spreadsheets you could create,' he said with a grin. 'You said you enjoyed making them.'

Yes, I could see the possibilities. But was this what I wanted to do with the next few years? Wasn't this just a neglected house in a little-known corner of Italy? Was I being unrealistic, to imagine myself staying here even longer? And worse than that, was I only considering it because of my relationship with Gio?

The kitchen of course was a disaster zone: a few battered wooden cupboards standing empty, with the doors hanging off the hinges, a massive stone sink and grime-crusted places where the cooker had once stood. There was a scullery with a terracotta-tiled floor, a rotting wooden worktop, a discarded enamel bowl and skeins of cobwebs hanging from the ceiling like lace. And yet there was something about the place that, rather dangerously, I was starting to like, to see its potential.

'It would take perhaps two years,' Gio said. 'Three, maybe more. But at the end of it, think what I would have saved, and created. And if you were there to help me, think what we could achieve between us.'

'And how would I do that if I'm living thousands of miles away? It would be a recipe for disaster. The paperwork, the bureaucracy, keeping on top of everything. How would I know what was going on?'

Gio shook his head and then he smiled. 'It's not as though I'm kidnapping you. And you don't seem in any rush to go back to London.'

'No, I'm not,' I said. 'Especially not at the moment.'

'And talking about that, I have had another idea,' Gio said.

'Yes, I thought you might,' I said.

We got back into the truck, and after about five minutes stopped outside a small, stone house on the edge of the town. It looked neat, the shutters closed, and had a small garden to the front with a parking space to the side.

'Here,' Gio said, 'if you want to stay you could rent this place. The owner has died, and the family are thinking of selling it, but they might also rent it out or use it for holiday lettings. Stefano assures me it is pleasant – he renovated it a few years ago and it was decorated throughout.'

'Goodness,' I said, my thoughts suddenly even more tangled.

This seemed a tempting option. Perhaps I could try this first, to see if I really liked living here, rather than just being on an extended holiday.

We got out of the truck, and I went to look around the garden which was small and neglected. There was a high stone wall at the back of the garden and what looked like a fig tree rambling up it. Fresh figs! How marvellous that would be. I could almost imagine myself, sitting outside in the sun, eating them. A carafe of local wine on the table, some olive-rich *pan de molche*, perhaps some cheese – a square Taleggio or nutty Asiago.

There was a patio made of stone slabs where I found a few empty terracotta pots, a lichen-peppered, wooden table and four chairs. I peered without success through the shuttered windows.

'We can see inside in a day or so if you like the idea. I am sure you would find it suitable.'

'Suitable for what? Me to live here? To move in?'

'Maybe, if that works for you,' he said.

Did it? Did I like this plan? Perhaps I did. Maybe this would be a temporary solution. To try living here, to forge new friendships and work out what I was going to do next.

Gio laughed and put an arm around me.

'Your face is a picture,' he said. 'I can almost see your thoughts racing around. There's no need to make a decision now. Just think about it.'

27

The Easter weekend was fast approaching, and Paulo needed some black truffles for the feast.

Apparently, the best time to go looking for them was at night. But after explaining what sort of truffles Paulo needed and where they were to be found, I could see from my mother's face that midnight foraging was not going to happen. But she was very keen to be involved regardless.

So, instead, we would go late in the afternoon when the heat of the day had cooled down. Alberto wasn't best pleased. I thought he must be concerned that his dog, Ascari, might not find any truffles and make him look foolish, but in the end, with time running short, it was agreed.

That Wednesday afternoon the weather was cool and damp, so Alberto was mollified. He said the scent would be more concentrated in colder weather, making it easier for Ascari to sniff them out.

We were all going to gather at Alberto's farmhouse at four o'clock. It was a low stone building some way up the hill, with numerous outhouses and ramshackle sheds.

Gio parked his truck in the yard, and we waited for Franco and Mum to arrive in his vintage Maserati. Franco drove in at a stately pace and went to open the passenger door for my mother as though she were a minor royal family member coming to open an event. She emerged wearing a tweed skirt, cashmere sweater and an artfully tied silk scarf. Not exactly the clothes for grubbing about in the woods.

Alberto was ready with Ascari who, as Alberto had proudly informed us, was a Lagotto Romagnolo – a breed famous for their ability to sniff out truffles. And he was obviously keen to get started. The dog, which looked like a small, woolly bear, barked and strained at his leash.

'Ascari, Ascari, no, *aspettare*! Wait!' Alberto said, giving the dog something from a plastic bag of dried treats in his pocket.

'It's getting a bit chilly,' I heard Mum call from the passenger seat of Franco's car. 'Perhaps I will wear my big coat.'

Franco fetched her Jaeger overcoat from the back seat and helped her put it on.

'And my gloves...' she said, fumbling in the pockets. 'Oh dear, I think they must be in the glove compartment. The long, brown leather ones. Would you be a dear and find them, Franco?'

Franco did as she'd asked, and then there was a brief discussion about whether she would need a hat too. In the end she re-tied her silk scarf over her hair and tightly under her chin, fussing about for a few minutes as the breeze threatened to whip it off again. After even more discussion, she accepted a yellow canvas sunhat from Franco to go over the top of it.

Meanwhile Ascari and Alberto were now even more keen to get going, and when Mum decided she would need to take her coat off again in order to put her gloves on, I saw Alberto roll his eyes.

'*Andiamo.* We will make a start,' he called out, and he and

Ascari disappeared into the trees behind the farmhouse. We could hear the dog barking joyfully all the way.

'Perhaps we should wait,' Gio said, watching with some amusement the pantomime that was Mum getting ready for a walk.

Mum pulled on her gloves and then her coat, buttoning it carefully up to the neck.

'I'm not sure about these shoes,' she said, looking down at her highly polished, lace-up brogues. 'It looks very muddy up there. Perhaps you were right, Franco – I should have worn boots. But of course I don't have any.'

'I have some spare ones in the car,' Franco said encouragingly, 'but they will be too big for you. I have large feet.'

'You certainly do,' Mum said rather archly and gave a mischievous grin.

I closed my eyes and took a deep breath.

From the woods we could hear a lot of excited barking and woofing and some encouraging shouts from Alberto.

'Well, I'll give them a try,' Mum said at last. 'I'll just sit in the car while you find them. If you don't mind?' She was looking up at Franco from under her lashes.

'*Certamente*! Of course,' Franco said cheerfully.

He opened the boot, and after a moment brought out a pair of muddy boots which he knocked against the ground to dislodge some of the dried mud. Meanwhile Mum had pulled off her gloves and unbuttoned her coat again. She plucked at the laces on her shoes for a few minutes until Franco came to help her, and then in a very odd, Cinderella-type moment, took the brogues off and slipped her feet into some enormous rubber boots.

Mum stood up and repeated the coat-off-and-gloves-on-first business, and then adjusted her scarf and sunhat combination.

'Well, I think I'm just about ready now,' she said brightly. 'These boots certainly are big.'

She took a couple of uncertain steps forwards, leaning on Franco's arm for balance. I tried hard not to giggle.

'Just call me Ms Baby Giraffe,' she murmured. 'I'm afraid I am going to hold everyone up. I need time to get my sea legs in these.'

'There is no rush,' Gio said kindly, coming to offer his arm as support on the other side.

Mum waved them both away. 'Let me give it a try on my own,' she said.

The sunhat slipped down over her eyes and she fussed about with it, rocking slightly as she re-tied the scarf for the third time, until it was like a garotte under her chin.

'Right, here we go,' she said. 'If Janice can walk up the Malvern Hills with her bunions, I am sure I can cope with size twelve boots.'

Franco and Gio hovered at her side as she took a tentative step.

'There – nothing to it. Oooooh!'

They caught her as she wobbled and almost fell over backwards.

'I am a silly thing,' she said. 'Let's try again.'

She managed three steps this time, her feet splayed out like a circus clown.

'I have a cane in the car, if you would like to use it?' Franco said helpfully.

'Oh, sure, offer me a Zimmer frame! I'm not quite at that stage just yet!' Mum replied waspishly.

At that moment Alberto, closely followed by Ascari, who evidently had his nose attuned to the delights in Alberto's pocket, came back into the yard.

Alberto ruffled his dog's curls with an enthusiastic hand.

'*Che buon cane!* What a good dog, Ascari,' Alberto said. 'The best dog, the cleverest dog. Look!'

Ascari sat at his master's feet, tongue lolling, as Alberto pulled a clod of earth about the size of a tennis ball out of his pocket.

'First tree. First smell! And he finds this!' Alberto said, brushing off the mud. 'Such a beautiful black truffle. Such a clever dog!'

He handed it over for us all to sniff. It was fruity, sort of earthy, almost chocolatey. Between us Ascari chomped noisily on what looked like the dried tip of a pig's ear.

'How marvellous,' Mum said, turning and plodding back towards the car, her sunhat well down over her brow. 'Well, that didn't take long. Wasn't that such fun? What is your dog eating now? Oh dear...'

'I think we need more than one, don't we?' I muttered to Gio.

He nodded, obviously biting his lip to stop himself from smiling, and we watched as Mum unbuttoned her coat, removed her gloves and hat, and sat back in the car to allow Franco to take the wellington boots again.

'I did enjoy that, dear,' she said with a sweet smile to Alberto, as Franco fastened her shoelaces. 'And your dog is very clever indeed. I couldn't be more impressed. I shall have quite the tale to tell Janice and Peggy when I next see them. Truffle hunting! Fancy that. You don't get the chance to do that in East Grinstead, even if your nephew is on the council. Now, then, Franco, let's go and have a brandy to warm up, shall we?'

We watched in amused silence as Franco drove away, Mum holding up the truffle with one hand and waving graciously out of the car window with the other.

'She is gone?' Alberto said, obviously confused.

'Just to let Paulo know we are finding some, I'm sure,' I said.

We turned to follow Alberto and Ascari back towards the

trees. Ascari, now his nose was, so to speak, tuned in, was very happy to carry on.

We watched as Alberto urged Ascari on up the hill, and to be fair the dog was as keen as mustard, but the minutes passed and he still didn't find anything.

'We go further up,' Alberto called back to us. 'We need to cross the brook. Not difficult.'

We hopped across a hedge and over a stile. It was getting steeper now, and there was the sound of running water from a small stream. We followed it up, further still, Ascari snuffling and seeking with all his might, encouraged on by Alberto's shouts.

I was wearing several layers of clothing, Zoe's walking boots which were slightly too big for my feet and had been padded out with thick socks and I was sweating.

'I hope he finds some,' I puffed as Gio and I paused for a moment so I could get my breath back. 'It would be a shame if we go back with only one.'

'Patience,' Gio said. 'Alberto knows where to look. There is a dry stream bed up here, where the water has washed away the soil from some of the tree roots. It's always a good place to look.'

We pressed on, with Gio pulling me up the steeper bit as though he were hauling a coal sack, and me trying not to seem too unfit. Alberto must have been in his seventies, and he was springing on ahead like a mountain goat. Perhaps there was something to be said for the Mediterranean diet after all.

After half an hour, when I was wishing I had brought a hip flask or at least some water, we reached the crest of a hill and the bed of the dried-up stream Gio had mentioned. Except it wasn't dried up. The recent rain had turned it to mud. Ascari was very excited as he snorted and sneezed amongst the exposed tree roots, and after a few minutes Alberto pushed him aside and used a thin trowel to dig out our second truffle. Another piece of dried pig's ear for Ascari. The quest was far from over, and evidently the fact that it was getting dark and it was starting to drizzle was no deterrent to either dog or master.

'Are you okay?' Gio asked as he pulled me through a broken-down hedge.

'Absolutely,' I said, biting back the words, *when can we go home.*

'We have two – one more should do it!' Alberto called across the muddy stream. '*Andiamo*, Ascari!'

Ascari certainly did *andiamo*, weaving in and out of the tree roots, his nose twitching madly and covered in mud.

We waited for a few minutes while the dog padded back and forth over one particular place, and then he started scrabbling eagerly in the earth, barking like a mad thing.

Alberto dragged him out of the way and started digging, while Ascari enthusiastically tried to help. Then, annoyed at being denied his prize yet again, and thinking that perhaps he would be better off on the other side of his master, Ascari took a leap around Alberto, barged into me and nearly knocked me flying. I stepped back, relieved when my boot found a footing. The last thing I wanted to do was fall flat in the mud. So far, I had kept up, been there for the hunt and rejoiced in the finds. I stood still, recovering my balance, and then took a step forward. Only to find I was now calf-deep in mud and the icy water from the stream was seeping over the top of my boot. Which was very unpleasant.

I took a step back with my other foot which in retrospect was a huge mistake, because both boots were now stuck. And with horror I realised I couldn't move either.

It was hard to extract water-filled boots from a foot of mud. And Italian mud seemed somehow different – not that my experience of any nationality of mud was great. It was as though my feet had been encased in concrete.

I stood, arms stretched out for balance, water streaming down my face, because by then of course it was raining properly, and wondered how I could extricate myself without looking a complete fool.

'Good dog, Ascari, *va bene!*' Alberto said happily as he handed another muddy lump to Gio. I didn't think either of them had realised my predicament. I gave a mighty heave of one leg and my boot came free from the mud with a gloopy, sucking noise. Which meant of course I was standing on one leg with no idea where to put the other foot.

'Er, I'm awfully pleased we found another one, but could someone give me a hand out of here?' I called politely.

Alberto and Gio turned. But it was the ever helpful Ascari who bounded through the mud towards me.

It was inevitable. Delighted with himself and still with the prospect of another piece of dried pig's ear, Ascari leapt up, both paws on my standing leg, and of course I went over like a sack of spuds.

I splatted full length into the mud with a despairing cry, just able to hear Alberto still praising his dog and, I thought, chuckling.

Gio pulled me up, and the mud and I parted company very reluctantly. I came out with a squelching, sucking noise, and he helped me back onto firmer ground where I stood dripping and shivering.

I spat out a mouthful of earth, and Gio handed me his handkerchief which I used to wipe the mud from my eyes.

'*Cara mia*! Are you hurt?' he said.

I was aware that behind him, Alberto was convulsing with laughter. Ascari, apparently pleased with his work, came and crunched his piggy treat enthusiastically in front of me. Jaws drooling.

'I hate to be a spoilsport, but have we got enough now?' I said.

* * *

I dripped and slid my way back down the hill to the farm, where Gio peeled off my sodden coat and unlaced my boots. Then Alberto found on old sack which he put onto the passenger seat of Gio's truck, and I got in. It was beyond unpleasant to sit down in soaking trousers, and I wondered how many baths and showers it would take to get all the mud off.

Alberto came to me with a huge grin on his face to show me the evening's haul.

'Ascari did well, hey? Look at these beauties!'

'Terrific,' I said, pulling a twig and a clod of earth out of my hair.

Alberto patted his dog enthusiastically and Ascari woofed.

'I think I had better take you home,' Gio said.

'You're trying not to laugh, aren't you?' I asked him.

'Absolutely not,' he said and then his voice cracked, and he started to chuckle. 'I'm sorry, I shouldn't laugh. As long as you are not hurt. I think you need a long shower, a hot meal and a strong drink. What do you say?'

I gingerly pulled the wet sleeves of my sweater away from my arms.

'I think those are excellent suggestions,' I said, 'but let's have the strong drink first.'

Gio leaned into the car and kissed me, and when he pulled back there was a smear of mud across his face.

'My brave truffle-hunter! You are sure you are not hurt?'

'Just a bit bruised,' I said. 'Those truffles had better be worth all this!'

28

Two days later was the start of the Easter weekend. There was a new excitement in the kitchen where Paulo seemed to have been spending twenty-three hours out of twenty-four at the stove.

'I have invited as many of my favourite people as I can,' Paulo was explaining. 'As we say here – *natale con i suoi, pasqua con chi vuoi*. Which means: Christmas with your relatives, Easter with who you want.'

'Tell me what I can do to help,' I said, 'and tell me what we are going to eat. It all smells wonderful.'

'So many things! Delicious dishes. I know you will love them. *Cosciotto di Agnello al forno con le patate* – roast lamb with rosemary, garlic, lemon and olive oil, accompanied by potatoes and green beans. There will be pasta with a generous helping of truffle shavings (and you will appreciate those more than anyone, I think). *Pasteriera napoletana* – a wonderful Easter treat flavoured with orange flower water. That's what I have been making for the last few days; it needs time to infuse. On Saturday night we will eat *casatiello* with cheese and pancetta. We will not be hungry – I can promise you. You and your mother will never want to leave. We will be together, eating and drinking each other's health, all night. Now, I have remembered, there *is* something you could do to help!'

'Anything,' I said, 'as long as there is no mud involved.'

'No mud at all. The weather will be fine; I think we can eat on the veranda. So, if you please, could you get it ready? Sweep it and then get Emilio to help you move the tables and chairs.' Paulo looked around. 'If he is still here... I hope he has not done one of his disappearing acts.'

'Not at all. He has been in town, in his father's office, working very hard on the website,' I said. 'And he said he would be back later to help you, and he wanted to take some pictures of the Easter feast to use on the website.'

'Then we must make it beautiful,' Paulo said firmly.

I went outside into the clear air, the breeze a little cold from the lake below us. But the sky was blue and the new leaves on the trees were fresh and green. Once again, I stood, taking in that matchless view, thinking about how far I had come since I had arrived here. Could I bear to leave this and go back to London? Would I be happy just being myself, where I had no real role any more except as a woman who used to be something, someone?

But no, that just wasn't right: there were still possibilities for me. I still *was* someone; I didn't need a glass-walled office, a PA, a meaningless award for doing my job every year to tell me that. I needed something more now, something different. Perhaps I needed this? An interesting thought.

I straightened up my shoulders, feeling more positive. Honestly, I'd been finding that, as time went on, I slumped a lot. My posture was terrible. Too much time hunched over a desk probably.

Remembering I was there to do something useful, I found the broom and started sweeping the veranda: a few dead leaves and twigs from last year which had blown in, and cobwebs from optimistic spiders. Then I pulled all the tables together to form one long row, and moved the wooden benches and chairs to either side. As Paulo had suspected, Emilio was nowhere to be found, but I enjoyed myself, setting everything out. It was almost as though I was creating a theatre, a stage ready for something.

Zoe came out with a bundle of fairy lights looped over one arm.

'Oh, good – you're here. Can you give me a hand with these? You can see the hooks on the ceiling. I would ask Paulo, but he is up to his elbows in food preparation.'

'You're so lucky, having your own personal chef.'

'Don't think I don't know that!' Zoe said.

She handed me one end of the lights and then of course the whole thing got tangled, and it took us a good hour, laughing and complaining, to sort them out, standing on the tables and looping them over the rusty hooks in the rafters.

'So, tell me what else is happening,' Zoe said. 'You have been so busy over the last few days. I haven't had much of a chance to catch up with you.'

I wobbled slightly on the table and grabbed at a beam. It was true, I had been busy: contacting the food growers and producers in the locality, outlining my plans for the tasting event, putting some orders in. It had all gone surprisingly easily.

'And what about Auntie Eleanor? I hardly see her either. I'm assuming she is going back to England soon. I thought she was only coming here for a week or so.'

I regained my balance and pulled the string of lights towards me.

'I don't know,' I said. 'I never see her either. Honestly, it's like having an evasive teenager around again. *Where are you going? When will you be back? Have you got your phone and your keys?*'

Zoe laughed. 'She and Franco make a handsome couple though; you have to agree. And he seems very chipper. I haven't seen him looking so well for a long time.'

'Or her actually. I mean, life in Winchester Hall was very comfortable, but I think she was bored out of her mind. Flower arranging and bingo sessions are not the way I would have imagined her spending her old age. But I know you are going to need us to vacate the premises soon – you have paying guests coming. Proper bookings.'

'Perhaps you can go and stay with Gio?'

'And Mum move in with Franco? I don't think that's a very good idea. No, we will both go home and think about what to do next. I need to sell my flat, get rid of a few things. That will take a while.'

Zoe nodded thoughtfully. 'Right,' she said at last. 'That's the last light fixed. Let's get down before one of us falls off this table and breaks a hip. I'll go and find the tablecloths. And the lanterns and the new box of candles.'

I helped her down onto a chair and she went back inside the trattoria. I, meanwhile, stood on the table for a moment longer, looking out from my even more elevated position at the lake and the mountains beyond it.

I saw Gio's truck pull into the car park. He got out and walked towards me, his hands in his pockets. He really shouldn't have done that: it made me...

'What on earth are you doing now?' he said, grinning up at me.

'Nothing,' I said in a stroppy teen voice.

'I don't want to see you fall again. Mud is one thing but...'

He chuckled and held out a hand, helping me down. And then he put his arms around me and kissed me.

'I've missed you,' he said, 'and so has Buffo.'

'I'm sure he hasn't!'

Gio nodded. 'He has, I can tell. He said to tell you he wants you to stay.'

'A likely tale.'

'No, it's true. He said you needed to be here otherwise he would be sad.'

'And you?'

'I would be sad too,' he said and kissed me again.

'You're making this very difficult,' I said, coming up for air.

'That is my intention,' he said, smiling down at me. 'So, what are you doing? Setting out the tables for the Easter feast?'

'Zoe has gone to get the cloths for the tables. You will be there, won't you?'

'*Certo*, of course. I will sit next to you and whisper in your ear and make you blush.'

'I'd rather you didn't,' I said, although my grin said something else.

'Then I will sit at the other end of the table and flirt with someone else.'

'I'd rather you didn't do that either.'

He caught hold of my hand. 'I wish you didn't have to go.'

I took a deep breath, realising just how hard it was going to be to leave. This place, this life, and yes, if I was honest – this man. I hadn't seen this coming at all, that day when I booked my flights, and ran out of my flat to the taxi. Nor on the drive to the airport when I had felt so uncertain of my future, but certain of my need to find a place of... sanctuary. And that is what this place had been. Not just for me but for my mother too. How strange. After all the years of feeling that we had nothing in common, this place had brought us together.

But soon it would be time to go back to London, time for her to return to Winchester Hall and her ordered life there. I had the awful feeling that neither of us was going to be very settled after this brief taste of freedom.

Everyone went to church in the morning. Even Mum, who was dressed up in her finest and who smiled regally as Franco handed her into the front seat of the Maserati Quattroporte, the bells from the village clanging out into the warm air. I had never been much of a church-goer, and so I stayed behind, sitting on the veranda with some coffee. Looking forward to the day ahead, to seeing Gio again, to meeting his family and his son who was also coming along.

Perhaps I would go to church one day when I felt more settled. Find out what all the fuss was about.

Then people started arriving for the Easter feast at about three o'clock. The weather had kept its promise, and it was pleasantly warm, the sky cloudless and blue above us. How lovely to be able to do this. I was pretty sure it wouldn't have been possible in London, even supposing I had the space. Another thing Italy did so well: dining al fresco.

There were so many introductions. Aunts and cousins and friends from the village. Gio's son, Francesco, was there too, slightly taller than his father with the same ready smile, the same charm. Gio's daughter, Isabelle, was still in London, unable to get time off from the hospital where she worked.

My mother was elegant in a beaded dress and pashmina, sitting next to Franco, who bent his head towards her, smiling, and just once kissing her hand when he thought no one was watching.

Everyone had brought something for the feast. Freshly prepared salads and bread. Wine. Bowls of fruit and platters of cheese. The tables, smart now with their starched white cloths, were full, people moving the dishes to make room for their plates and wine glasses.

The food was wonderful, the roast lamb tender and sweet with rosemary, the truffle shavings exquisite. Then the *pasteriera napoletana*, dusted with powdered sugar and studded with fruit. Mouth-watering.

Paulo explained. 'There are seven strands of pastry on the top, to commemorate the seven presents given by the people of Naples to the mermaid Parthenope. Flour, eggs, ricotta wheat, sugar, exotic spices and scents. Which the gods of the sea turned into this dessert.'

'It's wonderful,' I said. 'Absolutely delicious.'

There were a few children there too, slipping off their chairs when they had eaten, to play with Paulo's cat or run around the table laughing, while the grown-ups grabbed at them. And a couple of glorious teenage girls who tossed their dark hair at each other, and glowered over some lanky boy both of them had their sights on. And Emilio, taking pictures on his phone, and making notes in a little book he had taken to carrying around.

As the sun set, the fairy lights we had strung in the beams above us glowed in the darkness. The talk and the laughter were louder by then, fuelled by all the good local wine we had drunk. One little girl was asleep on her mother's lap, and a sleepy baby lay in a car seat on the ground next to her, gnawing at a fistful of bread.

I caught hold of Zoe's hand as she passed behind me, offering more wine.

'I've enjoyed this so much,' I said. 'Thank you for including me.'

She bent and kissed my cheek. 'Of course, it's been wonderful to have you here. Don't leave it so long next time.'

I looked down the long table at the people laughing and arguing and chatting. At Franco, his hand over my mother's; at Gio next to me, his arm along the back of my chair. And suddenly I felt the sting of tears.

It would be terrible to leave, to know all this was going to carry on without me. To miss the nailing heat of the Italian summer to come, the colour of the leaves when autumn came, the rain sweeping in across the lake. Even the cold winter winds. But more than that, it would be so painful to miss the friendship, the feeling of acceptance.

Franco, in his role as elder statesman at the head of the table, tapped his spoon against his wineglass for silence which came after a few seconds of people shushing each other.

'A thank you – *grazie mille* – to Paulo and to Zoe for this wonderful occasion. To old friends, to *very* old friends and to new friends.' He tipped his glass towards Mum and then towards me. 'We have a saying. *Chi si volta, e chi si gira, sempre a casa va finire.* No matter where you go, you will always end up at home.'

Mum dabbed at her tears then and smiled bravely up at Franco. I suddenly realised how hard this was for her too.

Franco patted her on the shoulder. 'I hope you and your lovely daughter will think of this as a second home. And don't cry. *La vita è come una fotografia. Se sorridi, viene meglio* life is like a photograph. If you smile it's better. We will miss you both.'

'Oh, stop it Franco, for heaven's sake, or I really will start crying,' Mum said, and everyone clapped and laughed.

I could see how it must feel to be a part of this, a large family, coming together occasionally to celebrate. Of course it wouldn't always be like this. After all this wasn't a Hollywood film, and sometimes there would be falling out or arguing, but essentially, they wanted to be together. It was something I had never known. And the one person I really wanted to see here was my son. Ben would have loved this; I was sure of it. I wanted it so badly, I could almost see him sitting here with us, laughing, making friends, enjoying the occasion.

That was what I would do next. I would go and see him. Meet his workmates and his partner – who I had only met once – and his friends. See what his life was like. I needed to do everything I could to make up for the years when I had spent too much time doing other things for other people and for myself. If these few weeks had taught me anything, it was that.

29

I was busy for the next few days, finalising the details of the taster evening. Paulo spent most of his time in the kitchen, occasionally asking for advice and opinions. Zoe and I gave the trattoria a thorough clean and even Emilio helped out, slapping fresh white paint onto the old walls. His website had been a terrific boost: the queries and reservations came in at a steady rate – also helped by the nuns in the convent Paulo had helped over the years, who handed out leaflets in the neighbouring towns. If there was one thing I had learned, it was that no one says no to a nun.

The meat supplier Paulo knew had brought some huge slabs of meat, lamb which had been reared up on the slopes above the lake (so, that was what people did with those flocks of sheep). He too was cheerful and looking forward to the feast.

Paulo was going to marinade the lamb for two days before he cooked it.

The day before, we were up before the sun to decorate the veranda with greenery and lights. Soon the tables were set with new cloths and ready; everything was going to be picture perfect.

'We are just about full,' Zoe said happily as we sat in the dawn light and polished wine glasses together. 'I can't believe it – over fifty guests! I've even had to put a few on a waiting list in case there are any cancellations. There will also be some tables out here; the weather has been so warm, and it looks as though it's going to be a lovely day. I just hope the rest of the food arrives on time.'

'It will,' I said firmly. 'I double checked with everyone. It's all on my spreadsheet.'

As I spoke a van pulled into the driveway, kicking up a fine trail of dust from the gravel which swirled in the headlights.

The woman I recognised from the bakery in the town got out, and pulled out a tray of beautiful focaccias, studded with sea salt and sprigs of rosemary, followed by another tray of crispy breadsticks wrapped in a linen cloth. For someone who had only known breadsticks to come in paper wrappers, this was a delight.

She came and embraced Zoe and even shook my hand. I didn't think I had realised how big a deal this was for the local people. I should have done, because life was difficult here with the young people leaving the area to find work elsewhere. So many of the houses were boarded up and empty.

There had already been deliveries of lots of fruit and vegetables. Not pre-packaged in plastic bags or trays but stacked in enticing baskets which swamped the kitchen table.

Later that morning a battered, dusty truck arrived. On the side in curly writing, I could just make out: Formaggi Deliziosi.

'It's the cheese,' Zoe said happily. 'My favourite part of the meal.'

A young man jumped down from the cab. He glanced at a sheaf of paperwork in his hand.

'*La signora* Harrington? Delivery,' he said. '*Formaggi*. Cheeses.'

'Marvellous,' I said. 'Just bring it all in. I'll open the door for you.'

He looked a bit blank. '*Se sei sicuro.*'

Which meant – 'if you are sure'. An odd thing to say.

'Of course,' I replied, frowning slightly.

The young man shook his head and opened the back of the van.

It was packed with all sorts of parcels and cheeses wrapped in cloth or tissue paper.

'Goodness me, you're very busy today,' I said cheerfully. '*Molto occupato.* You have lots of deliveries.'

He gave me another look and didn't say anything.

And then he started unloading. Three metal trays of cheese – huge slabs of something very pungent – two wooden crates and a plastic tray.

'This can't be all for us,' I said, feeling a bit panicky.

He held out his paperwork for me to sign, which of course I couldn't do as I was laden down with several chunks of what smelled like gorgonzola.

'*Cinquanta chili.* Fifty kilos. The assortment you wanted. *È tutto qui.* It's all here,' he said.

'No, I ordered five kilos,' I said, dumping my overpowering packages on a nearby table. '*Cinque chili.* Only five.'

He held out the order form. I grabbed it. And looked at the price. Even in unfamiliar Italian writing done with a scratchy pen, it was a huge amount.

'Fifty kilos. Not five,' I repeated. My voice tailing off into disbelief.

Zoe grabbed it from me. 'I don't think this can be right,' she said. 'We were expecting our guests to have some elegant little slivers of local cheeses at the end of the meal, beautifully presented with edible flowers and some little glasses of port. We have fifty guests. I don't think each of them will be wanting a kilo of assorted cheeses on their plates. Do you?'

'It would be a stretch, even for me,' I said faintly. 'Oh, good grief. But I was trying to sort out so many things at once… Zoe, I'm so sorry. My mistake. Obviously I will pick up the bill.'

Zoe breathed a sigh. 'I'd really appreciate that, but it doesn't solve the problem of what we are going to do with it all.'

'How much could the nuns shift at the convent?' I said hopefully. 'Can he take some of it back? Explain it was my mistake?'

'We'll have to find out,' Zoe said.

She sprinted off to catch the van up and had a brisk, rapid-fire discussion with the driver. A few seconds later, he drove away.

'He says they don't take second-hand cheese,' she said. 'It's all ours.'

'I only carried the gorgonzola,' I said, 'and I can still smell it. I didn't touch any of the others. Anyway, if this is the only thing that goes wrong, it will all be fine,' I said, speaking more confidently that I felt. 'The only thing left is the handmade chocolates. And it isn't possible to over-order chocolate, is it?'

I was wrong.

Three minutes later another van pulled up: *Cioccolato dal Cielo.* Chocolate from heaven. Actually, it wasn't from heaven; it was from a new place along the far side of the lake which had only been in business for two months. Which probably explained why their van was new and brilliantly clean.

A cheerful-looking young woman hopped out and came to embrace us both.

'*Grazie mille! Grazie mille!* Thank you so much! *È il nostro ordine più grande! Non posso ringraziarti abbastanza.*'

'She says it's the biggest delivery they've ever had; she can't thank us enough. I've got a bad feeling about this,' Zoe said. 'How much did you order?'

'Enough for three chocolates for each customer. I didn't want to seem stingy.'

The young woman opened the doors of her van and staggered out with two massive cardboard boxes which she put onto a collapsible trolley.

'Trust me, I don't think we are going to seem stingy,' Zoe said.

I felt a bit faint. 'I think I ordered two kilos, or 150 chocolates. They are quite big.'

'They must be the size of house bricks if that is 150 chocolates, and I don't suppose they will accept second-hand chocolates back either,' Zoe said, rather tersely. Which was understandable.

I was about to hyperventilate. 'Oh god, I'm so sorry. I'll pay for this too. It'll be fine; I'm sure we will get through some. Perhaps the nuns at the convent can have a cheese and chocolate festival?'

'I don't think so,' Zoe said rather crossly. 'Paulo is going to have a fit.'

We followed the young woman into the trattoria, helping her and her trolley up the steps. And then we put the boxes, which smelled a jolly sight more inviting than the cheese, onto a worktop.

Then I hurried her away, back to her van. She was all smiles and handshakes. I had obviously made her day.

Back in the kitchen Paulo was still standing looking at the cheese, his mouth slightly open.

'What am I supposed to do with all this?' he said at last. 'Make the biggest fondue in Italy?'

'I'm sorry, I'm sorry. It's all my fault,' I said, trying to stand between him and the chocolate mountain that was being delivered. 'Is fondue popular around here?' I asked, grasping at straws.

Paulo picked up a package and sniffed it.

'Not,' he said tersely, 'with gorgonzola.'

He sounded very annoyed, and I couldn't blame him.

'No. You'd need a lot of bread,' I said, with a weak smile.

Paulo stalked off back to the stove, his back rigid with annoyance.

I felt terrible. They had been so kind to me, and now this had happened. I'd been so sure I'd known what I was doing, that I was efficient and oh-so-clever, and I was none of those things. Me and my blasted spreadsheets.

I needed to sort something out. Think. *Think.*

'So, how much do we have?' I asked, seeing that Zoe was looking at the invoice from the chocolate makers.

'We needed 150. We have over a thousand,' she said and sat down rather heavily on a kitchen chair.

Then she dropped her head into her hands, and for a horrible moment I thought she was going to cry. How could I have done this to her, just ploughing ahead, sure of my own abilities? For some people, it would be a small problem, but for people like Paulo and Zoe this was really significant. How could I have steamed in here with my ideas, not thinking how it might affect them?

My mind raced, frantically searching for solutions...

Everyone liked chocolate, didn't they?

There was a leaflet on the top of the first box describing the contents.

Caramello, sorpresa di lamponi, pistachio, tartufa al cioccolato, tartufo allo champagne.

'What's *sorpresa di lamponi*?' I asked.

Zoe looked up, her eyes haggard. 'Raspberry surprise.'

'It's all a bit of a surprise, isn't it?' I said, trying to inject some levity into an awful situation. All I had wanted was to help them out with this taster evening idea, and now I had made even more work for them. Even more stress.

'It's such a waste of food – that's what I don't like. And if you think we can get through over eight hundred freshly made chocolates before they go stale, well, you're mad.'

'I'm going to work something out,' I said firmly. 'None of this will go to waste.'

'How?'

'Trust me,' I said confidently.

At that moment Mum wandered in, looking for coffee as usual.

'What is that terrible smell?' she said. 'Has something died in here?'

30

'Gio. It's me. Have you got a minute? I need to ask a favour.'

I had escaped to my room and found my mobile.

'Yes, *cara*, of course. What's the matter? You sound worried,' he said.

'Do you remember that night we went out to the lake for dinner, and there was a woman there. You said she owned an artists' materials shop?'

There was a pause while Gio thought about this. 'You mean Lucrezia?'

Oh god, please don't let her be a Borgia.

'Could you take me over to her shop?' I asked. 'Now. I wouldn't ask but it's very important.'

'Yes, I suppose I could. What has happened?'

'I'll tell you when I see you. I've ordered a bit too much chocolate. And cheese. I need a plan.'

'Life is never dull with you around, is it?' he said.

'Unfortunately, no. Please hurry?'

'I will give Buffo his food and then I will be right with you,' Gio said. '*Calmati.* Calm yourself.'

'Does Buffo like cheese? Because I have forty-nine kilos of the stuff going spare.'

Gio gave a disbelieving laugh. 'He's greedy but not that greedy.'

* * *

Lucrezia's shop was about a twenty-minute drive away, and I took the opportunity to fill Gio in with my ordering disasters. He could immediately understand the problem. He knew so much more than I did about what it was to live here, of how Paulo would fear the embarrassment in front of his friends and family.

'I feel terrible. All this was my idea, and now I have given them a huge amount of stress and work to do.'

'So, you have a plan?' he asked.

'A lot of the cheese will go to the convent and to some of the shelters in the surrounding towns. Please could you help me with that too? But the chocolates are going to go stale in a few days, and they aren't packaged, so I have to shift them as soon as possible. They are far too good to waste. Unless you can come up with some idea?'

'A lot of places would accept some of the cheese – I am sure,' Gio said, pulling up at the side of the road. 'Here we are. Let's go and see if Lucrezia can help out.'

The shop was small but filled with all sorts of interesting things. Looking in the window, I could see artists' palates and paints. Canvases in all sizes and tools for card-making and cake decorating. How people made sugar rose bouquets and convincing looking pets from sugar paste, I couldn't begin to imagine.

'I need cellophane bags,' I said. 'I'm going to make gift bags to give away after the meal.'

'Yes, I can see that might work,' Gio said, opening the door and setting off a jingling shop bell.

'Let's hope so.'

* * *

Yes, it might have been a good idea, but it took me hours. And served me right really.

I found what I was looking for and then went back to the trattoria where Paulo and Zoe were in the middle of a quiet but obvious argument. For which I blamed myself.

I began work that evening when they had closed up and gone to bed. I had helped out as much as possible – serving behind the bar and clearing tables – but the atmosphere in the trattoria was very subdued. From what I could see, Paulo and Zoe were barely speaking to each other.

My plan was to put ten chocolates into each of the cellophane bags and tie them with some rather natty ribbon, patterned with the Italian flag, which I had also found in Lucrezia's shop. She really did have everything there, and it had been very hard not to allow myself to get carried away. Would I ever start making a wall hanging from pom-poms? Or a spring wreath from paper flowers? Or fabric bunting? Probably not.

Then, just after midnight and inspired by my own efforts, I went and wrestled with the new computer. I wanted to personalise the bags, explain where the chocolates came from and thank people for attending the taster evening. But I realised I was used to asking other people, with more technical knowledge than I had, to sort that kind of problem out. It took me hours.

I had thought I was pretty computer literate, but as is always the way, the printer seemed to know there was some urgency to my task and refused to co-operate. It mashed up several sheets of card, and then insisted the paper tray was empty when it obviously wasn't. Then it wanted more ink, a search which took a good half an hour. It was almost spiteful. Perhaps all printers had a built-in stroppiness? I'd never known one that did just as it was told. I was embarrassed to say that by three-fifteen in the morning, I had called it a few choice names. And then, because it had obviously taken that badly, I apologised to it, and we reached an uneasy truce.

Printing onto card, punching the holes for the ribbon ties and cutting each label out took a very long time. And somehow a few of them got smeared with chocolate and had to be done again. I couldn't think how that had happened…

At last, just after four-thirty in the morning, I finished. The relief I felt was as great as my tiredness, and I will admit to tasting quite a few chocolates through the night, so I felt a bit queasy too. But it was done. And the cellophane bags looked terrific, really attractive. I was sure the remaining chocolates would get eaten. I just hoped I had saved the day. Of course, the cheese mountain still needed to be addressed, but that could wait.

I lugged the chocolates into one of the cool stores, closed the door and then fell into bed, where I dreamed of a massive fondue. And chocolate. And I woke up with a headache.

* * *

The guests arrived in the early evening, as the sun was setting behind the hills, throwing the lake below us into shadow. It had been a busy and very warm day and Paulo had not set foot outside the kitchen since early morning.

'If this is a failure, you must never let me do this again,' I heard him mutter to Zoe. 'Never. I cannot feel my feet, and my back is breaking. I have not cooked for so many people at once for years. And what if people laugh at me? This is a simple trattoria; we are not looking for Michelin stars.'

'It will be wonderful, Paulo. Have faith in yourself,' Zoe murmured, rubbing his arm.

He turned to throw me a resentful look which made me feel even worse.

Zoe, Emilio and I were dressed in black trousers and white shirts, ready to start serving the diners. I'd admit I was nervous. I had done quite a bit since I had come here – I could even knock up a few cocktails quite efficiently – but what I did this evening was going to be important. Not just to Paulo and Zoe, but for the area. There had even been a couple of local reporters, questioning where the food had come from – was it organic? Did local producers deserve more support from the government?

There was the occasional wafting whiff of the cheeses, which had been taken out of the cold room and hidden away into the office to allow them to come to room temperature. Paulo's cat was nearly crazy, trying to sneak in there, and very annoyed at being left outside.

Paulo had marinated the lamb in red wine, garlic and fresh herbs for the previous two days, and slow-cooked it overnight. The aroma in the kitchen that day was even more delicious than usual. He had brought in two heated trolleys from somewhere, and all the serving dishes and plates were already warming up.

We could hear the excited chatter from the trattoria where the guests were assembling, enjoying Prosecco and some little bowls of olives, which were apparently grown along the lakeside, and had been seasoned with orange peel.

'The mayor has arrived,' Zoe hissed as she came hurrying back into the kitchen.

'I didn't know there was a mayor?' I said.

'It's Alberto. But he takes these things very seriously,' Zoe replied.

'Especially if there is food involved,' Paulo shouted across the kitchen.

'And Gio is here,' Zoe added. 'Tell him to come and help.'

I went out and saw Gio looking very smart in a dark suit and white shirt. I didn't think he was exactly dressed for serving food, but I went and caught him by the elbow and pulled him into the kitchen.

'Can you help? I said. 'I'm sorry to ask. I thought I had hired two waitresses, but they haven't arrived.'

'Perhaps you forgot? Or maybe you ordered ten?' Paulo muttered as he assembled the appetiser course. Little plates of locally cured prosciutto on crostini, garnished with slivers of pear and strands of rocket leaves.

'It's seven o'clock. People have started sitting down. Are we ready?' Zoe asked.

Gio shrugged off his jacket and came to stand beside me.

'Just tell me what to do,' he said.

I threw him a grateful look. 'What's Italian for you're a star?'

'*Sei una stella*,' he said with a grin.

'Well, you are.'

We took the plates out and served them to the diners, enjoying their *oooh*s of appreciation. Alberto and his companion were seated at a prominent table, a gold chain, which could have graced the neck of any Medici prince, around Alberto's neck. Next to him my mother and Franco were in their finest; Stephano and Maria on his other side. They were laughing and chattering away like extras in an Agatha Christie murder mystery.

Gio served bottles of the chosen wines to each table like a pro.

I hurried back to the kitchen where Paulo was sorting out the next course: the *primo*. He had spent hours making the *tortelli con tartufo nero*, using the black truffles we had found up on the hillside.

'We had so much *parmigiana* – I made a velvet cream to serve with it,' he said as I passed him. 'So, perhaps it's not all bad news.'

Certainly, the bowls of pasta looked delicious, garnished with sprigs of greenery and drops of vinaigrette. The guests thought so too.

My mother caught my arm as I passed her.

'I must make this when I go back,' she said. 'It looks so simple. I wouldn't make the *tortelli* myself of course, but I know they sell them in Waitrose. Do you think I could buy truffles in Winchester? That would be one in the eye for Sue, who thinks she is a culinary expert. You're doing awfully well you know. That scallop gratin course was fantastic. I wished it had been twice the size, but Franco said there was still a lot of other things to come. Everyone is amazed at the food. Some people have been putting pictures up on Instagram already. #italian-food. #delicious. Your organisational skills haven't left you then?'

I looked down at her and she smiled, a twinkle in her eye, and suddenly I felt a burst of love for her. She was so indominable, so feisty. And she looked marvellous. She was an inspiration.

'I will fill you in on the details another time, but let's just say I have made a mess of things in several areas.'

Mum raised her eyebrows. 'I didn't think you ever made mistakes.'

'Well, I do,' I said.

Back in the kitchen Paulo was nearing a meltdown, wailing over his lamb, the star of the *secondo* course. It looked perfectly alright to me: pink and succulent on a bed of crushed new potatoes and mint leaves.

'I have lost my *jus*,' he kept shouting. 'Where is it? Has someone stolen it?'

Plates were flashing past at a great rate into the stone sink, where Emilio's new girlfriend, Bianca, was washing up. From the dark looks she was throwing Emilio, I didn't give this relationship much of a chance after that evening.

* * *

Despite the problems, the evening was a triumph for Paulo. I didn't think I had ever felt so relieved about anything.

He came in to the trattoria while the guests were finishing up their *dolce* – panna cotta, caramel sauce and berries – and looking forward to their coffee and chocolates. He was quite taken aback when he received a standing ovation from everyone.

Zoe went and hugged him; there were flashes as people took pictures on their phones; and the two local reporters who had booked in unknown to us, interviewed him at some length.

'I am so glad all that is over,' Paulo said, sitting down at last with a large glass of brandy. 'But people keep asking me when the next one will be. Next one? I swore never to do this again!'

Zoe hugged him. 'You said if it was a disaster you wouldn't, but it has been such a success. Do you know we had twenty people on the waiting list? And Emilio says there have been loads of emails through the website. People asking if we do accommodation too.'

'I can't tell you how relieved I am, after all the mistakes I made,' I said.

Paulo flapped a hand at me. 'It was okay after all. We managed. But it might be a while before I do this again!'

Behind him, the phone rang.

'It's nearly midnight. Who on earth is ringing at this hour?' Zoe said, going to answer it.

She came back a few minutes later, her eyes round with excitement.

'That was the local radio station; they want to interview you, Paulo!'

31

Mum and I arranged to leave Italy a week later.

First there were flights to be found, farewells to be said, visits for coffee and cake with a few of our new acquaintances who all wanted to know when we would return. The woman who ran the bakery came round the counter to embrace me like an old friend, and presented me with a small box of *maritozzi* – which were the best cream buns ever invented. Two elderly ladies stopped me in the supermarket, nodding and smiling, *fai un buon viaggio* – wishing me a good trip.

Stefano, Franco's friend, left a punnet of tomatoes and a card on my doorstep, hoping my mother and I would return soon.

Two days before we left, Alberto and his wife, Maria, invited us round to their house for lunch. By then I had found out that Maria had never been a ballerina, despite her still trim figure and perfect posture. *Ballerina esotico* meant something else entirely. But she was charming and chatty and very curious about Gio.

It was after lunch and we were in her greenhouse, which she had insisted I needed to see. There were plants which she said needed watering. And I could help her. Of course, what she really wanted was to find out more about how Gio and I were getting on.

She slanted an eyebrow at me and winked.

'All my friends have been wondering what he was up to; some of them were jealous of course, but also glad that he had at last found someone to make him smile.'

'Well, if I have done that then I am happy,' I said.

'His wife was always a difficult woman, but beautiful of course. I think Gio *ha la pazienza di un santo* – had the patience of a saint. She was away for such a long time, flitting in and out, leaving Gio to bring up the children.'

'And what was she like? Really?'

Maria thought for a moment.

'Charming. If she had been here today, she would have made you feel as though you were best friends already. She would talk to you about your life and your thoughts, and you would probably have liked her. But she was selfish. Always dissatisfied. Even her children were not enough to keep her here.'

At last, I realised why the atmosphere between Gio and I had turned frosty on that first drive together from the airport. That foolish, flippant, throwaway comment I'd made. I had let him believe that my work was more important to me than my family. I hoped he realised now that I was different, that I did care about Ben and always had. I'd just hidden it under a layer of insecurity.

Maria was still talking. 'Never the sign of another woman in his life. And then one day, there she was, back in the village for good. And he looked after her. No man could have been kinder, despite everything. And when she died, I think he was genuinely sad. He went into himself. Hidden away in his house on the mountain. You have brought him back to life, I think.'

'I didn't know that,' I said, pretending to examine some seedlings.

'Oh yes, for years, we would occasionally see him at the trattoria, sometimes out in the country, painting. But now, *è magico* – it's like magic. He has the old sparkle back in his eyes.'

'I'm glad to think I have done something for him. He has been so kind to me.'

'You will not leave him alone again, will you? I think you will find he needs you. And Uncle Franco—' Maria clapped her hands in delight. 'Never has that man been more happy. You and your mother have been like *una boccata d'aria fresca* – a breath of fresh air. And what you did for Paulo, it's been wonderful to see.'

'I didn't realise... I didn't expect that...' I said, rather emotional. I had been so wrapped up in the way this place had changed me, I hadn't considered that we might also be having an effect on other people.

Maria patted my arm. 'Come back soon, you have friends here, and you are part of a new family.'

'I will,' I said. 'I don't think I could stay away for long.'

'I have travelled all over the world. I have danced in theatres, on ships, in clubs— ah, *beh, basta così* – enough of my chatter. But this little place is special. It has *cuore* – heart. People care for each other, watch out for each other. You know how it is.'

Actually, I didn't know how it was at all. Life for me had been strangely solitary considering I lived in such a big city. Perhaps that was what I needed: to feel a part of a community. I thought of my apartment block, and the other people who lived there. Some of them I had never met. But then had I ever made much of an effort? Probably not, it worked both ways after all. I still had a lot to learn.

And then I thought of Gio. The last few days we had together were perfect and at the same time sad for both of us. I spent most of my time with him, in his house, just being together with him, while outside the spring weather blossomed into wonderful sunny days.

We drove up into the mountains alongside a tumbling river, past beautiful villages with weathered wooden shutters. We explored – I borrowed Zoe's walking boots again, which had by then dried out – and we saw the ancient carvings done by people who had lived, fought, farmed and hunted there for thousands of years. I didn't think I had walked so far for ages, but it was worth it. It was breathtaking in every sense of the word. The views of the mountains, the clear, crisp air. That day the world opened up for me. And I was filled with a new determination to see it.

* * *

And then at last, the day came when we would have to leave.

I woke up, encircled by Gio's arms, and the first thing I saw was Buffo, sitting on the windowsill outside. He miaowed soundlessly at me through the glass. Behind him, that wonderful view. The trees. The mountains beyond. It seemed impossible that by the end of the day I would be back in the concrete canyons of London.

'I am going to miss you,' Gio said. 'The days won't be the same without you.'

'I will miss you too,' I said.

'You will think about what I said?'

'Of course. I've thought about little else,' I replied.

'Are you sure I can't drive you to the airport?'

'Mum's booked a car. I think it would be for the best,' I said.

'If you are sure?'

Well, no, I wasn't sure, but Mum had insisted, and anyway I didn't think she would have been very happy to be stuffed in the back of Gio's truck when she had become used to the grandeur of Franco's Quattroporte.

We returned to the trattoria where Zoe and Paulo were preparing for another day. Paulo was in the kitchen, and Zoe was wiping down the dew from the tables under the veranda.

'You're all packed?' she asked.

'I am. I hope Mum is too.'

'She is. I'm warning you – she's not happy,' Zoe said, pulling a face.

'Nor am I, actually. But we have to go. We both have things to sort out, things to do, things to think about.'

'Don't think too long,' Zoe said. She came forward to hug me, her cheek warm against mine. 'Thank you. Thank you so much.'

'So,' said a cross voice behind us. 'You really are making me go back, just when I was enjoying myself for the first time in years.'

I turned to see Mum, stylish in a green linen dress and jacket but with an expression that could only be compared to a slapped arse.

'I'm not making you do anything,' I said.

She harrumphed a little and looked away. 'First you deposited me in that mausoleum—'

'I didn't deposit you; you chose it after a long and exhaustive search.'

'—and now you are going to drag me back there. To continue the fossilisation procedure.'

'I've told you. We have to think about what we are going to do next. This is hard for me too you know.'

'Oh, for heaven's sake, let's just get it over with,' Mum said impatiently, hoisting her handbag onto her arm. She rummaged inside it. 'Passport, ticket, wallet, spectacles, phone – all here. Do you know, when I was younger, I honestly believed that I would figure everything out. Then I realised as I got older that I wouldn't, but I didn't much care. Now I realise I do.'

A familiar car pulled into the drive, and Franco, very dapper in a dark-blue blazer and crisply pressed slacks, got out. He came over, his hands out towards Mum, and he hugged her.

'Ah, Gio. *Come sta*? Eleanor, Clover – a safe journey,' he said, sounding rather croaky. 'Are you sure I cannot drive you to the airport?'

'Absolutely not, Franco. It would make me too sad,' Mum said.

She didn't sound very happy at all. Well, this was going to be a fun journey.

We turned as the taxi pulled into the drive, and my heart sank even further.

Gio and Paulo helped to load up the car with our luggage while the driver stood tactfully to one side and puffed at a cigarette. And then there were hugs and kisses and farewells. Paulo came out from the kitchen to embrace us and say goodbye, even Emilio stood looking regretful (presumably because his occasional replacement as a sous chef was leaving). Still, he was more than happy with the cash I had given him for his work on the website, and from what he had showed me, it was looking very professional. There were recently added pictures of the tasting evening, where Alberto, in his mayoral chain, was raising a glass of a particularly fine Barolo to the camera while next to him my mother was caught mid-laugh, looking a bit crazy. She wouldn't thank Emilio for that when she saw it.

As we drove down the hill and away from the trattoria, we realised people were waiting for us in the village. Waving as we passed. The woman from the bakery, Stephano, Alberto and Maria, even the man from the hardware store was standing on the pavement, smoking and looking slightly less moody than usual.

Behind me I could hear Mum, opening her handbag and

doing a bit of rustling around, blowing her nose and sniffing. I felt awful.

Was it good to have come here, or had it been a mistake? Had it, in the long run, just made us both feel that our lives were unsatisfactory?

No, it had been the right thing to do. To look at the years left to us with fresh eyes, to wonder about the possibilities and potential. That was a good thing.

I turned in my seat to my mother. 'Are you okay?'

She looked out of the car window at the lake, passing swiftly by.

'No, I'm not,' she sighed. 'Italy is not playing fair with us this morning. It's looking far too beautiful. I wish it was raining.'

We reached the airport in good time; the roads were more familiar now. The soaring beauty of the lake behind us, we passed though towns and factories and back into civilisation.

We got rid of our bags and found the airport lounge.

'I've never thought to say it this early in the day, but I think I need a drink,' Mum said. 'I can just imagine what it's going to be like. *Shades of the prison-house begin to...* —something something. That was that miserable chap Wordsworth, wasn't it? I learned it in school. I feel quite depressed. All of a sudden.'

I brought her a glass of wine and sat down beside her. I patted her hand.

'You might be pleased to see a few familiar faces,' I said.

'No, I won't. Janice will still be banging on about her bunions, and Peggy will want to tell me in excruciating detail about how her son, the recycling Tsar, is changing things. Sue will have stored up enough bile to tranquilise an elephant. It's all too awful.'

'But you can tell them all about Franco,' I said. 'That will shut them up.'

She gave a little smile and took out her lipstick and compact mirror.

'Yes, it will, won't it?' she said. 'That trumps anything they may have to tell me about the new fire regulations or changes to the menu. That awful sausage casserole – I'd be happy never to see that again. After all, I've eaten wild rabbit. And enjoyed it. They will be absolutely appalled. I don't care what they think, I've always had a sophisticated palate.'

'Anyway. Cheer up. I'm coming back,' I said, 'and if you want to, you can come with me.'

Her eyes brightened. 'Really?'

'Really. It's not going to be easy or quick, but I'm not putting up with things the way they used to be. And I'm not letting you do it either. We are going to seize the day. We're both pretty fit, especially you. I'm going to work something out, you wait and see.'

Mum put her lipstick away, clicked her bag closed and crossed her elegant legs.

'I shall await developments with interest,' she said, raising her wine glass towards me.

32

We collected my car from the long-stay car park, after paying an enormous fee, and I drove Mum back to Winchester Hall. I'd suggested she come to stay with me for a few days, but she wasn't having any of it. I had the sneaky suspicion she was almost looking forward to bragging about her holiday and Franco, and, if nothing else, getting out her cards and starting up the Texas Hold 'Em Poker group. I almost felt sorry for the other residents.

She sailed ahead of me as I trundled her suitcases into her suite, and almost immediately there was a knock. A sparse, grey-haired woman in an ugly crimplene dress peered round the door.

'So, you're back safe, in civilisation again. You poor thing – you look exhausted. And this must be Clover, your daughter. I thought you said she was fifty; she looks much older than that.'

Mum sighed. 'Hello, Sue, *stronzo*, how nice to see you, and yes, this is Clover. Do be kind. She's been working through a few issues recently. As you can probably tell by her footwear.'

'Oh, nice one, Mum,' I muttered.

Mum turned back to her open suitcase and pulled out a few things.

'So did you have fun?' Sue said, her eyes like boot buttons.

'Tremendous fun,' Mum said, 'and I learned a lot of Italian.'

'Well, we have all missed you. The place seemed a lot quieter without you here, racketing about and spreading cheer among us all.'

Mum gave a tight smile and went to hang up some clothes.

'And there is going to be a recital tonight,' Sue continued. 'From the college students. At seven-thirty. They are doing songs from the shows again. It was such a success last time, but of course you missed it. Janice said she'd never heard anything like their performance of "Bloody Mary (is the girl I love)". None of us remembered the celery sticks in *South Pacific*. Or the condoms. Still, they have to learn somewhere don't they. And the Easter bonnet event was fun too, but you missed that as well, didn't you. Kath wore hers all week, even to church on Easter Day. She looked like a drag queen. Dear me, you really are out of the loop.'

'Am I, Sue? *Testa di cazzo!* Well, I will be sure to catch up now I am back,' Mum said, throwing me a look.

'And the blessed eco-campaigner Peggy took over with the Sunday afternoon teas because you weren't here. We had such a lovely time. Her sandwiches were from Waitrose, and they were the best I have eaten in – well, since I came here. (I hope she recycled the wrappers properly, or we will be getting a visit from the recycling Tsar.) And she had Cadbury mini-egg nest cakes too, because it was Easter. Such a treat. Seems to me you have a bit of a rival. You must have missed English food; I mean, what do the Italians know about cuisine apart from pasta and pizza? I expect you found it very hard. All that garlic.'

'Well, no, actually, Sue. I have eaten better than I have in years,' Mum said. 'I had *pappardelle di coniglio*. It was so tasty. Far better than the sausage casserole we will be having tonight.'

Sue bridled and fiddled with her glasses, which were strung on an annoying little chain around her neck.

'Goodness me, what's that?' she asked.

'Wild rabbit,' Mum said airily. 'Absolutely delicious.'

Sue blanched a little. She turned to look at me. 'Really? Rabbit?'

I nodded enthusiastically.

'And I was taken out to dinner or lunch nearly every day by a charming man I met there. Franco. Very attractive and athletic for his age. He had a vintage car. A Maserati Quattroformaggio. So comfortable.'

I turned away to hide a smile.

'Franco?' Sue said. 'Like General Franco?'

'More like Franco Nero,' Mum said, 'in *Camelot*. We had such a special friendship, and I had the best sex I've had for years. That's probably why I look so tired. We shared a dozen oysters one night, but only one of them worked.'

Sue staggered back out of the door and off down the hallway at a shambling trot.

'Well, that didn't take you long,' I said, laughing.

Mum pressed her lips together, to hide her smile. 'Interfering old fart.'

'So, sausage casserole and songs from the shows to look forward to this evening.'

Mum slammed the wardrobe door closed. 'I'd rather stick pins in my eyes.'

'Yes, I think I would too,' I said.

She turned to face me. 'You have to do something, and soon. The prospect of living here for any longer than I have to is too ghastly.'

There was another knock on the door. Another elderly looking lady with a walking stick and Velcro slippers came in, looking around her with interest as though Mum was hiding something.

'Eleanor! How wonderful you are back. And Clover, how nice to see you again. I've just been talking to Sue. She says you had a wonderful time in Italy.'

'Janice. *Che palle*! How are your bunions?' Mum said brightly. 'Are you persevering with those toe correctors? I met a ballerina while I was away. She had to have surgery on hers and her toenails were always falling off.'

'How awful for her. Art can be a cruel mistress. But you must come over for a cup of tea and then you can tell me all about your adventures.' Janice threw me a darting glance. 'Confidentially, of course. We can have a good old girl's natter. I have some KitKats too.'

Mum pulled a packet out of her hand luggage.

'I've developed quite a taste for these actually,' she said. 'Pan di Stelle. They are Italian.'

'Goodness, quite the cosmopolitan!' Janice said.

'I've had a few of those too,' Mum said proudly. 'I wonder if there is any triple sec in the bar.'

'Well, I'll leave you to unpack,' Janice said rather weakly, 'and I'll see you later. Songs from the shows this evening. Shall I save you a seat next to me?'

Mum sighed rather theatrically. 'Two nights ago, a very handsome man serenaded me with "Brindisi" from *Traviata*. By Giuseppe Verdi, who was Italian. "*Let's drink to an evening of laughter and song.*" I don't think college students in suspenders singing the "Time Warp" is really going to cut it for me, to be honest. Do you?'

'No, I suppose not,' Janice said. 'Well, I'll see you later.'

Mum gave her a little wave. '*Per favore, vai via*! See you later!'

I waited until the door had closed behind her and then I burst out laughing.

'Mum, you really are terrible!'

She laughed. 'I am, aren't I? I'm so glad Alberto and Stefano taught me all those Italian insults.' Then she sighed. 'Oh well.'

I shook my head. 'This holiday has really been a wakeup call for both of us, hasn't it? And people will say we are old enough to know better.'

Mum gave me a look. 'Trust me, I will never be old enough to know better.'

* * *

I was still chuckling as I reached my flat. Mum might be out of sorts having returned home, but I had the distinct impression she was going to have a lot of fun teasing the other residents for a few days. At least that would take her mind off things.

Inside my apartment was at least tidy, and, more importantly, empty. Jack was not there and there was no sign he had been there recently, apart from the vague drift of his aftershave.

There was a pile of letters in my post box, the usual flyers from the local takeaways we had used and some catalogues, from companies selling the sort of thermal vests and shoes I would not be seen dead in. But more interestingly there was a letter from a local estate agency, Battenberg and Tunis. Surely with those surnames they would have been better off selling cakes.

Apparently, there was a high demand for property in my location. If I was interested in selling, they would assure me of their most discreet and prompt service. Well, what a coincidence!

There was hardly any food apart from some exhausted looking cheese and claggy-looking milk in the fridge. A sliced loaf and some fish fingers (secret vice, hidden behind the ice container) were in the freezer, plus an empty bottle of vodka. I took it out and stared at it.

What was it that made people do that? Usually men. It never ceased to amaze me that anyone would finish something off and carefully replace the empty container. That probably took more effort than just dropping it on the floor. And why? Did they think that magically it would be replenished?

I prised off two slices of bread to defrost, put some fish fingers in the oven and made myself a sandwich. I would have added some mayonnaise too, but with no surprise I found the empty jar in the larder.

I sat with my very unsophisticated supper in my lap and put the television on. It was Eastenders, and now a different woman was shouting, '*Get outta my pub!*' I did a bit of desultory channel-hopping and tried to get into some wildlife thing about Australia.

Apparently, as ferocious predators and scavengers, Tasmanian devils could eat 40 per cent of their body weight in a day.

I sighed. *Same, Tasmanian devil, same.*

Then there was a subtitled series about French detectives, who would have got on much quicker if they had stopped smoking and drinking pastis in dark bars all the time. I turned the television off again and went to pour a very large glass of wine.

Inside my apartment it was quiet, but it was a different sort of quiet. I could still hear the polite gurgle of the fridge freezer, the muffled roar of the traffic in the street below. The occasional car horn or someone shouting. There was none of the deep, restful silence of the barn at the trattoria. How odd. How had I not noticed this before?

I closed my eyes and wondered what Gio was doing. We had exchanged texts while I waited at the airport. He was missing me; I was missing him. He hoped we would have a good flight.

It was nine-thirty. Perhaps I should go to bed and put an end to this day?

My mobile rang. Unknown number. I was almost outraged; it was nine o'clock. I took a big swig of my wine and answered.

'Clover! My dear old friend! How wonderful to hear from you!'

'You rang me. Who is this?'

'It's Nick,' came the reply.

I knew exactly who it was, but I wasn't having any of it.

'Nick who?' I said. 'If you are trying to flog me insurance, I'm not interested.'

There was a familiar chuckle from him.

'Nick Crane, of course. From XS. Jack told me you had been away. I thought I would reach out, see how the land lies.'

I could feel a familiar clench of unease in the pit of my stomach.

'What do you want?' I asked.

'I just wanted a catch-up. We've all been wondering how you are, how your holiday went. Now you've had time to get over the shock of what happened.'

'I had a great holiday, thanks.'

'Good. Good. You deserved it. We are all ploughing on here at XS, arses to the grindstone. Nina is working for me now. You were right about her: she really is very competent. A bit taciturn sometimes, but very efficient.'

I remembered Nina as being very chatty, a great one for inter-office gossip and information. Perhaps working for Nick had changed all that.

'What do you want?' I repeated.

Nick chuckled. 'Well, what do *you* want? That's the thing, isn't it? Jack gave me your new phone number and your address in Italy. I hope you got my letter. Now you are back, we can talk money and bonuses. Interesting things.'

I took another sip of my wine and wished for a moment I smoked. This would be a good time to light a cigarette, leisurely, and blow smoke over the phone to affirm my contempt for him.

'Oh, yes?' I said.

'You know we want you to come back as a specialist consultant. There's a 15 per cent upgrade on the table – perhaps I could wrestle them up to 20 – plus the usual benefits, plus a consultancy sign-on fee.'

I felt myself relax; I had the upper hand now and I was beginning to enjoy myself. I'd known Nick Crane for long enough to recognise the desperation in his tone.

'Is that all?' I said.

He laughed. 'It's a very generous offer, Clover. And I think Sven would be happy for you to use his *hytte*. That's his holiday place near Blindleia. He's very keen to see you back on board.'

'Why, has he got a boat?'

Nick clicked his tongue. 'No, you misunderstand, sweetheart. The Olafsen deal is reaching its last stages, and Sven is absolutely set on this: he wants you back in the saddle, leading the charge.'

'He has horses too?'

'Oh, for... no, listen. Sven Olafsen wants you to come back to the team, to finish off the deal.'

'Ah, I see. Yes, you said that in your letter.'

There was an uneasy pause which I let roll on.

'Look,' Nick said, 'I hope there are no hard feelings about what happened? I was just the messenger; I told them at the time it was short-sighted. I knew it was a mistake to let you go—'

'Make me redundant.'

'Okay, make you redundant. But it's all changed now. There is a place for you at XS, in a very senior role. Look, sweetheart, Clover, you have XS by the squishies now.'

'What an elegant turn of phrase, Nick. And stop calling me sweetheart.'

'I'm sorry. Look, we've been friends for years, you know that.'

'No, I don't remember it like that at all.'

Nick gave an exasperated sigh. 'Colleagues then. Teammates. Us against them. Look, I was asked to let you go; just as I've been asked to get you back. The whole deal depends on this. You know what a tosser Sven Olafsen is.'

I know what a tosser you are.

'So, let me get this straight. A 15 per cent pay rise. Maybe 20 if I push. Use of the company hut in Norway. Extras.'

Nick breathed a sigh of relief. 'Exactly. Your own office, a personal coffee machine and you can have Nina back.'

'A sign-on bonus, perks, use of the executive toilet I expect.'

'Anything,' Nick said. 'I know we could make it work.'

'You mean the executive toilet is broken?'

He gave a frustrated whine. 'No, of course not. Look, Clover, let's cut to the nitty-gritty. If you could see me, you would know I'm actually on my knees. Begging. I have to get back to Sven by the end of the week with good news.'

'Oh dear,' I said, finishing my wine and topping up the glass. Which was an okay Merlot. What I really wanted at that moment was some freshly opened Bollinger.

'Just tell me what it would take for you to come back.'

I thought for a moment.

'Nick, I have learned something about myself in the weeks I have been away.'

'Of course you have. That's what holidays are all about, aren't they?'

'I spend decades working and building up my career, and then in just a few weeks I understood I needed to rethink everything. I thought I knew what I wanted, but now I realise I didn't. I want to decide what is important for me from now on, rather than what is important to other people like you. Who, let's be fair, didn't give me a second thought after I left, except then Sven Olafsen cracked the whip. And all of this has made me think about my priorities.'

'That's the beauty of some time off,' Nick replied. 'Time to think, to reflect. On how much you miss the cut and thrust of deals. On how much you still have to give?' Nick said hopefully (and rather patronisingly, I thought).

People said things like that when they were booted off reality shows, didn't they? They always had 'a lot left to give'. Which always made me think, well, why didn't you give it in the first place? Then you wouldn't have been voted off the cooking/dancing/singing show.

'I do have a lot left to give—'

'Thank god for that,' he sighed.

'But not to you or XS or Sven, or any other weaselly company that comes knocking on my door. If you offered me the keys to the executive jet, a round-the-world cruise on the Queen Mary 2 and a fistful of dollars, I would still have the same answer. No. And what I really, really want is for you to understand that, and tell the XS board that too. I'm going to spend the rest of my life doing things I enjoy with people I like. With friends. And with family.'

'I didn't think you had any friends. Or family,' he blustered.

'And there you have it, Nick. You don't really know me at all, do you?'

I ended the call at that point, trying to imagine Nick Crane, begging on his knees, fluff from the carpet on his trousers, the toes of his horrible shoes curling up against the floor.

33

In London it was raining. Everywhere was just as crowded and noisy as I'd remembered. My extended holiday really was over, and I needed to firm up plans for my next steps.

The sale of the flat went through only a month later, to a pair of solicitors who magically were able to work at top speed. Which confirmed every suspicion I had ever had about the legal side of a house purchase usually being deliberately drawn out to justify exorbitant fees. I arranged for most of my belongings to go into storage.

By then my mother was champing at the bit to leave Winchester Hall. The frequency of her phone calls confirmed that. News of her holiday romance had filtered fast through the gossip channels.

The final straw had been when Douglas, he of the habitual cravat-wearing, had made a clumsy pass at her, in the grandly named King Alfred Function Room, just after the latest entertainment. A selection of Gilbert and Sullivan from the local operatic group.

'He had the nerve to lay hands on me,' Mum said, outraged on her latest phone call, 'and they were very cold and clammy. I would have kneed him in a specific area, but I think marriage to Judith has long since shrivelled that part of his anatomy. So, I slapped his face instead.'

This led to Douglas's wife Judith making a formal complaint to the management, followed by a furious stand-up row in the dining room just before a Sunday morning brunch, an occasion apparently overlaid with the aroma of kippers.

Mum recounted the event with a certain belligerent pride.

'She called me a trollop and accused me of trying to seduce Douglas! And I said it would have taken a braver woman than I to prise Douglas out of his polyester slacks. And she said I had no business trying to entice another woman's husband into my – what did she call it – *lair of lechery*. Isn't that marvellous? And I asked if she had forgotten to take her medication that morning, because she was obviously not quite the ticket. Then she deliberately knocked the crystal vase of flowers on my table over, threw a piece of toast at me and called me a Jezebel. I wish you had been there to see it. Anyway, since then we have been on '*no speaks*' which is quite a relief, because now I don't have to listen to any more of her tedious tales about how important Douglas was during their time in Rhodesia. And I expect all he did was sharpen pencils in the Embassy. Dull, dull, dull.'

'So, did you start up the poker school?'

Mum sighed. 'I did try, but half of them have got memory problems and the other half thought I was trying to start a gambling den. Sue berated me in the garden, telling me that the love of money was the root of all evil, and I was in danger of *piercing myself through with many sorrows*. And I said what about all your premium bonds then. She's always bragging she has won fifty pounds, but she says they are an investment. It's not gambling, apparently. And I said they weren't an investment, and in the end, I goggled it—'

'Googled.'

'—and I was right. So, she said she would pray for me. And I said *facia di culo* which means your face looks like your bottom. Which under the circumstances I thought was quite restrained. So, what's happening with you?'

'Most of my things are going into storage and I've found a holiday cottage to rent on a weekly basis near Basingstoke.'

'Good god. Basingstoke. And?'

'And then I thought we could go back to Italy. To see if we still like it there.'

'About bloody time,' Mum said. 'If I stay here much longer, I will probably be arrested for GMC.'

'That's the General Medical Council; I think you mean GBH,' I said. 'Grievous bodily harm. Look, I'll check some flights. So, is any time not good for you?'

There was a rustling of paper. 'I have nothing in my diary, except Introduction to Basket Weaving on Tuesday and still life art classes which are starting on 3 September. The day war broke out. Which is probably appropriate because the rumour is that Douglas is going to pose. Hopefully with his clothes on. Can you just imagine the alternative?'

'I'll get back to you,' I laughed.

Mum went suddenly quiet, looking off into the distance. 'Ah me, *che bella macchina*,' she said, looking oddly sad.

'What does that mean?' I asked, wondering why she might be talking of machines.

'What a beautiful car. Franco taught me that one... and I haven't had the chance to use it.'

* * *

We returned to Italy two weeks after that. Mum: with too much luggage and a spring in her step. Me: feeling nervous and more excited than I had felt for years. And Gio – smiling and even more handsome than I had remembered – was there to meet us. He had even cleaned the cardboard boxes and painting materials out of his car specially for the occasion. He enfolded me into a big hug, holding me against him for a long time as though he hadn't thought about much else since I'd left. Mum gave a discreet cough behind us and Gio laughed and kissed her cheek. And then he handed Mum into the back seat as though she were a duchess.

'Well, how wonderful to be back,' Mum said as we drove alongside the lake again. 'I feel as though I have been in suspended animation for the last few weeks. And it's my birthday soon.'

'Then we will celebrate,' Gio said. He squeezed my hand. 'Uncle Franco is so excited to think he will see you again today. He has been very sad without you.'

And I have been sad without him,' Mum said with a bitter-sweet sigh. 'I couldn't be more pleased to hear that though. It's wonderful to be missed.'

Zoe, Paulo and Franco were outside the trattoria, sitting on the veranda out of the bright afternoon sun. As we arrived, they all stood up and Zoe came running over to greet us.

'You're back!' she said hugging me. 'I never really knew if you meant it when you said you would return.'

'Well, here we are,' I said. I was grinning so much my face was aching.

I turned to see Mum and Franco hugging and talking over each other, and I think both of them were rather emotional.

Gio came to put his arm across my shoulders and then hug me again.

'I am taking them with us to your new house, but they wanted to come here first,' he said. 'Stephano has made sure everything is ready for you, and I think Maria went in to freshen the place up.'

At that moment another vehicle pulled into the car park and Alberto, Stephano and Maria got out, hurrying to greet us and welcome us back.

I looked around me, rather overwhelmed by the moment. The friendly faces, all so pleased to see us, the beautiful day, the marvellous view across the lake were just as I'd remembered, and yet that day it all seemed sharper, better. The air was warm and clear, the chatter loud and welcoming. It wasn't long before someone called for some Prosecco to celebrate our return.

'Welcome back,' Franco said, and I think there really were tears in his eyes. 'You are very welcome.'

Zoe handed out the glasses and there, in the car park, under the cheerful Italian sun, we clinked our drinks together, and I really did feel as though I had come home.

EPILOGUE

A lot happened after the day that Mum and I took a leap of faith and left England. Some of it was surprisingly easy. Parts of it – the bureaucracy, the form filling – were more difficult. But with the help of our friends, we managed it.

* * *

Mum and I moved into the rental house which Stephano had renovated, and each day we strolled into the town to buy *pane Toscano* or herb-topped *focaccia*, and sometimes sweet *brioche col tuppo*, from the bakery.

About a week after we had settled in, Zoe and Paulo threw a surprise party to celebrate our return and also Mum's eightieth birthday, and it felt as though the whole town came. The lights on the veranda glowed out across the tables as the summer evening darkened and a couple of tiny bats swooped and twirled across the sky.

There was always someone to talk to, someone doing the rounds with carafes of wine or platters of food, and always, not far from me, there was lovely Gio. Looking out for me, his eyes filled with affection. Actually caring that I was happy.

Mum and Franco sat together chatting and enjoying planning their next adventure. I hoped he wasn't teaching her too many new insults or swear words.

'Isn't this marvellous?' Mum said when I went to sit next to her. 'Everyone is so kind and friendly. Winchester Hall feels like a lifetime away. Do you know I heard that Janice took over my old suite of rooms. She moved in the day after I left. Talk about dead men's shoes! Well, I wish her luck. I wouldn't be back there for all the garlic in Italy.'

'Funny isn't it,' I said, 'to find ourselves here, at this stage in our lives. I don't think either of us could possibly have imagined this.'

'Well, you know what they say: if you don't go after what you want, you'll never have it.'

I laughed. 'And what else do they say, these wise people?'

'If you don't ask, no one will ever say yes. And my personal favourite: if you don't step forward, you'll always be in the same place. There is just one thing which would make this even more perfect.'

'And what's that?'

'Oh, you'll see. All in good time. Do you know, I have realised I shall die here,' Mum said cheerfully. 'Oh, don't look like that. There's nothing wrong with me – I just realised the other day that I would. That I would end up in a box in that funny little church, hopefully with people sobbing into handkerchiefs and telling each other how marvellous I was.'

'That's a bit morbid,' I said.

'We all have to go at some point, and where better than here?'

'Well, not for some time, I hope, after all the fuss you made about leaving.'

'I didn't make a fuss!'

I laughed. 'Not much, but I do remember it rather differently.'

'Would you be very offended if I moved in with Franco one day soon?' Mum said. 'Our little house is lovely of course, but we are getting on so well again and I don't want anything to spoil that. I think he will ask me, and I would like to.'

'Of course not, I'm glad to see you so happy.'

'And won't you want to move in with your young man? Not that it's any of my business, but it would be nice for you, wouldn't it?'

I looked across at where Gio was talking and laughing with the man from the hardware shop and my heart did a little leap of happiness.

'We'll see,' I said.

Gio came towards me, a big smile on his face, and took my hand.

'We have another surprise for you,' he said. 'One I think you will like. Your mother and I have been plotting behind your back.'

'What's that?' I said, rather nervously, 'what have you been doing?'

At that moment a taxi pulled into the driveway of the trattoria, and of course everyone stopped talking and turned to look.

And a moment later Ben got out of the back seat and rushed towards me. I stood there, unable to speak, my mouth open with the shock.

My mother squeezed my arm and sniffed back her tears. 'I said there was one more thing to make this perfect, didn't I?'

Ben enfolded me in a big hug – the thing I had missed and wanted for so long. Behind him Brianna stood, smiling, even more golden and glorious than I had remembered.

I started to sob. Tears of happiness and shock.

'What on earth— Ben!'

'Hi, Mum. Nice surprise?'

For a moment I couldn't catch my breath. I couldn't speak.

'But how?'

'Blame Granny and your friends of course. It was her idea,' he said. 'She organised it all. The emails have been flying across the Atlantic for a while now.'

I turned to stare at my mother who was dabbing at her eyes with a handkerchief and looking very emotional.

'You've been emailing?'

She tilted her head to one side. 'Well, not me, technically. Emilio has been such an enormous help with the computer. He's a really clever chap. Despite the questionable dress sense. And Gio helped too, of course, typing up my words.'

I turned to look at Ben and started to cry again.

'This is the best day of my life,' I said.

'So far,' Mum said firmly. 'The best day of your life so far.'

Then there were all the questions to be asked and answered. How had their journey been? How long were they staying for? What did they think of Italy?

At last Ben and Brianna took their bags into the converted barn where I had stayed, and after a while came back out to join the party.

'You look great, Mum,' Ben said. 'You and Granny both do. It looks like Italy suits you.'

'It does,' I said, sighing happily.

It was so wonderful to have him there, instead of being thousands of miles apart. I could just reach out and touch his arm, see first-hand the affection between him and Brianna. Who knew? Perhaps one day soon, I would need to buy a hat.

'So, how do you spend your time?' Brianna asked. 'It looks like a beautiful place. Is there a lot to do here?'

I did try and tell her that, no, there really wasn't much to do, but they seemed to find that rather wonderful. And they were right, truthfully. Maybe there comes a time in everyone's life when doing nothing, just being, was okay for a while.

Ben reached over the table for the cheese platter.

'And you are enjoying life? Granny said you and Gio were renovating a house. That doesn't sound like you at all. Can we see it?'

'Of course, tomorrow. But there is still a lot to do. You could help if you want to.'

'I'd like that,' Ben said, and he refilled Brianna's wine glass before his own. 'And I want to hear all your news. And meet all your friends – they seem a fun bunch.'

'Do you play Texas Hold 'Em Poker?' my mother asked with a glint in her eye.

* * *

About a month before Mum and I had returned to Italy, Gio had bought the abandoned house, which was actually called Villa di Russo after the family who had built it, and it was six months after, that the work started on the restoration. He wanted me to be involved, with ideas for the best ways to organise the rooms, suggestions about decorating and planning. I had to learn Italian very quickly. It was sometimes exasperating, sometimes exciting.

Scaffolding went up, skips were hired and filled with rubble and rotten plaster, and gradually, slowly, the house was brought back to its former beauty. The builders worked for months, repairing the roof, the broken floorboards and shutters, and installing proper electricity, new plumbing and heating.

After a year the beautiful glass veranda was cleaned and repaired, and the horrible kitchen was restored with new wooden units, polished granite worktops and a vast utility room. There was new plastering. New skirting boards and doors. The building gradually came back to life.

After another year, we started to clear the garden of rubble and rubbish, and old paths appeared underneath the neglected grass. Building inspectors from every government department came with sheaves of paperwork, and had long heated discussions with Stephano and his workmates.

Sometimes it seemed as though it would never be finished. There were weeks at a time when nothing much happened: people were on holiday or busy with another job, or just didn't turn up. Then out of the blue the builders would return, without any sort of explanation, and start work again.

As Stephano was fond of saying: *niente che valga la pena di avere è facile.* Nothing worth having comes easily. Which I supposed was a good way to look at life in general, not just the slow transformation of Villa di Russo.

It had taken me a long time to find my happy place in the world and taken my mother even longer. It was good to be able to grasp the opportunity, the friendship and the companionship that life in Italy, in that unremarkable, funny little town, had brought me.

I had learned to cook. I sketched, and I painted; after all, I had a good teacher. I explored the countryside, and for the first time I had been looking after myself. Not just my physical wellbeing with visits to the gym or the doctor, but concentrating on being content, doing things I enjoyed. Being with people who made me feel good about myself and my choices.

I wished I had done it earlier; my life would probably have been very different. But perhaps, in the grand scheme of things, everything had just worked out exactly as it should.

ACKNOWLEDGMENTS

Thank you to so many people who helped and supported me while I was writing this book.

Firstly, to Jane Ayres, who saw me through some very dark and impossible days. Also, to James, Claudia, Freya, David, and their families who have been so reassuring, loving and encouraging.

To the invaluable team at Boldwood Books, especially Emily Ruston who was so kind when I needed it most.

To my wonderful agent, Broo Doherty, who has always been so considerate and supportive.

Also, to the many friends and fellow writers I have made through the RNA and The Ross Writers group. Never forgetting my wider writing circle who are always so generous with their time and enthusiasm. Particularly Judy Leigh, Ian Wilfred, Sarah Bennett, Lynda Stacey, Diane Saxon, Jessica Redland and all the members of the Boldwood Books' Book and Tonic group.

Finally, thank you to all the readers around the world who have left me such lovely and enthusiastic reviews. You make it all worthwhile.

MORE FROM MADDIE PLEASE

We hope you enjoyed reading *A Vintage Vacation*. If you did, please leave a review.

If you'd like to gift a copy, this book is also available as an ebook, large print, hardback, digital audio download and audiobook CD.

Sign up to Maddie Please's mailing list for news, competitions and updates on future books.

http://bit.ly/MaddiePleaseNewsletter

Explore more feel-good reads from Maddie Please.

ABOUT THE AUTHOR

Maddie Please is the author of bestselling joyous tales of older women. She had a career as a dentist and now lives in Herefordshire where she enjoys box sets, red wine and Christmas.

Follow Maddie on social media:

- facebook.com/maddieplease
- twitter.com/maddieplease1
- instagram.com/maddieplease1
- bookbub.com/authors/maddie-please

Boldwood

Boldwood Books is an award-winning fiction publishing company seeking out the best stories from around the world.

Find out more at www.boldwoodbooks.com

Join our reader community for brilliant books, competitions and offers!

Follow us
@BoldwoodBooks
@BookandTonic

Sign up to our weekly deals newsletter

https://bit.ly/BoldwoodBNewsletter

Made in the USA
Middletown, DE
27 May 2023